THE VIKING DECEPTION

A James Acton Thriller

Also by J. Robert Kennedy

James Acton Thrillers

The Protocol
Brass Monkey
Broken Dove
The Templar's Relic
Flags of Sin
The Arab Fall
The Circle of Eight
The Venice Code
Pompeii's Ghosts
Amazon Burning
The Riddle
Blood Relics
Sins of the Titanic
Saint Peter's Soldiers
The Thirteenth Legion
Raging Sun
Wages of Sin
Wrath of the Gods
The Templar's Revenge
The Nazi's Engineer
Atlantis Lost
The Cylon Curse
The Viking Deception

Special Agent Dylan Kane Thrillers

Rogue Operator
Containment Failure
Cold Warriors
Death to America
Black Widow
The Agenda
Retribution

Delta Force Unleashed Thrillers

Payback
Infidels
The Lazarus Moment
Kill Chain
Forgotten

Templar Detective Thrillers

The Templar Detective
The Templar Detective and the Parisian Adulteress
The Templar Detective and the Sergeant's Secret
The Templar Detective and the Unholy Exorcist

Detective Shakespeare Mysteries

Depraved Difference
Tick Tock
The Redeemer

Zander Varga, Vampire Detective

The Turned

THE VIKING DECEPTION

A James Acton Thriller

J. ROBERT KENNEDY

CreateSpace

ISBN: 9781998005444

First Edition

10 9 8 7 6 5 4 3 2 1

For Jamal Khashoggi.

Murdered for daring to have a voice.

THE VIKING DECEPTION

A James Acton Thriller

"I assure you that the reports that suggest that Jamal Khashoggi went missing in the Consulate in Istanbul or that the Kingdom's authorities have detained him or killed him are absolutely false, and baseless."

Prince Khaled bin Salman on the disappearance of Saudi journalist Jamal Khashoggi
October 9, 2018

"The individuals who did this did this outside the scope of their authority. There obviously was a tremendous mistake made, and what compounded the mistake was the attempt to try to cover up. That is unacceptable in any government."

Saudi Arabia Foreign Minister Adel al-Jubeir
October 22, 2018

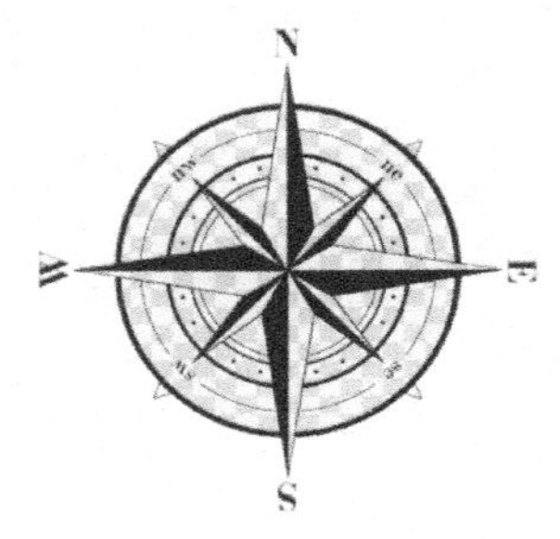

AUTHOR'S NOTE

The tragic murder of Jamal Khashoggi at the hands of the Saudi regime is referred to herein. No disrespect is intended. Instead, these references are meant to prove the plausibility that such actions could be undertaken by those involved.

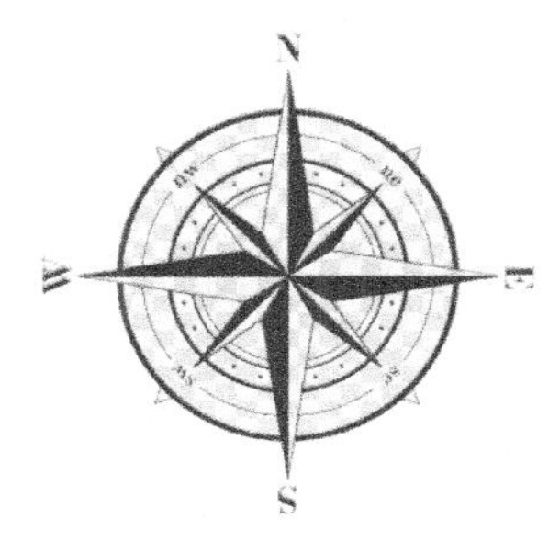

PREFACE

On the afternoon of October 2, 2018, Jamal Khashoggi entered the Saudi Arabian Consulate in Istanbul, Turkey. He never left alive. Earlier, a team of fifteen hitmen, described by the Saudi regime at first as tourists, landed in Istanbul, at least one with a bone saw.

Typical tourist gear, for certain.

He was brutally murdered, his body dissolved with chemicals, and the coverup, however inept, began.

Was Khashoggi scared when he entered the sovereign territory of the country he criticized? We assume so from statements made by his fiancée. And she was the reason he was there. This isn't a statement of blame, but merely fact. He loved her. He wanted to marry her. He needed paperwork from the Saudi government to make it happen.

And he died for it.

And now, one must ask who in their right mind would set foot in a Saudi Arabian facility, anywhere in the world?

But what if you had no choice?

What if the consequences of choosing not to, were worse?

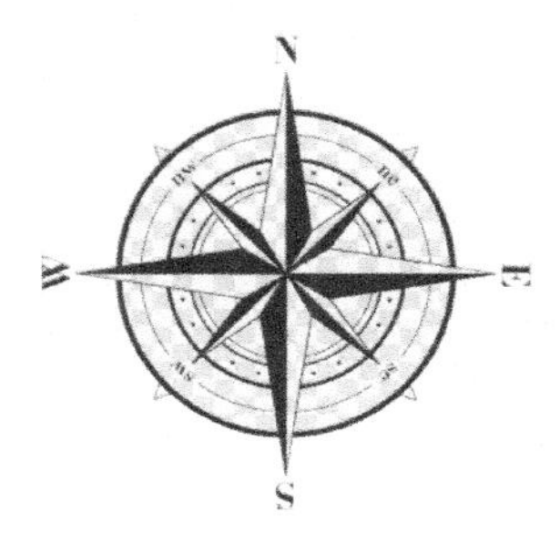

Stockholm University

Stockholm, Sweden

One day from now

Elsa Andersson scratched the back of her neck, all four fingers raking against the skin as she wondered what was going on. The text message she received had been from Professor Karlsson's phone. She had double-checked the number, something that had proven entirely unnecessary as he was in her contacts list, with more messages exchanged than with anyone else including her boyfriend.

She frowned at the thought of him.

There's no future there.

She was tired of wasting her time with boys. She wanted a man. Professor Karlsson was definitely a man, and if he wasn't married, and perhaps twenty years younger, she'd consider making a play for him.

She loved brilliant minds.

Though sleeping with a man old enough to be her grandfather wasn't exactly appealing to her.

And neither was the infantile moron she now bedded.

She sighed as the elevators opened, her scratch turning into a massage, though a rather ineffectual one. She was worried about the professor. She hadn't reached him all day, thus his message had been a tremendous relief. He had somehow guessed where she was, which now that she thought of it, was a bit of a leap.

Why would he think I'd be at the university at this hour?

The only reason she was here was that he hadn't shown up all day, and the remains delivered earlier had to be processed. Normally, they would have worked on it together at a more reasonable hour, but with his lack of communication all day, she had decided action had to be taken, regardless of the consequences.

Yet he had known she was here. That much was certain from his message.

Meet me in the lobby right away.

But he wasn't there. A quick check with security confirmed he hadn't been and left. He had never been.

Could he have been referring to a different lobby?

Her eyebrows rose at the thought as she slowly made her way to the lab at the end of the hallway. It was a possibility, though she couldn't fathom what lobby he might have been referring to, nor why he would think she was somewhere that had one.

None of it made sense, and it had her even more concerned than she already had been. Calls and messages had gone unanswered all day, even to his home, though if he wasn't there, that wasn't unusual. Mrs. Karlsson never answered when she called for some reason. He was to have met with an old friend of his, Professor James Acton, an archaeology professor from the United States, along with the man's wife, Laura Palmer, also a professor of archaeology.

If that's not a recipe for boredom, I don't know what is.

The two professors were to meet with Karlsson this morning then tour the dig site, but they never showed. None of them did, and all day she had worked under the hypothesis they had found something better to do. After all, they were all academics, and that type was notorious for losing track of time when a good discussion was underway.

She frowned at the thought.

You're *an academic.*

She paused, staring into nothing.

Am I going to become like them?

She shuddered at the thought, resuming her tired trek to the lab. She hoped she would remain the vital, vivacious, exciting person she now was, then again, at this moment, she could think of nothing more exciting than the remains she was now about to process.

She reached the door and fished under her hoodie for her pass, her mind returning to the task at hand, Professor Karlsson's idiosyncrasies put on hold.

He can text me again if he actually shows up.

She swiped her pass then entered her personal code for the lab, something she still remembered to this day being issued. It had been one of the prouder moments of her life. The trust the professor had shown in her had been an emotional revelation. She was one of the few he allowed into his lab unaccompanied. In fact, there were less than a handful of students with the access she had.

The door clicked, the sound always sending goosebumps through her body, and she pushed against the door, a slight hiss sounding, the room pressurized to keep foreign contaminants out should there be something truly delicate inside. The door swung open and she gasped at the sight that greeted her.

"What's going on here?"

A man was standing over the body of another, staring at her, shocked at having been caught. She froze, the door swinging shut behind her as her jaw dropped with the recognition of who the murderer standing before her was.

It was the same man whom she had Googled just yesterday.

"Professor Acton?" She stared at the body, recognizing one of the security guards. "Oh my God! Is he dead?"

Something behind her caused her to flinch and as she turned, she caught a glimpse of a woman she recognized as Professor Acton's wife. She pressed something into her back.

"Move and you die."

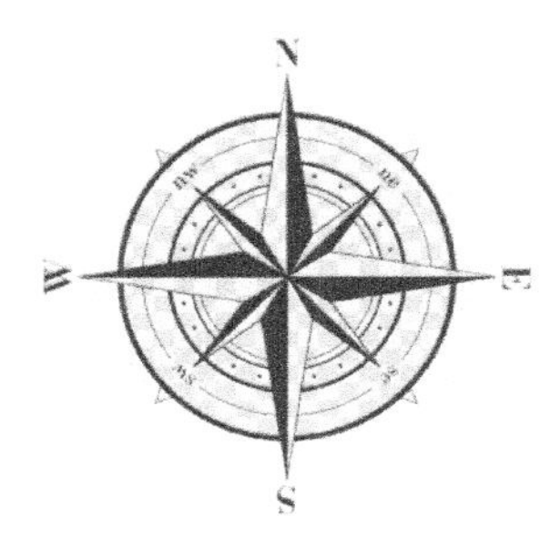

Al Lixbuna, Islamic Iberia

Caliphate of Córdoba

(Modern Day Lisbon, Portugal)

989 AD

Fatima Halabi's heart raced as her lips pressed against his, his thick beard and mustache tickling her face, the shocking blond hair just one of a myriad of things that attracted her to his forbidden embrace. For it *was* forbidden. Her love was not hers to give, nor were her favors. Those all belonged to her father. He alone could barter her future, her feminine assets, to the eventual betterment of their family's position in the Caliphate.

And she had resigned herself, willingly, to that fate.

Until a month ago.

She had seen the Vikings before. Fierce, proud men, their striking hair, so different, the first thing one noticed when they mixed with the locals. And their clothing, so distinctly different from the flowing robes she was so accustomed to seeing, fascinated her. It immediately had her wondering what Viking women wore.

And that was the question that had started this entire affair, an affair that had to stop, yet an affair she couldn't resist continuing.

"What do Viking women wear?"

It had been an innocent enough question, though asked out of turn. It wasn't her place to speak to male guests, and her father had admonished her, apologizing to their honored visitor, Prince Magnus Hamundarson, for her breach of protocol.

Yet Magnus hadn't minded. In fact, he had brushed off the apology as unnecessary, and eagerly answered the question, addressing her directly, rather than the others gathered in the room.

He had treated her as an equal, something no man had ever done.

And it had empowered her, if only for those few, precious moments.

It was a feeling she began to crave, and she had done something foolish. Dangerous. Rebellious.

She had sent him a message.

An innocent message.

If she weren't Muslim and female.

If sent to a Muslim man, she would fully expect him to reveal her transgression to her father immediately upon receipt.

Yet she hadn't feared that from this man.

He was different.

He respected her without knowing her.

The response had been swift, and discrete, Magnus thankfully recognizing the risk she was taking. It made sense. He had been here many times, from what she had been told, and he even spoke and wrote Arabic, though not with the proficiency of a native.

He understood her culture.

Messages continued to be exchanged, her infatuation with the man growing with each one, then a treacherous escalation had been proposed.

A meeting, in person, just the two of them.

It had been the most exciting, erotic, passionate night of her life, and she had fallen madly in love with the man whose arms now enveloped her tightly, infusing a sense of safety and serenity like she had never felt before.

She pushed away, staring up into his vivid blue eyes. "I've missed you."

He smiled at her. "And I you."

"I didn't think I'd ever see you again."

Magnus pushed several stray hairs back under her hijab. "Nor I."

Fatima rested her cheek against his chest, the pounding of his heart comforting. "I can't stand being apart from you. Every moment is torture."

His chest expanded as he took a deep breath. "I'm afraid I have bad news."

She pushed away, just enough to stare up at him, her entire body tensing as she prepared for something tragic to be revealed. "What is it? Please tell me you're not leaving."

He frowned. "I am. In two days."

A single cry escaped, tears flowing down her cheeks as she imagined her life without him. "Will you be back?"

He sighed. "I will try, but it would be at least a year, perhaps longer."

Her shoulders slumped, her cheek returning to his chest. "By then it will be too late."

"What do you mean?"

A lump formed in the back of her throat, painful, restricting, and she had to gasp out the words. "A messenger arrived this morning. That's why I had to see you."

Magnus took her by the shoulders, holding her out so he could see her tear-streaked face. "A messenger?"

She nodded. "My future husband will arrive tomorrow."

Magnus drew a quick breath, his jaw dropping, genuinely hurt by the news. "Husband?"

Her shoulders sagged in his arms, her strength abandoning her. "My father has arranged my marriage to Sheik Al-Musawi. The wedding is to occur the day after he arrives."

Magnus' arms dropped to his side, the break in his embrace crushing her. "Do you love him?"

Her eyes widened and she reached out for his hands. "Love him? I've never even met him! I know nothing of him beyond that he is twenty years my senior and extremely powerful." Shame washed over her at her next words, her head sagging toward her chest as her eyes burned. "I am to be his fourth wife."

"Disgusting!"

A brief ember of anger flared at his words. "It's my culture!"

He lowered his voice, his outrage pushed aside. "I know, I'm sorry. Sometimes I forget how different we are." He pinched her chin, raising her gaze to his. "Can you say no?"

Fatima's eyes widened. "Are you mad? To refuse one's father in these circumstances is unheard of. I will have to marry him. I have no choice. The decision has already been made."

Magnus' eyes bored into hers. "But I thought you loved me?"

Her shoulders shook as her tears flowed once more. "Oh, I do. Never doubt that, my love. You are the only man I have ever loved, and you will be the only man I ever love. This man I am being forced to take as my husband will never have my heart as you have mine." She reached up and squeezed the back of his neck. "I love you more than any woman has ever loved a man, and that will never change."

He smiled, and she could see the love in his eyes, feel it in his hands as he cupped her face in them, the skin rough from a life hard lived. "Then we can't let this happen."

Her eyes narrowed. "What do you mean?"

His voice became earnest as he leaned closer. "You must come with me when I leave."

Her eyes widened. "You're mad!"

He chuckled. "That may be, but it is your love that drives me mad, and I cannot live knowing you are with another man, a man whom you despise."

She shook her head, her eyes still wide. "But if I go with you, then my family will pursue us. It could mean war!"

Magnus grunted. "I don't fear war, and your family will find that we Vikings are not to be trifled with."

She patted his chest, shaking her head with finality. "No, I can't have people dying because of me. It would be selfish, and an abomination in the eyes of Allah." She drew a slow breath, exhaling loudly. "Though I hate what my father has done, I still love him, as I love my mother and my brother, all of whom support this arrangement. To run away would be to dishonor them, and to see them die because of my actions, would be unbearable." She frowned, grasping his hands in hers. "I fear our destinies lie apart, my love, and there is nothing we can do about it."

Magnus held her tight, saying nothing, as they shared one last moment together. She would miss this, and she'd never find this feeling in the arms of the elder sheik, in the arms of a stranger that would take her into his bed for a business deal.

"What if I told you there was a way?"

She closed her eyes. "Then I would say that this is a dream, for I cannot fathom any solution to our situation."

He held her out, staring into her eyes, his smile melting her to her core. "Do you trust me?"

"With my life, you know that!"

His smile broadened. "Are you willing to sacrifice ever seeing your family again to be with me?"

The question was something she hadn't expected, something until a moment ago she had never considered an answer to. To never see her family again was something simply unfathomable. They were her life. They were everything she knew.

Yet once she married, she would return with her new husband to his home outside Mecca, and the chances of ever seeing her family again were slim. Perhaps she might see them a few more times in her life if there were a purpose, but the prospect of seeing them fewer times than could be counted on her fingers was devastating. Could she sacrifice the possibility of seeing them a few last times, over the course of her entire life, for one far happier all the other days? She closed her eyes, her heart hammering at her decision.

"I am."

He drew a breath, his chest expanding as she saw the relief spread throughout him. "Then trust me now. Go to your family, pretend you are happy with the arrangement, but be prepared to act when you receive my message."

She nodded, his instructions suddenly making this very real.

It terrified her.

He held up a finger, his expression becoming serious. "Pack *nothing.* Take *nothing.* No one must suspect you planned on leaving. Understood?"

She acknowledged him with a trembling nod. "I-I do, but what do you have planned?"

He grabbed her, holding her tight to his chest as his voice cracked. "A way for us to be together for the rest of our lives, and for your family to never know."

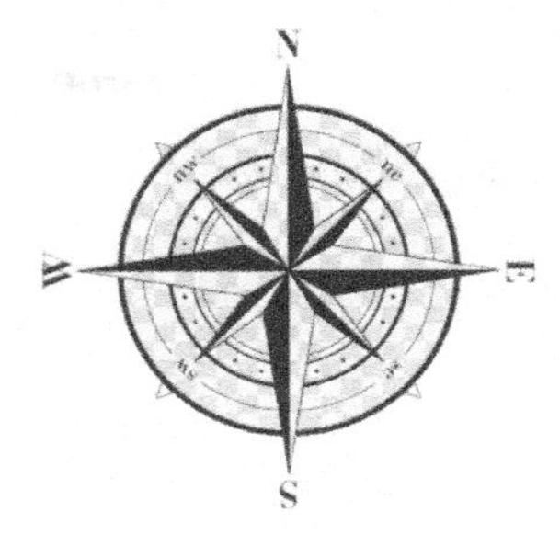

Outside Sigtuna, Sweden

Present Day

Professor Viggo Karlsson leaned back in his chair, the laptop in front of him showing a picture of a runestone they had discovered only this week, zoomed in on the final line of tightly clustered characters. His yellow ruled notebook, filled with chicken scratches and doodles, contained a quick translation of the ancient Norse inscription.

"Done?"

He flinched, forgetting he wasn't alone, his top student, Elsa Andersson, sitting across from him in the tight quarters provided by a trailer set up on the dig site. They had been here every day for weeks, excavating an ancient Viking burial ground north of Stockholm that preliminary estimates suggested dated around the turn of the first millennium. It was an exciting find under normal circumstances, but these weren't normal.

For they had found an anomaly, an anomaly that couldn't be easily explained. His hope was that the runestone discovered with the aberration could give at least context to what they had found.

His stomach growled.

"Did I forget to eat?"

Elsa tilted her head toward the microwave. "Yes. Do you want me to reheat what you left in there over an hour ago?"

He chuckled. "Would you?"

She rose, hitting the Express button, the microwave kicking in to excite the molecules constituting his forgotten pasta lunch. "So, what does it say?"

"It's a recipe for penne alfredo."

"Huh?"

The microwave beeped and she pulled his lunch out. She gave him a look, holding up the thin box. "Penne alfredo."

He snickered. "Exactly. The translation worked up an appetite, so…"

"It's a recipe for it. Got it. You know, Professor, you're not exactly funny."

He shrugged, attacking his forgotten pasta, then his thermos filled with a smoothie concoction his wife had prepared this morning in the hopes of helping him eat a little better and get his cholesterol under control.

Cholesterol. I'll die from natural causes before those numbers kill me.

He wiped his mouth clean with a napkin, then tossed the empty box in the garbage can behind him. "I think I'm hysterical, so if you want to get your PhD, you'll best laugh at my jokes."

Elsa regarded him for a moment. "You're an ass."

He grinned. "I am, aren't I? But don't tell my wife. She thinks she's cured me of my youth."

Elsa held a hand up. "I swear, your secret is safe with me." She pointed at his chicken scratches. "So, what does it say?"

He cleared his throat, leaning closer to the pad. "Now, this is very rough, but it appears to be a tombstone of sorts, marking the final resting place of Prince Magnus Hamundarson, and his wife Fatima Halabi."

Elsa's eyes narrowed. "Fatima Halabi?"

He nodded. "Yes. It was a phonetic translation, obviously, and I did make a bit of a logic leap based upon what was found on her."

"I think your leap will be forgiven, Professor. There's little doubt of its origin, and if you're right about her name, little doubt of where she came from."

He had to agree with his student, though he wasn't willing to commit to their interpretation of what they had found just yet. "We'll do DNA testing to confirm their ancestry, but I think we can safely say we have found a member of Viking royalty, along with his wife. His *Muslim* wife."

Elsa leaned back in her chair, shaking her head. "This is unbelievable. I never thought this could be possible. To be honest, until I took your class, I never knew the Vikings had any contact with Islam. I always thought they were in the north, and the Muslims were in the south."

"True for the most part, though our ancestors were known to have sacked cities as far down the Atlantic coast as modern-day Spain, where the Muslims had established their Caliphate. As you know, Muslims ruled much of the Iberian Peninsula until they were finally driven out in 1492.

Before that, our Viking forebears not only invaded, but traded extensively."

Elsa gestured toward the dig outside. "What do you think happened? This Viking prince fell in love on one of these trade missions? Or did he take her as his thrall then force her into marriage?"

Karlsson frowned. "I doubt we'll ever know. We're lucky to have found the runestone to know as much as we do. If it weren't for that, there's no way we'd know they were married, or what their names were. Instead, we'd simply have the burnt remains of him, and hers buried with him, left to wonder what could have possibly put these two completely different individuals together in their final resting places." He stared at the runestone sitting on a nearby work table. "You know who would love this?"

Elsa shrugged. "Who?"

"Jim Acton."

"Who?"

"You don't know who Professor James Acton is?"

She shrugged again. "Should I?"

"Yes, you should. Google him, or whatever it is you kids do, then feel shame for your ignorance."

She stuck her tongue out at him then pulled out her phone, her thumb tapping away. "If I don't know who he is, it's only because you didn't bother to teach me about him."

He smiled at her as he dialed his old friend. "You've got me there." His call was picked up on the third ring.

"Hello?"

He smiled as he recognized Acton's voice, despite it being years since he'd heard it. "Hi, Jim, Viggo Karlsson here."

"Viggo, you old dog, is that you?"

Karlsson's smile broadened. "It is, it is. How are you, my old friend?"

"Excellent. You?"

"Fantastic."

"To what do I owe the pleasure? You sound excited about something."

Karlsson grunted. "Is it that obvious?"

"You sound like you just had another kid." There was a pause. "You didn't, did you?"

Karlsson chuckled. "I'm a little too old to be starting over. But I am excited about something, something I think you'd enjoy seeing."

"What?"

"A ring."

"A ring? As in one ring to rule them all?"

Karlsson paused. "Excuse me?"

"Never mind, just my inner geek being channeled, though you do need to get out more, Viggo."

"My wife keeps saying the same thing."

"So, what's this ring you've found? What's so special about it?"

Karlsson picked it up from the table, holding it up to the light. "I found it on the finger of a woman that was buried alongside a Viking prince almost a thousand years ago."

"Oh? That's not odd. What is it you aren't telling me?"

"You're right, it's not odd, but there's more."

"I knew it."

He smiled at the eagerness he now detected in Acton's voice. "There was a runestone near the grave."

"And being an expert, you translated it."

"I have. Roughly. I'll delve deeper into it now that I have the gist, but I have names."

"Yes?"

"Prince Magnus Hamundarson, and his wife, Fatima Halabi."

There was a burst of static as a quick breath was drawn on the other end of the line. "Fatima? Are you sure?"

"Yes."

"Not exactly a Viking name, now is it?"

"Not at all."

"That's an Arabic name."

"It is."

"Are you suggesting a Viking married an Arab?"

Karlsson smiled. "I am. And I can get even more specific than that."

Acton groaned. "You're killing me, Viggo! Spill it!"

He chuckled. "There was an inscription on the ring."

"What did it say?"

"For Allah."

"I'll be there tomorrow."

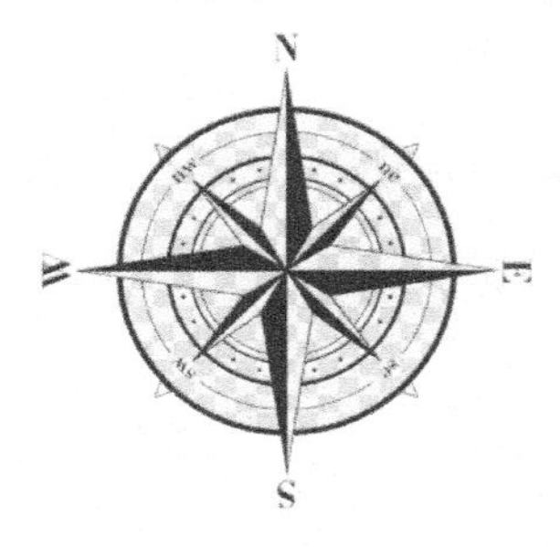

Al Lixbuna, Islamic Iberia

Caliphate of Córdoba

989 AD

Fatima forced a smile. Her family was clearly ecstatic about the upcoming wedding. She was marrying upward, and that could help drag her family slightly higher on the social scale. The dowry she was receiving was satisfactory, though with her position as Sheik Al-Musawi's fourth wife, it wasn't substantial, indicative of how little value her future husband felt she brought to the pairing.

She was certain the same amount could have secured her the position of first wife to a family of equal stature to her own, but as she had learned in her short life, women were commodities to be bartered, and if it weren't for Magnus, she might be happy to play her part in improving her family's station.

But she wasn't, and it was tearing her apart.

She loved her family with all her heart. Her father was a good man, a hardworking man, a man with a respectable business trading goods throughout the Caliphate. She loved her mother and all her siblings, especially her little sister Samira.

Oh, how I would miss you!

She didn't know what Magnus' plan was, but he was powerful among the Vikings. She knew little of them, and the prospect of perhaps spending the rest of her days among them was terrifying, though with Magnus' love, she would adapt, and learn how to fit in with his people.

But the cold!

It was something she couldn't fathom. Magnus had spoken of how cold it was for much of the year, and when she had compared it to the desert night, he had laughed. He had failed miserably at explaining snow to her, something she had only seen at the top of mountains, and never at her feet. It sounded fascinating, and she did look forward to seeing it.

But to be cold for the rest of her life?

"That's what fires are for." He had grinned. "And there are ways to warm each other."

They had made love, Magnus warming her to her core, and she ached for more nights like that, cold or not.

Yet she still feared whether she could fit in with them. They were so different. Their skin was whiter than any she had seen, most had hair so golden, she longed for her own dark hair to someday be as blond.

I wonder if living there will change it.

Where her family was from, everyone had dark hair, dark eyes, dark skin—though not as dark as some she had seen from the African continent. When her father had moved them from their homeland to Iberia where the end of the trade route he used to transport his goods was located, she hadn't been happy about it. Yet once she discovered there was land beyond the desert, she had embraced their new home.

It was incredible here, and she loved it. As the years passed, her memories of home faded, and with it the harshness was forgotten. At times she did wish to see it again. The friends she had left behind, and the extended family, were dearly missed.

She sighed. That would be one advantage of marrying Sheik Al-Musawi. She would be returning closer to home. And though it meant leaving all her family here behind, their elevated position could, perhaps one day, allow them to return and enjoy the fruits of their labor, reunited once again.

And how many years will that be?

But at least she would have the chance.

If her beloved Magnus was correct, and he had a way for them to be together, then it had to mean leaving everything she had ever known and loved behind, and traveling to the frigid lands these strange Vikings called home.

And what would she do there? She knew only a smattering of words, most of which couldn't be repeated in public. Magnus spoke very passable Arabic, facilitating trade between their peoples, but none of the others spoke it, meaning he might be the only one she would have to talk to.

You'll learn.

And she would. After all, she had quickly mastered the local tongue upon their arrival here, so Norse would merely be a matter of time.

Are you really considering this?

She stared out the window she sat in front of, the sunbaked city she had called home most of her life spread out before her, the ocean in the distance a sparkling blue, a storm on the horizon. Could she leave all this? She glanced over at her family, entertaining her future husband who had paid little attention to her beyond the obligatory greeting. Could she leave all of them?

Her shoulders rolled inward and shook.

Keep it together, otherwise the others will ask questions.

She drew a deep breath, forcing her shoulders back. She stared across the room, her family and friends of her parents gathered, smiles and laughter punctuating the telling of stories and exploits, her future husband the guest of honor and center of attention. He was decades her senior. Far more than the twenty years she had been told, and she wondered if her father had been as surprised as she was. Their greetings suggested they had never met each other, and the very idea her father would marry her off to a complete stranger had hurt her.

She regarded the man, a frown creasing her face as she did so. His skin was mottled with scars and pockmarks, and his teeth were black and rotting. His clothes were as fine as any she had ever seen, and he was undoubtedly wealthy, yet he appeared a pig of a man, and she couldn't picture ever giving herself to him.

Not willingly.

Not as she had with Magnus.

She tingled with the memory.

It had been forbidden, dangerous, and because of it, all the more thrilling. She had given her virgin self to him willingly, and he had shown her how wonderful the act of love could be between those who truly had feelings for each other.

She shuddered as she wondered how the sheik would react when he discovered she wasn't a virgin on their wedding night.

He'll kill you.

She had heard of childhood accidents, and a myriad of possibilities played out in her head as she tried to settle on one that was believable, though none seemed plausible. Could it be that those stories she had heard were all lies to cover up the truth?

She wondered what her mother would say if she were to tell her. Would she tell her father, risking the death of her daughter for dishonoring the family, or would she come up with a tale to tell should the discovery be made, a tale she would back.

None of that would matter if you left with Magnus.

This was true, though she didn't want to leave to escape her problems. She wanted to leave because she loved the man she was leaving with, and wanted to spend the rest of her life with him, to have his babies, to raise those children to be adults, to be Vikings.

She frowned.

I wonder what color their hair will be.

She paused with a troubling thought.

Would her new Viking family accept their children if they were different?

Her eyes burned and she quickly turned her head back to the window, nearly gasping at what she saw. A man, his hair a bright blond, crouched directly under the window. He held up his hand, a piece of folded paper grasped between his thumb and forefinger. She glanced back at the room, everyone laughing at something said by her future husband, and was thankful that even on this day that was supposed to be so special in her life, nobody here paid any attention to the young woman sitting alone by the window.

Her hand darted out and she took the piece of paper, quickly tucking it against her side. She checked again to see if she had been noticed, still finding herself ignored. She unfolded the paper and trembled at the words written by her love.

Leave with him now! Bring nothing!

Acton/Palmer Residence

St. Paul, Maryland

Present Day

"What has you so excited?"

Archaeology Professor James Acton rushed past his wife, Archaeology Professor Laura Palmer. "We're going to Stockholm."

Her eyebrows shot up. "Sweden?"

"Unless they moved it."

Her eyes narrowed. "What's in Sweden?"

Acton shrugged as he pulled his suitcase from the closet. "Delicious meatballs and beautiful blondes?"

She grunted. "You better be focusing on the meatballs, mister."

He flashed her a toothy smile. "I'll be focusing on the ring that Viggo just discovered adorning the finger of a woman named Fatima, *wife* of Viking Prince Magnus, buried with honors—a runestone marking the site—and with an inscription on the ring."

Laura rose from her perch in the corner, putting down her eReader, now giving him her full attention. "What did it say?"

"One ring to rule them all—"

"I'm going to boot you in the Swedish meatballs if you don't tell me."

He angled his boys away from her on instinct. "For Allah."

Her eyes shot wide. "Bloody hell! She was Muslim?"

"Yes! At least it appears so. I assume they'll do DNA testing to at least see where she was originally descended from."

Laura fetched her own suitcase then paused. "Wait. That doesn't make sense. Muslims don't wear wedding bands."

Acton nodded. "Right, but they do wear engagement rings."

"So, this was an engagement ring."

Acton shrugged. "I assume so."

"Then what is a Viking doing giving his bride-to-be an *Islamic* engagement ring?"

Acton stood straight, his head cocked to the side as he thought for a moment. "Huh. Good question. And I'm sure we'll come up with dozens more by the time we get there."

Laura resumed packing. "It was nice of him to invite you. When was the last time you saw him?"

Acton removed a pair of shorts he had tossed in the suitcase, remembering where it was he was going, and what time of year it was. "Five years? Maybe six? It was his twenty-fifth wedding anniversary, so whenever that was."

Laura zipped up her suitcase. "I win." She winked at him then sat on the bed and grabbed her phone from the nightstand. "I'll arrange a plane.

You should tell Greg that we're leaving town. You have a class to teach on Tuesday."

Acton shook his head. "We'll just pop over, spend a few days, then head back. I'm just curious to see the site and what they've found. If we end up staying longer, I'll let Greg know."

She shrugged. "Suit yourself." She held up a finger, her call to their travel agent answered, a private plane quickly arranged through their lease-share network. Acton was a poor professor, but Laura, though a professor as well, was anything but. Her late brother had made a fortune selling his Internet business shortly before his death, and had left everything to her.

She was worth more than he could fathom, though one would never know it to see her. She, like him, lived a modest lifestyle, using her—their—money to make travel more comfortable and frequent than the average person could afford, funding their own archaeological dig sites when necessary, helping friends in need, and desperate though deserving students. They lived in his humble home bought before they met, and she still had her flat in London for when they were in England.

There were no yachts, no estates, and no gold cutlery in the kitchen drawers.

Life was simple, though with none of the restrictions most faced. Life was good, though if they were dirt poor, it still would be so long as she was at his side.

Laura put the phone down. "Everything's arranged. We can still have dinner with Tommy and Mai tonight, then catch our plane and be there in the morning, local time. We'll spend two days rewriting history, then be back before anyone knows we were gone."

Acton frowned. "We need more friends."

Laura pshawed. "I'd rather have the few *good* friends we have, than dozens of shallow acquaintances."

Acton chewed his cheek. "I suppose." His eyes widened. "Maybe on our way back we can pop in and see Hugh."

Laura smiled at the prospect of seeing their old friend, Hugh Reading, a former Scotland Yard Detective Chief Inspector who had tried to arrest them when they first met. Now an Interpol Agent based in London, he had become a dear friend over the years. "That's a wonderful idea. But we'll definitely be late, then."

Acton sighed. "Stupid job, always getting in the way."

Laura laughed. "You can always quit. It's not like we need the money."

He eyed her. "I'll quit the day you quit."

She lay down on the bed, propping her head up with an elbow. "You're right. We'd both be miserable without our careers."

"I think I could live without the career, but I could never give up my students."

Laura sighed, and Acton knew why. She had given up a lot to move to Maryland and live with him after they got married. She still occasionally taught at her old school in London, though only as a guest lecturer, and her new position at the Smithsonian hardly filled the void, her time with students limited. There was nothing like standing at the front of a classroom with kids that were empty vessels to fill with knowledge.

He smiled at her as he zipped up his suitcase. "Regrets?"

She chuckled. "I've had a few?"

He hopped on the bed, scooching over to be closer. "How about we remind each other why being separated by thousands of miles was interfering with our sex life."

She pushed him onto his back and rolled on top of him. "You've got two hours to remind me, then we have to start dinner."

Acton's eyes widened. "Two hours? I'm an old man, remember."

She leaned closer. "I'm not." She kissed him, and he opened his mouth slightly, his heart already hammering with excitement.

Thank God for that!

Al Lixbuna, Islamic Iberia

Caliphate of Córdoba

989 AD

Fatima tucked the note from Magnus up her sleeve then rose. Her mother took notice, for the first time in hours, Fatima was certain, and beckoned her over.

She obeyed.

"What are you doing sitting over there? You should be with us. This is an important day."

"Yes, Mother." She gripped two of her fingers with her other hand, staring at the floor. "I'm not feeling well."

Her mother rose, the back of her hand immediately on Fatima's forehead. "What's wrong? Are you sick?"

Fatima shook her head. "I'm just overwhelmed with everything." She searched for the right words, her mother still feeling her face. "With the joy of it all. I hope you understand."

Her mother beamed a smile at her, Fatima's reasoning behind her sudden illness apparently an acceptable one. "I understand. I was overwhelmed myself on this day." She patted her hand. "Go lie down, then return when you feel better. The festivities will continue all day."

Fatima gave her mother a weak smile, and the thought of leaving her grew all the more painful at the love she had just been shown. Her mother truly did love her, and obviously felt this was a good match for her. And perhaps she was right. The sheik was so old, he might not live much longer, and she could find herself a widow in short order. Perhaps another man, a better man, would take over responsibility for her, and she could enjoy the remainder of her days, with her family still in her life.

She genuinely didn't feel well now.

She dragged herself to her room, closing the door behind her, sitting in the chair by the window, her heart heavy with what she was about to do—leave everything she had ever known and ever loved, for an uncertain future in a strange land with even stranger people.

She closed her eyes and imagined Magnus, his smile warming her heart, their bodies intertwined in passion.

Then she pictured tomorrow's husband mounting her, kissing her with his rotting mouth.

Bile threatened to overwhelm her.

You have no choice.

Yet she did. There was only one correct choice. She had to stay for the sake of her family. She had no choice in the matter. Her happiness didn't enter the equation.

Yet what was it that Magnus had said?

"A way for us to be together for the rest of our lives, and for your family to never know."

She hadn't an inkling of what he had planned, but she did trust him, and if her family would never know, then what harm would there be? If they didn't know she was with Magnus, then there should be no dishonor, no betrayal.

No broken marriage.

Yet what could his plan possibly be that would mean their happiness along with her family's honor preserved?

She had no idea, but she had to find out. She rose, staring at the room that had been hers for most of her life, then made for the door. She paused, staring at the tiny figurine of a horse sitting next to her bed, a gift from her little sister last year, Magnus' words echoing in her head.

"Take nothing."

But she had to have something to remember her sister by, the precious girl innocent in all this, her mind so simple she'd never understand why her big sister had left her.

She grabbed it, sticking it in her pocket before cautiously opening the door. The hallway was clear, and she stepped out of her room, closing the door gently.

Somebody tugged at her arm. "Where are you going?"

She nearly soiled herself at the tiny voice behind her.

It was Samira.

She gathered herself then turned to face her little sister. "I'm going to get some fresh air."

"Can I come with you?"

Fatima so wished she could. She shook her head. "No. Go back to the party. I'll be there in a little bit."

Samira hugged her legs then smiled up at her. "I'm so happy for you. I can't wait until I get married."

Fatima's heart broke, and she questioned everything she was doing, every selfish thought she had been dominated by these past two days.

You can still change your mind.

She patted Samira on the top of her head. "Go join the party."

"Okay." Samira let go of her grip and began a little dance.

Fatima hurried for the rear entrance before she lost complete control. She stole one last look at her sister, then nearly cried out in horror as the precious creature bent over and picked up a piece of paper from the floor.

The paper with her terse instructions from Magnus.

The paper that must have slipped from her sleeve when Samira tugged on it.

She opened her mouth to call to her, but it was too late.

She had already skipped around the corner, back toward the party.

Oh no! What do I do?

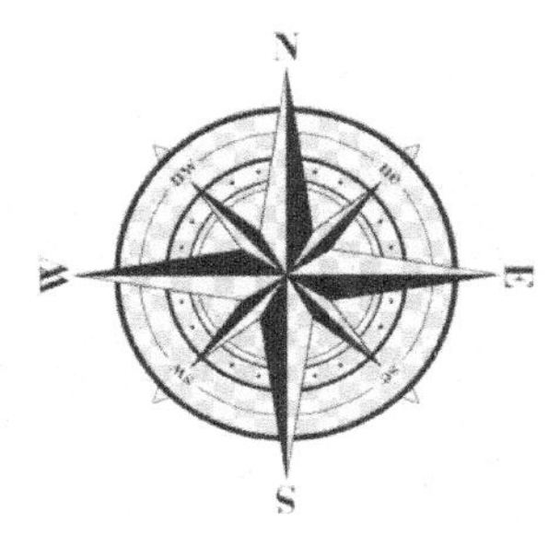

Karlsson Residence

Stockholm, Sweden

Present Day

Viggo Karlsson sat in his Stressless Voyager recliner, his feet up, his eyes half closed as two fingers of Good ol' Sailor Vodka rested on the left arm, the remote control for the TV on his right. He was exhausted but content. It had been a good day, and his friend was arriving tomorrow morning. It was a reunion he was looking forward to.

"Why don't you go to bed?"

His head lolled to the side and he smiled at his wife, Mira. "Trying to get rid of me?"

She grunted. "You've been gone most of the evening."

He returned the chair to an upright position. "I'm sorry, dear, but it was a big day at the dig."

"It always is."

He regarded her. "Do I detect a hint of frustration?"

She looked up from her book. "You detect a hint of something, that's for sure."

His eyes narrowed and he put his drink on the end table, leaning closer to her. "What is it? What's wrong?"

She huffed, shoving her bookmark into the pages and snapping the book shut. "I'm old."

He stared at her blankly. "Huh?"

"I realize I don't look like I used to when we first met, and men have needs, and maybe I just don't interest you anymore."

His eyes widened. "Huh?" He could think of nothing else to say.

"I realize why you'd want to spend as much time with her as possible. I mean, she's gorgeous. Far more so than I ever was. I could even understand it if you were to have an affair with her. After all, you're a man. Why, I think—"

He held up a hand, cutting her off. "Are you talking about Elsa?"

She stared at him. "Of course I am. Why, is there another?"

He laughed, rising from his chair and taking a knee in front of her. He took her hands in his and held them to his chest, but not before giving them a kiss. "You silly, *not* old woman. Elsa is beautiful, yes, but she's a kid. I'm over twice her age."

She scowled at him. "I should say closer to thrice."

He laughed. "Exactly! I have no eyes for anyone but you, my dear, and never doubt that. I don't spend time with *Elsa*, I spend time at my dig site with my *students*. It just happens that my most senior student is Elsa. Next year it could be some handsome gentleman that might catch *your* fancy."

She smiled slightly. "Now *that* sounds promising."

He chuckled, gripping her hands tightly. "So, you're okay? *We're* okay?"

"I'm sorry. I guess I'm just feeling sorry for myself." She sighed. "I should never have retired early."

"Yes, you should have. You just shouldn't have stopped working on your book. When was the last time you wrote anything?"

She shrugged. "Months, I guess." She groaned, leaning her head back. "I'm going crazy in this house. I need to do something."

"Then I suggest you start writing again. You were always happy behind the keyboard."

She sighed, then nodded. "You're right. I think I will. There's a lot I'd like to share before I meet my maker, and I'm not getting any younger."

He smiled then rose, groaning from the aches and pains that had rapidly formed just by taking a knee.

"Are you okay?"

He grunted. "*I'm* the one who's getting old. I *am* ten months older than you."

She laughed. "You did like them young, Professor."

He shook his head, returning to his chair, then realized he had forgotten to mention the big news of the day. "Speaking of young professors, I forgot to mention that Jim Acton is arriving tomorrow morning to tour the site. He's bringing his new wife, Laura Palmer."

She brightened at the news. "That's wonderful! Will I get a chance to see them?"

His tension eased at her improved mood. "Of course. They'll be here for two nights. We'll have dinner with them, I'm sure, at least one of those nights, if not both. I know he'd love to see you."

She sighed. "It's been a while." She held up her aging hands. "I look so old!"

He wagged a finger at her. "Don't you start again!"

She frowned. "Fine, you're right."

The phone rang and he glanced at the call display, not recognizing the number. He answered. "Hello?"

"Hello, Professor Karlsson, my name is Abdullah Al-Jubeir. I am the Chargé D'affaires at the Saudi Arabian Embassy in Stockholm. I apologize for the late hour, but I would like to arrange a meeting with you at your earliest convenience."

His eyes widened slightly. "I'm not sure what for. What could we possibly have to discuss?"

"I think you'll find we have much to discuss. Your recent find, for one thing."

Karlsson tensed and his stomach churned. "H-how do you know about that?"

"One of your students blogged about it and one of our staff noticed."

"But we only just found it." His eyes narrowed. "And why is your staff monitoring my students?"

The man laughed. "Oh, it's nothing so nefarious, I assure you. We use Google Alerts for anything that might be of interest to the Kingdom. The discovery of an Islamic artifact in Sweden certainly does qualify, don't you think? At least from an intellectual standpoint?"

Karlsson pursed his lips. "I suppose so. Again, I fail to see what we have to discuss."

"The Ambassador is eager to meet with you, and congratulate you on your discovery. It shows how our two cultures have been linked for over a millennium, and in these troubled times, I think anything that can peacefully link our two societies is something to be celebrated, and not hidden away, don't you agree?"

Karlsson wasn't certain he did. "I suppose so."

"Wonderful! Could you come tomorrow morning, nine o'clock?"

Karlsson frowned. "Yes, I suppose so."

"Excellent. The Ambassador will be so pleased. Have a good evening, Professor."

The call ended and he hung up the phone, staring at it for several moments.

"Who was that?"

He flinched then looked at his wife. "The Saudi Embassy."

Her mouth opened slightly. "What did *they* want?"

"*They* want to meet."

She paled slightly. "Meet? About what?"

"About our discovery. The ring, I guess."

She shook her head vehemently. "Absolutely not! You can't meet with those people. They're barbarians!"

He frowned. "Now, now, we shouldn't say things like that."

"But it's true! You know what they did to that poor man in Turkey. He went inside their embassy and he never came out." She held up a finger. "Correction. He *did* come out. In pieces!"

He sighed. She was right. These were not people who could be trusted. But he was an academic, not an activist journalist. A Swedish citizen, born and raised, not a Saudi citizen. This was Sweden, not Turkey. He had never criticized the Saudi regime. There was no reason for them to do anything to him. "I'm sure I have nothing to worry about."

"Are you willing to take that risk?"

He frowned, another more likely outcome occurring to him. "I'm not sure it's wise to upset these people."

"Why? Because they could hurt you? Kill you?"

He smiled slightly. "No, nothing so harsh. But they *do* control a lot of money, and wield a lot of power. Upsetting them by not showing up, might get me blackballed somehow. Do you realize how many foreign students we have at the university? How much they pay for their tuition? It helps fund so many of our programs, it might be the University President that I have to fear." He shook his head. "No, I have to go. And besides, there's nothing to worry about. I'll go, see what they have to say, then meet Jim and Laura at the airport." He smiled. "I'll use them as my excuse to leave."

His wife stared at him as if he had grown a second head. "I still think you're a fool."

"But you love me anyway."

She grunted. "I suppose." She jabbed a finger at the air between them. "Just don't go getting yourself killed on me. I'm bored enough as it is!"

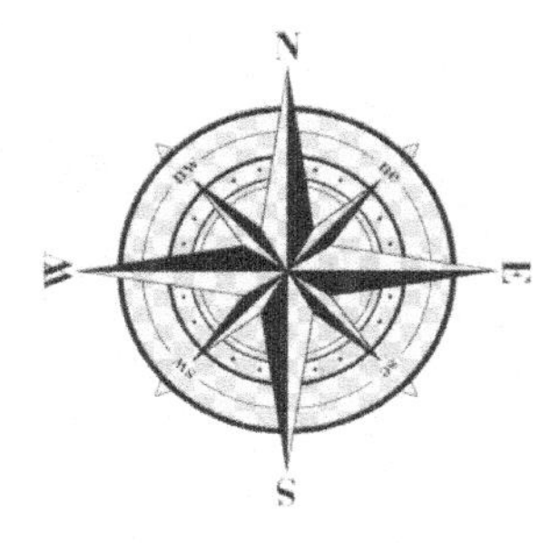

Al Lixbuna, Islamic Iberia

Caliphate of Córdoba

989 AD

Rafiq Halabi laughed at another story from his future brother-in-law, a story he had little doubt was a complete fabrication. Yet it was his duty to be the good host, his duty as the eldest son to support his father in any decision he made.

Even if it meant losing his sister to this decrepit, disgusting man.

He was a boor, yet the difference he could make in all their lives was tremendous, and undeniable. His wealth far exceeded theirs, and if everything went according to plan, Rafiq stood to gain the most, for as the eldest, he would inherit everything when his father finally passed. It wasn't that he wanted to hasten that occurrence. Not at all. He loved his father, and was content to be second to him in all things. And with this masterful arrangement, their family was about to become much more important than they currently were. Though respected business people, they had little status.

But all that was about to change, thanks to his father's cunning ability to recognize an opportunity, and his sister's breathtaking beauty—beauty enough to tempt an old sheik into taking on another wife after one of his had died.

His eyes scanned the room for Fatima, narrowing at not spotting her. Samira skipped into the room, a smile on her face. He beckoned her over. "Where's your sister?"

"She went to get fresh air."

She skipped away, circling the room as only one so young could be forgiven for. He rose, excusing himself, then headed for the courtyard. Fatima was nowhere to be found, and his concern grew, though he wasn't sure why. He strode over to the front gate, two guards snapping to attention.

"Did you see my sister?"

One of the men pointed down the street to their left. "She went that way just a few minutes ago."

Rafiq's eyes narrowed as he peered down the street, not spotting her. It was not only out of character for her to go off, it was forbidden. If she wanted to leave the house, she needed to be escorted by a male relation. That was usually him, as their father was too busy, or one of several "cousins" hired to make life more accommodating.

"She left unescorted?"

The guard hesitated. "Yes."

Rafiq drew an angry breath. "And you let her?"

The man shook his head, taking a step back. "No, she said her cousin was meeting her. She pointed at him."

"And you saw him?"

The man trembled, his eyes darting about, focusing anywhere but on his interrogator. "I, umm, saw a man, but…"

"But what?"

"She, umm, walked past him and met another man."

Rage surged through his body at the very notion of his sister meeting a man who wasn't a relation. "Who?"

The guard shrugged. "I don't know, but he had blond hair. He must be one of those Vikings."

Rafiq was taken aback. Why would a Viking meet with his sister? And more importantly, why would his sister meet with a Viking. None of it made any sense. His father had been conducting business with the Vikings for years, and for almost a month with Prince Magnus. Magnus had even been to their home on multiple occasions as a guest, and though he had addressed his sister directly several times, Rafiq had dismissed the impropriety as a cultural difference, and not worthy of threatening a lucrative business relationship.

But none of that explained why Fatima would meet with one of Magnus' people, or Magnus himself.

Little girls can be foolish.

He trusted Fatima, yet she had seemed fascinated with the novel Viking. Could he be taking advantage of the trust his family had placed in him? Could he be taking advantage of his naïve sister?

"That can't be permitted!" he hissed, sprinting in the direction his sister had headed, the possibility of losing everything they were working toward in the house behind him terrifying.

All because of some silly, naïve little girl.

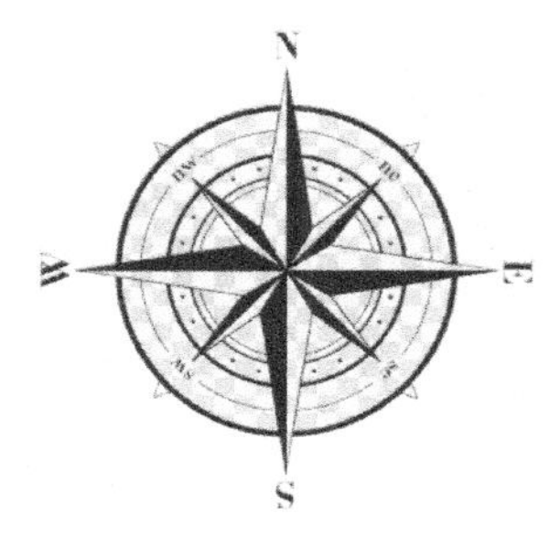

Stockholm Bromma Airport

Stockholm, Sweden

Present Day

Acton frowned as he stepped down from their private jet and onto the tarmac. He had expected Karlsson to meet them when they arrived, though he was an old man and it was a chilly day. He turned to Laura.

"He must be inside where it's warm."

She shivered. "Then he sounds far smarter than us."

He chuckled as they scurried toward the terminal reserved for private charters, groaning with pleasure at the warmth that greeted them inside.

And still, there was no sign of Karlsson.

Acton checked his phone for messages, finding none from Karlsson or any of his people, Laura doing the same. A quick check at the counter found no messages left for them.

"Could he have got confused and thought we were meeting at the hotel?"

Acton shrugged. "I can't see how there could be any misunderstanding, but perhaps. He was always *very* academic, if you know what I mean. How about we go there then try to find him. It'll be a lot more comfortable than waiting around here."

Laura agreed, and a rental vehicle was quickly arranged, their arrival at the hotel swift and efficient, the Nobis Hotel the finest of establishments. And again, they found no Karlsson, and no messages.

"I'm getting a little concerned." Acton brought up the website for Stockholm University, and after a few transfers, was speaking with one of Karlsson's grad students at the dig site, Elsa Andersson.

"I'm sorry, Professor Acton, we haven't seen him all morning. Wasn't he supposed to meet you?"

"He was, but he didn't."

"That's odd. I'll try texting him, though I'm sure you already have."

"We have, many times. Do you have his home number? I'd like to call his wife."

"Yes, absolutely." She provided the number and he jotted it down on a piece of hotel stationery. "I'll let you know if I hear from him."

"Thank you." Acton immediately dialed Karlsson's wife. "Hello, Mira. This is Jim Acton. How are you?"

"Oh, hi Jim, I wasn't expecting to hear from you. Viggo said we'd be doing dinner tonight. Did that old fool mess up our plans again?"

Acton chuckled, feeling slightly better at the revelation that his old friend might simply be confused instead of missing. "Well, he must have gotten really mixed up, because he forgot to meet us at the airport, and we can't reach him."

There was a pause. "Oh…"

He sensed something in her tone that had him concerned. "What is it?"

"Viggo received a phone call last night."

Acton's eyes narrowed. "From whom?"

"From the Saudi Embassy."

His eyebrows shot up. "What did they want?"

"The Ambassador wanted to meet him. This morning at nine o'clock." He heard a quick intake of breath. "You don't think…"

Acton was terrified to voice what he was thinking. "I'm sure I don't. He probably got sidetracked with something and lost track of time. Don't worry. We'll try to track him down, and if you hear from him, tell him to call."

"I will, Jim. I'm so sorry about this."

"No need to apologize. I'm sure it's completely innocent. I'll talk to you soon."

He ended the call and briefly recapped the conversation for Laura.

"What do we do?"

Acton sighed, shaking his head. "Given the Saudis' recent history, I think we have to assume the worst."

"Surely they wouldn't repeat such a stupid thing?"

Acton grunted. "Were there really any consequences?"

She frowned. "I suppose not. So, what do we do? Report it?"

Acton tapped his chin, slowly shaking his head. "No, that could take hours. Law enforcement probably would just hang up, telling us to wait forty-eight hours." He pursed his lips then smiled slightly as an idea occurred to him. Then he frowned at the idiocy of it.

"I know that look. What are you thinking?"

He blasted his frustration through his lips. "Well, I was thinking there's still a chance to save him, if he's still alive."

"How?"

"By letting them know we know they have him."

Laura's eyes widened. "And just how are we going to do that?"

"I'm going to go inside."

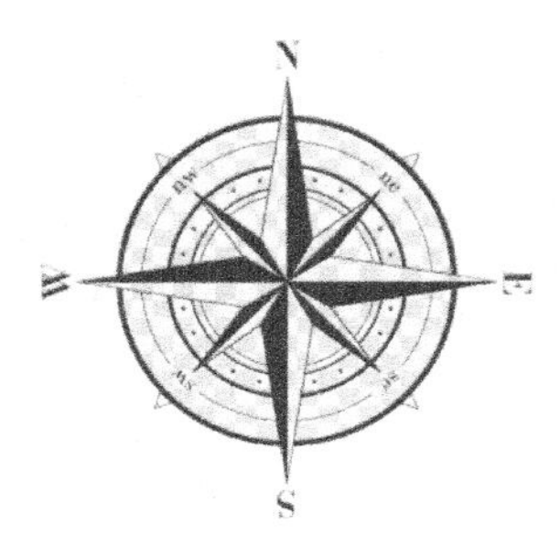

Al Lixbuna, Islamic Iberia

Caliphate of Córdoba

989 AD

Fatima kept her face down and turned her head strategically to avoid the eyes of those who might challenge her being in the streets with the Viking, though none who took notice appeared willing to confront the muscled man with brilliant beard. Yet despite this, with each step away from her certain past and toward an uncertain future, her heart hammered harder.

And she grew faint.

What are you doing?

It wasn't too late. She could turn around and run home. Nobody knew she was gone except the guards, and if she returned before no one else noticed, they would say nothing, for they should never have let her go alone.

Their punishment would be worse than hers.

Magnus' messenger kept urging her forward with a beckoning hand, but rarely looked back at her, perhaps uncomfortable being with an unrelated woman.

But that's not his culture.

It was one of the reasons she had been so intrigued by these Vikings. The fact they treated her far better than her own relations, suggested to her, perhaps incorrectly, that women were partners rather than property where they came from. She prayed it was so, but in all honesty, wasn't concerned with such things, as long as she could be with Magnus.

She spotted him near the edge of the cliff overlooking the roaring ocean below and her heart leaped, energy surging through her, spurring her reluctant legs forward and past the messenger. As she neared him, though, she slowed. His face was stern, his eyes glaring at her, none of the love she had come to expect in view. He stepped behind a large stone and out of sight. She slowed to a walk then cautiously rounded the rock, uncertain as to what had changed, only knowing that her stomach was now in knots, and self-doubt ruled her.

"Magnus?"

He turned to face her, his smile broad, his eyes bright, and she sighed with relief as he held out his arms for her. She rushed into them and they embraced if only for a moment. He pushed her away, holding her shoulders.

"We have little time. Do you still trust me?"

"Of course, my love."

He bent over and picked up something lying unnoticed on the ground. "Then listen carefully."

Rafiq came to a halt at the edge of town, the ocean ahead, the waves crashing against the cliff face a constant reminder of its strength. He loved the water, and swam in it whenever he had an opportunity, and never turned down an invitation to go to sea if his duties permitted it.

Yet those opportunities were rare, and would be even more so if he didn't find his sister.

A sister nowhere to be seen.

He scanned the entire area, not for her, but for the striking blond hair of her Viking companion, yet saw no one. He turned his attention to the dozens walking in the area, some moving with purpose, some strolling with no obvious cares.

Then he heard shouting.

"We can never be together!"

He turned toward the argument, the accented Arabic recognized at once as that of Prince Magnus. He stormed out from behind a large rock, then spun on his heel, stabbing a finger at someone.

"That was never my intention, you silly girl! We can never be! It would dishonor not only your family, but mine as well, and I would never risk my people's business for a woman."

"But Magnus, please, don't go!"

His stomach writhed with anger and horror at his sister's voice, the foolish girl hidden by the rock. He wanted to go to her, to grab her by the scruff of the neck and haul her home for the shame she was bringing to her family, but he resisted. Nobody could see her. Nobody knew who she was. If he were lucky, this entire incident might play out with no one the wiser, and his family honor might yet be preserved.

"I'm done with you, silly girl. Make *no* attempt to contact me again!" Magnus stormed off toward the port to the north where his trading fleet was moored, and Rafiq took several tentative steps toward his sister's hiding place, each passing moment suggesting her dishonorable actions might yet go undiscovered, those witness to the altercation already resuming their business.

"If you will not have me, then no one will!"

He gasped as his sister stepped into view, everyone turning toward her once again, this time the source of the other half of the conversation in full view. Rage flared in his chest at her stupidity, at her betrayal, at her naïve selfishness.

Then she stepped off the cliff, her scream bloodcurdling as it quickly faded.

"Fatima!" He stood frozen in place, unable to move, exchanging shocked glances with those around him. He finally tore loose from whatever held his feet in place and stumbled toward the edge of the cliff. As he neared its treacherous edge, he slowed, his fear of heights threatening to overwhelm him. He came to an abrupt halt a good half-dozen paces from the edge, then willed himself closer as others approached, their concerned utterances going unnoticed. He dropped to his knees, crawling to the drop-off, his heart hammering, sweat beading on his forehead as he finally screwed up the courage to peer over at the churning waters below.

But there was nothing to see beyond water and rock and a post jutting from the edge with a ring at the end, its purpose unknown, its rusted surface suggesting many years since its installation.

There could be no doubt.

She was gone.

He rolled onto his back, tears streaking his face as he stared up at the heavens. "Fatima, what have you done!"

"Look!"

Someone nearby was pointing out to sea, and he rolled back on his stomach, hope surging anew at the prospect of his sister being alive in the waters below, though it quickly faded at the sight of what had attracted the onlooker's attention.

A lone Viking ship, heading away from the cliff, its sail raised and filled with the wind.

For a moment, he thought of calling to them, to beckon them back to search for his sister below, but it would be a useless effort. They would never hear him, and they could never get close enough to the cliff face to rescue her regardless.

She was dead, her lifeless body likely hammering against the rock below, unseen, her soul already condemned to eternal damnation for throwing away Allah's most precious gift.

Life.

Why did you do it, Fatima, why?

Yet he knew why. She couldn't face life with Sheik Al-Musawi, away from her family, relegated to the position of fourth wife. Before hearing the argument of moments ago, he never would have considered the concept of love in the equation. What did love have to do with marriage? At least at the beginning. Even his own parents came from an arranged marriage. They loved each other now, of that, he had no doubt, but he was certain there was no love there when they first met. How could there be?

And his sister had met few men in her brief life to even entertain the concept of marriage, let alone marriage based on love. She always knew her destiny, though he was certain she did have her own misguided fantasies of what her future husband might be like, and those imaginings certainly never would have included the pig of a man Al-Musawi was.

He did feel bad for her.

Genuinely.

Though none of that was an excuse to commit suicide, and publicly humiliate the family in the process.

He pushed to his feet and slowly edged away from the cliff, the Viking ship silhouetted in the distance, then headed for home, wondering what he could possibly do to save his family from the fury his news would undoubtedly bring from her future husband.

A man so powerful, he could crush their family with a casual word.

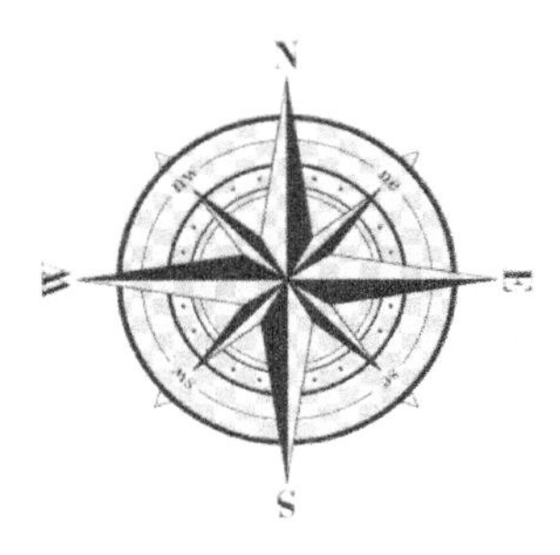

Embassy of Saudi Arabia

Stockholm, Sweden

Present Day

Acton stepped through the doors directly facing the street of the Saudi Arabian Embassy, his phone gripped in his hand for all to see, a call connected to Laura who was nearby in their rental, the doors locked, the engine idling. With her driving skills, he had little doubt she could reach the police station that wasn't far from her location before anyone could stop her.

A smartly dressed young man with a cleanly shaved face smiled at him from behind an ornate desk. "Good morning, sir, how may I help you?"

"My name is Professor James Acton. I need to speak with the Ambassador."

The man's eyes flared momentarily. "Do you have an appointment?"

Acton shook his head. "No, but my friend, Professor Viggo Karlsson did, at nine o'clock this morning. I'd like to meet with him to discuss his whereabouts."

The man's knuckles whitened as his fists clenched atop the desk for a moment. "I'm afraid the Ambassador is a very busy man, and all of his appointments are arranged through his Chargé D'affaires, Mr. Al-Jubeir."

"Then I'd like to see him."

"I'm afraid Mr. Al-Jubeir is a very busy man as well, and isn't available."

"Well, this is very perplexing. My friend hasn't been seen since he entered here, and if he were meeting with the Ambassador, then that would suggest they are still meeting. If I could see my friend, then that would be sufficient."

The man was clearly flummoxed, uncertain of what to do. "Ahh, I'm afraid you're mistaken. The Ambassador left for business in the Kingdom earlier."

"Then I'll meet with Mr. Al-Jubeir."

"I'm afraid he accompanied him."

"Then that means any meeting with my friend has concluded, yet no one has seen him since. Where is he?"

"I'm not sure, though I'm certain he isn't on the premises." He pointed at a sign-in book. "According to this, he's already left."

Acton stepped closer. "May I?"

The man closed the book. "I'm afraid I can't permit that."

"Why not? Anyone signing in can see the names listed."

"Only those who have legitimate business with the Kingdom. You do not."

"So, you're refusing to confirm—"

"Is there a problem here?"

The man leaped to his feet, bowing his head, but Acton cut off any reply.

"Yes. I'm looking for Professor Karlsson."

The man's eyebrows shot up, as if he recognized the name. "Yes, of course. I spoke to him last night." He extended his hand. "I'm Abdullah Al-Jubeir, the Ambassador's Chargé D'affaires."

Acton smiled slightly at the receptionist, who quickly looked away, having been caught in a lie. "Interesting, I was led to believe you had just left for Saudi Arabia with the Ambassador."

Al-Jubeir glanced at his underling, though didn't miss a beat. "Change of plans. I was needed here." He clasped his hands behind his back. "How may I help you?"

"I'm looking for my friend, Professor Karlsson."

The man's eyes narrowed as he tilted his head slightly. "Why would you be looking for him here?"

"Because you had a meeting with him, and he hasn't been seen since."

Al-Jubeir frowned. "The Ambassador and I met with him as scheduled at nine this morning, had a pleasant discussion, then he left about half an hour later."

Acton regarded the man. He was smooth. Very smooth.

Too smooth.

"If that's the case, then why has no one been able to reach him since?"

Al-Jubeir shrugged. "I have no idea. I'm sure there is some innocent explanation, however."

Acton motioned toward a nearby security camera. "I'm sure you have footage of him leaving, and perhaps even footage outside. It might help us track him down."

"Us?"

"His wife is concerned."

Al-Jubeir paused, eying him for a moment. "Forgive me, but I didn't get your name."

"It's immaterial."

"Professor James Acton."

Acton silently damned the receptionist's exceptional memory.

Al-Jubeir extended an arm toward the bowels of the embassy. "Perhaps we should discuss this matter somewhere more private, Professor."

Acton tensed, though attempted to remain calm on the exterior. "I don't think so. I'll be leaving now."

Al-Jubeir held up a finger. "Professor, I think we really should continue our conversation."

Acton held up his phone. "Say 'hello,' dear."

Laura's voice replied through the speaker. "Hello."

"Are you still recording everything?"

"I am, and it's all been streamed to the cloud, just in case."

Al-Jubeir turned slightly red, glaring at the phone. "And what is the meaning of this?"

"A little insurance, if you will. Your country doesn't exactly have a good track record of letting people leave, now does it?"

Al-Jubeir's nostrils flared and his fists clenched. Acton decided it was best to beat a hasty retreat.

"I'll be leaving now. If I'm not on the street in two minutes, call the police."

Laura's reply was immediate. "I will. Two minutes, starting now."

Acton headed for the exit, finding it blocked by two men in suits that hadn't been there when he arrived. They ignored him, instead staring at Al-Jubeir. Acton turned back to face the man.

"Questions are already being asked about Professor Karlsson. He's not well known. With *my* connections, and the fact I'm an American citizen, born and bred, you'll find my not showing up on the street in ninety seconds will prove most unfortunate for you."

Al-Jubeir flicked his wrist and the doors were opened. Acton bowed his head.

"Thank you." He turned and walked with purpose toward the doors, desperately controlling his urge to run. He held his breath as he approached the exit, the street and Swedish territory directly outside the door. He slowly exhaled as his feet cleared the threshold, saying a silent prayer of thanks. He held his phone to his lips. "I'm out."

"On my way."

Acton headed left, toward where Laura would be coming from, his heart hammering as he spotted their rental round the corner. She came to a halt and he yanked open the passenger side door, hopping in. Laura hammered on the accelerator, slamming him into the back of his seat as he reached for his seatbelt. He took one last look at the embassy and shuddered as he spotted Al-Jubeir standing on the sidewalk, staring at him, a phone to his ear.

That can't be good.

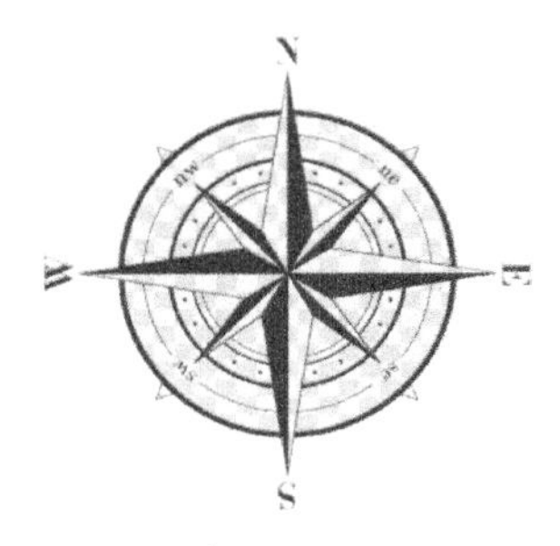

Al Lixbuna, Islamic Iberia

Caliphate of Córdoba

989 AD

Fatima screamed at the top of her lungs as she slid down the rope toward the boat floating below. As she picked up speed, nearing the deck of the Viking ship bobbing in the waters, she spotted the men on the deck below gripping what appeared to be a second rope. She followed it with her eyes and noticed it above her head, just out of reach, and she realized they must be keeping the rope she was on taut.

That meant it was all one rope, looped around a ring at the stern of the boat, and apparently another one positioned atop the cliff.

This calmed her, if only slightly. She hit the deck hard, two of the crew catching her, bringing her to an abrupt halt, but before she could say a word of thanks or even catch her breath, a dagger was drawn. Her eyes bulged as the man grabbed the harness Magnus had fit her with then hooked to the rope only minutes ago. He cut her loose then rushed her below deck, a dark robe held up behind her, blocking most of the light from above.

An order was shouted by someone above, and she could hear the men raise the sail. She inched forward, her curiosity too much, and watched as the men cut the rope she had slid down, securing one end to the ship as the other was let loose to drag behind it. Within moments it became taut, and she realized what was happening.

They were dragging one end of the entire rope, still looped at the top of the cliff, and once they had pulled it past the halfway point, it would slip out of the ring above, fall to the sea below, and these men would reel it in.

Leaving no evidence behind of what they had done.

What she and Magnus had done.

She took a step toward the deck, wanting to confirm her suspicions were true, when she was grabbed by the shoulder. The man said something in Norse then jabbed a finger toward the floor, indicating she was to stay put. She nodded, stepping back into the shadows and out of sight.

A shout of triumph was heard on the deck and she caught a glimpse of the rope being hauled in by the crew, her guess confirmed.

Ingenious!

She again peered out from the robe still held by one of the men, and her heart ached at the site behind them. At least a dozen people were atop the cliff, and one of them, she was sure, was Rafiq, rushing to the edge, his flowing robes and familiar figure unmistakable to her.

And the fact he was there almost made her faint.

For there was no reason for it.

Unless he knew.

And if he did, there was no way they would escape with their lives.

Valhallavagen Street

Stockholm, Sweden

Present Day

"What do you think?"

Acton shook his head, frowning at the road as Laura expertly guided them away from the embassy and along a pre-planned route programmed into the car's GPS—a route that took them past several important locations such as police stations, as well as the American and British embassies. "I think they have him."

Laura cursed. "So do I. Do you think he's dead?"

A pit formed in Acton's stomach. "If past experience is any indication, then yes, but the question is why? Why would they kill a Swedish archaeology professor? It makes no sense!"

"Little makes sense with these people."

Acton grunted. "True, though there's usually at least a thread of logic. In this case, I can't see any."

"Maybe he's not dead."

Acton nodded. "Perhaps, but if he isn't, why hold him?"

"They want something from him."

It was a possibility, and the only plausible explanation so far that had his friend still alive. "*If* he's alive, then I agree. Let's operate under that assumption. He's alive, and they want something from him. It must be the ring. That's the only thing that he has that could possibly be linked to Saudi Arabia."

"That's not entirely correct."

Acton's eyes narrowed and he tore his eyes away from the road to look at his wife. "What?"

"The body the ring was found on, this Fatima. If we assume she's Muslim, then maybe they want her as well. Or instead."

Acton chewed his cheek for a moment as he grabbed onto the dash, Laura shuddering them to a halt for a red light that had bested her. "But do they know who she is?"

Laura shook her head. "I can't see how. Perhaps with DNA testing they might be able to trace her lineage, but it's been a thousand years, and there could be tens of thousands of relations by now."

"But if there's royal blood—"

Laura hammered on the gas again, reminding Acton of the first night they had met, and how her driving skills had saved their lives. Though they hadn't, really. The man who had tried to kill them that night was now a friend, and had explained to him how he was toying with them the entire time, putting on a show for his corrupt taskmaster.

Though he did compliment her on her driving, her skills honed on the track with her late brother's Porsche.

Acton pried his fingernails from the dash and instead worked his imaginary brake. "But if she has royal blood, how could they possibly know? I doubt they've done the DNA testing yet."

Laura eased off the gas as they approached the first police station on their route. "Stay or go?"

Acton glanced behind them, finding no evidence of pursuit. "Go."

She resumed their route, giving them more time to gather their thoughts. "There's no way the DNA testing is back yet, and most likely hasn't even been started. I think this has everything to do with the ring."

Acton grunted. "Or fanaticism."

Laura stole a quick glance at him. "No Christian scientist will possess any ancient Muslim artifact?"

Acton shrugged. "I wonder if they know Viggo is atheist."

Laura chuckled. "If it's fanatics, all they care about is that you're different from them." She eased off the gas slightly as they approached the British Embassy. "Stay or go?"

Acton crouched down to check his side mirror. "Go." He gestured at the speedometer. "I think you can ease off now. I don't think they're following us."

Laura lifted her lead foot off the accelerator.

Slightly.

"Do you think they're going to try anything?"

Acton glanced at her. "With us?" He shook his head. "No, but we need to let the authorities know what we know."

"There's another police station coming up."

Acton pursed his lips, debating what to do. "No, two crazy tourists spouting conspiracy theories won't get us anywhere."

"Then what?"

"I can only think of Mira. She can get the university involved, and anyone else we can think of. We can hopefully have a shit storm brewing before tonight's newscasts."

Laura frowned. "Could that just panic them?"

"I think they're already panicked by me being there. If he's already dead, then my guess is they began the process of disposing of his body before I even got there. But if he's still alive, then this might just keep him that way until they figure out how to extricate themselves from this situation." He sighed. "I have to think they don't want a repeat of Istanbul."

A burst of air erupted from Laura's lips. "I doubt they learned anything except to have the fall guys lined up ahead of time."

Acton's phone, still gripped tightly in his hand, vibrated. He checked the call display to see it was a blocked number. He held it up for Laura. "I wonder who that could be?"

"Answer it."

He swiped his thumb, putting it on speaker. "Hello?"

"Jim, is that you?"

Acton's jaw dropped and his heart slammed as Laura eased off the gas, her attention now split between the road and Karlsson's voice. "Yes, Viggo, it's me! Are you okay?"

Another voice, an altered voice, replied. "Your friend is alive. How long he stays that way is entirely up to you."

Acton's body tensed. "What do you want?"

"We want the ring."

Acton's eyes narrowed. "Why?"

"That is none of your concern. Get us the ring, and your friend lives."

Acton stared at the phone, his eyes wide. "How? I don't even know where it is!"

"Instructions will be sent to your phone. Tell anyone of what has happened, and your friend dies." There was a pause before the words that sent a chill down his spine. "And so do you and your wife."

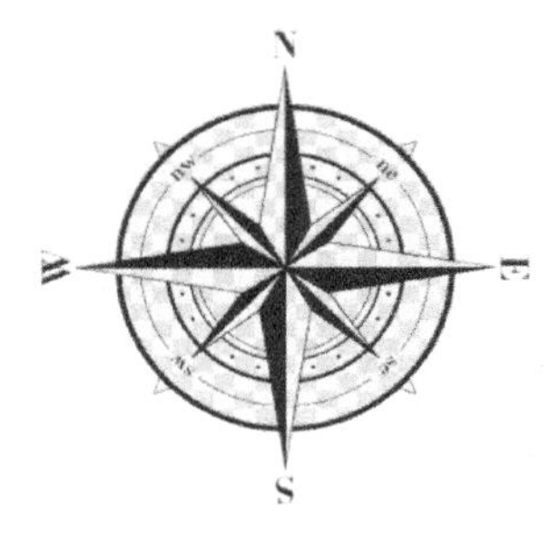

Al Lixbuna, Islamic Iberia

Caliphate of Córdoba

989 AD

Rafiq ignored the curious looks of the guards that had failed in their duty to protect his sister from herself, instead shuffling past them, stunned, his cheeks stained with dried tears, still uncertain of what to say. He had to figure out some way to save his family, and at first, he was inclined to claim she had fallen off the cliff, rather than having thrown herself willingly into the sea below.

Though if the lie were discovered, yet more shame would be heaped upon the family, and the sheik's anger might know no bounds, punishing them even more severely.

But he could claim ignorance as to the reason. No one could prove he heard any of what was exchanged. He could claim she had a fight with the Viking, about what, he didn't know, then threw herself off the cliff in a fit of despair.

Because she didn't want to leave her family!

He almost smiled at the thought. *That* was a totally plausible reason for what she had done. Though it could never be forgiven, it might be enough to ease the sheik's anger. Rafiq wasn't certain what had taken place. From the words spoken, it suggested his sister had it in her mind there was some connection between herself and the Viking Magnus, and he had dismissed her advances outright. As far as Rafiq was concerned, it appeared Magnus had done everything within his power to act honorably, and his sister was to blame for everything that had happened.

You poor, silly girl.

His mother saw him first, the party still in full swing, and her smile quickly faded as she recognized his anguish. She leaped to her feet, reaching for him.

"What is it? What's wrong?"

He closed his eyes, his shoulders heaving as his chin dropped to his chest. "Fatima is dead."

His mother screamed then collapsed, everyone suddenly on their feet as he was bombarded with questions. It was all he could do to sob out the same words repeatedly.

"Fatima is dead."

His father and Sheik Al-Musawi pulled him from the throng of women and children, into the corner of the room.

"Everyone shut up!" ordered his father, his own tears welling. He turned to his son. "Tell me, son, what happened?"

"I'm not sure, exactly, but for some reason, she had a meeting with the Viking Prince Magnus. There was a brief argument, though I heard none of it, then she…"

His father shook him by the shoulder. "What, son, what?"

"She jumped off the cliff and into the ocean below."

His mother cried out again, joined by the rest of the women and children in the room, and he found himself swaying as the reality of the situation came crushing down on him.

His sister was dead.

And it was his fault.

If he hadn't stood by, more concerned about saving his family's honor than rushing to his distraught sister's side, she would be alive right now. Instead, he had stood, waiting for those who had witnessed the argument to disperse.

He stepped over to the window and sat on the ledge, struggling to regain control of his emotions as the sheik exploded in rage, exactly as he had feared, shouting at his father about the dishonor, about the shame of it all, about how he had wasted his time traveling all this distance.

And how he would ruin the family.

It was too much.

See what you've done, Fatima?

Samira tugged on his arm.

"Not now, Samira."

She held something out in her hand, a crumpled piece of paper. "What does it say?"

He eyed her hand then sighed, taking the paper and unfolding it.

Leave with him now! Bring nothing!

It was written in Arabic, though with an unpracticed hand.

But its words changed everything. He took his little sister by the hand. "Where did you get this?"

She pointed toward the hallway leading to the bedrooms. "It was on the floor."

"Show me."

Samira led him out of the room, a room drowning in grief and rage, a room he had to escape. She pointed at the floor in front of Fatima's room. "It was on the floor, right there."

"When did you find it?"

"Before Fatima went for fresh air."

"Did she say anything else?"

Samira shrugged. "I don't remember." She stared up at him. "Why is everyone so sad? Is Fatima okay?"

He nodded. "Go to your room and wait for Mother."

"But I don't want to—"

He pointed a finger down the hall. "Now!"

She burst into tears and sped away. He felt bad for losing his temper, but he didn't have time for childish antics. He stepped into Fatima's room and carefully looked around for anything that might give him a clue as to what had happened, and what the note could mean.

He was about to leave the sparse room when he paused.

Where is it?

The carved figurine of a horse, at an almost impossibly small scale, was missing. It was always proudly displayed, a gift from Samira to

Fatima just last year. Samira had been so proud to present it to her sister, and Fatima so happy to receive it, that it was always the first thing she ever showed guests.

And it was gone.

Why would she take that with her?

There was the possibility that someone else had taken it, but if that were the case, then it would be the first time since it had been in Fatima's possession.

No one touched it.

And it was always on display here, in this room.

He sat in the corner, staring at the note, processing what precious little information he had. He had seen her arguing with Magnus, so obviously the note was from him. But why would he tell her to bring nothing? And then why would she defy him by taking something despite his specific instructions?

The snippets of the argument he had heard suggested she wanted to be with him, which would mean going with him, and he wanted nothing to do with it.

"If you will not have me, then no one will!"

Her final words were chilling, yet they spoke volumes. It was obvious that she was in love with this Viking, and was unwilling to marry the sheik. And it was also obvious that her feelings for Magnus weren't mutual.

Then why send the note?

Magnus had been adamant he wasn't interested, though if that were true, then there would have been no reason to meet her, especially as he and his fleet were leaving tomorrow morning, their trading expedition complete. He could have simply left without seeing her, and whatever feelings his sister had for the man would be left unrequited, and any drama would have been avoided.

Bring nothing.

It was those two words that didn't fit. Why would he care if she brought anything? And why would he have summoned her in the first place? Why meet at the cliff in full view of everyone? There were always people near the cliff.

None of it made any sense.

He needed answers. He needed to know why his sister had killed herself. His family had to provide an explanation to the sheik who had traveled so far to wed Fatima, and who would now be leaving emptyhanded.

He'll keep the dowry, I'm sure.

And if the marriage were to never take place—as it now never would—everything would be ruined. His father was counting on the lucrative shipping contracts his new son-in-law would bring them, contracts that would line their pockets for years to come. Their entire future, *his* entire future, had jumped off that cliff today, and he had to know why.

And there was only one man who might know the answers to the questions that consumed him.

Magnus.

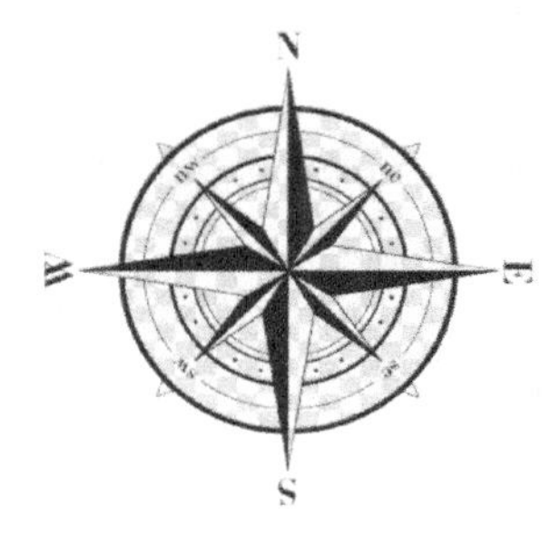

Nobis Hotel

Stockholm, Sweden

Present Day

Acton tossed his phone on the bed and Laura did the same as they entered their hotel room. They had driven in silence the rest of the way, abandoning their pre-planned route now that there was no point. Acton took Laura by the hand and led her to the bathroom where he closed the door then turned on the shower.

"You don't think they've bugged our room, do you?"

Acton shook his head. "No. Not yet, anyway. I'm more concerned with our devices being hacked. You've seen what Tommy can do. I'm sure they've got their own whiz kids."

Laura stared at the door, the only thing between them and two cellphones, eReaders, tablets, and laptops. When it came to tech, they didn't travel lightly. "So, what do we do?"

"We wait for their instructions, then decide, I guess."

"We have to go to the authorities." Laura regarded him, her eyes narrowing. "Don't we?"

"They have him already, and they have diplomatic immunity."

"That doesn't cover kidnapping."

"No, but right now he's alive. He can be thrown in front of a bus, found drowned in a bathtub, or OD'd with a needle in his arm. They didn't make the same mistake they made in Istanbul. This time they kept him alive, and can kill him in any number of ways that leave them in the clear."

Laura sighed. "You're right, of course. There's no way we can trust that the local authorities haven't been infiltrated somehow."

"Exactly. We can't risk locals, but maybe we can risk someone else."

"Hugh?"

Acton shook his head. "No, he'd have to use official channels, and Interpol I'm sure is infested with Saudis."

Laura smiled. "Dylan."

Acton nodded. Dylan Kane was a former student of his, a CIA Special Agent who had proven useful on multiple occasions. "If we can get word to him, he might be able to help us."

"You better send him the message right away. We don't know when they might hack our phones."

Acton pursed his lips, tapping his chin. "Can we risk sending him a message through that secure app he installed? What if they've already done it?"

Laura folded her arms, leaning on the counter. "I wish Tommy was here. He'd know what to do." A smile spread. "I have an idea."

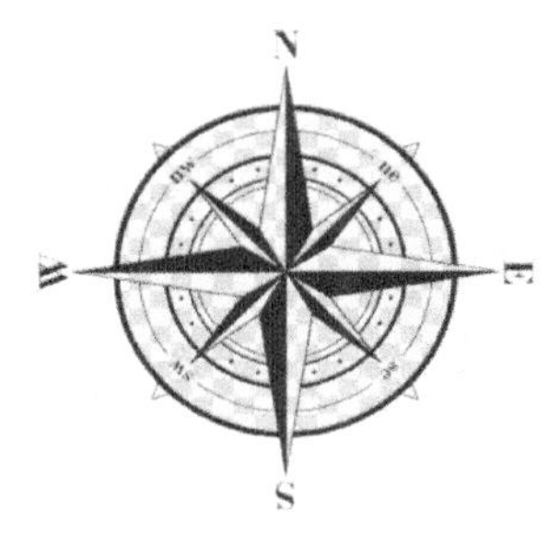

Al Lixbuna, Islamic Iberia

Caliphate of Córdoba

989 AD

Rafiq waited for Magnus to be summoned, an opportunity provided to watch the men busy themselves preparing to leave, one of the vessels with the distinctive Viking sail already leaving the port.

Yet they weren't to leave until tomorrow.

And who would depart at dusk rather than dawn?

These Vikings were a strange people, their ways so different from his, that he found they had little in common beyond the desire to trade. His recognition several years ago of the fact they might become important trading partners had led him to learn as much about them as possible, including their odd language from a traveler who had spent several years living among them. Though he would never consider himself fluent, his Norse was as good as Magnus' Arabic, and it was why his family's business had been chosen by the Vikings upon their arrival.

He had been the only one able to greet them in their native tongue.

Magnus finally appeared, extending his hand. "Rafiq! What brings you here, my friend?"

Rafiq frowned, the man's charming personality always winning him over, despite his determination to not trust the man so different from everything he knew. "I thought you weren't leaving until tomorrow?"

Magnus glanced over his shoulder at the work carried out behind him. "That was my intention, but our business here is concluded, so I decided we should leave when ready. The men are eager to get home."

Rafiq nodded, disappointed that the explanation was sound. He wanted this man to be guilty of something, something that might explain why his sister had killed herself, yet he could think of no way to find out anything without being direct. "I'm afraid I have bad news with respect to my sister."

Magnus' eyes narrowed. "What's happened?"

"You don't know?"

Magnus' eyes flared slightly. "Evidently."

"She committed suicide."

Magnus' eyes widened and his jaw dropped. "But that can't be! Why would she do such a thing?"

Rafiq drew a breath, knowing this was the moment he had been waiting for. "I was hoping you could tell me."

This appeared to catch Magnus off guard, his eyes narrowing with confusion as he took a slight step back. "Why would I know? I barely knew her except to see her at your home when your father showed me the honor of his hospitality."

Rafiq's chest tightened at the lie. "Then why did you see her not one hour ago, only moments before she threw herself off the cliff and into the ocean?" He held up the note. "Why did you send for her?"

Magnus' eyes widened at the sight of the paper, then sighed, dropping his head while gripping his forehead. "Fine, I suppose there's no harm in you knowing now that she's dead."

Rafiq tensed, surprised the man would reveal his secrets so easily. "What? What is it I don't know? What are you keeping from me?"

Magnus frowned, finally lifting his head and staring at Rafiq. "Your sister was in love with me."

Rafiq's eyes bulged as his suspicions were confirmed. Yet it made no sense. There had never been any opportunity for such emotions to develop. "I don't believe it."

Magnus lowered his voice, as if to protect Rafiq's family's honor. "It's true, I'm afraid." He held up a hand. "And I must assure you that nothing dishonorable happened. It was simply the curiosity of a young woman who was intrigued by something different. I spotted her staring at me when I first came to your house and thought nothing of it, but she began having notes sent to me, then tried to gain my attention on subsequent visits. I, of course, ignored all her advances, as I wouldn't dishonor your father that way, but she persisted."

Rafiq's chest ached and his stomach churned at the explanation, an explanation he found plausible knowing his foolish little sister. "And is that why you met her today?"

"Yes. She had sent me a message, demanding we meet, otherwise she would tell your father that I had been, well, inappropriate with her. I agreed to meet, I made my position clear, then I left." He gestured at his men, rushing about. "I thought it best to leave sooner rather than later, in case she made good on her threat."

"She didn't."

Magnus nodded, regret on his face. "In a way, I wish she had. Though it would have resulted in difficulties for me, at least she would be alive to be reasoned with." He gripped Rafiq's shoulder. "You have my condolences, my friend."

"Thank you." Rafiq paused. "Why did you tell her to bring nothing?"

Magnus frowned, his head shaking slowly. "In addition to the messages, she began sending gifts. I feared she might bring me something, and I didn't want that."

Rafiq's shoulders slumped at another perfectly reasonable explanation. He shook Magnus' hand. "I wish you a safe journey home, and I apologize on behalf of my family for any trouble my sister may have caused you."

Magnus smiled slightly. "No apology is necessary. I'm sure we have all done foolish things in matters of the heart."

Rafiq frowned. "This is true." He stepped onto the dock and looked down at Magnus. "May Allah protect you on your voyage, Viking."

Magnus bowed slightly and Rafiq turned, watching another Viking ship set sail.

And he paused.

He turned back to Magnus. "One more thing."

"Yes?"

"I saw one of your ships by the cliff. Why was it there?"

Magnus' eyes widened slightly. "Excuse me?"

"One of your ships was near the cliff."

"Oh yes, I forgot about that. I sent one of the ships home earlier with a sick man in the hope he'll get to see his family one last time before he dies."

Rafiq nodded, again the explanation plausible. "And will he make it?"

Magnus shook his head, a frown creasing his face. "I fear it's doubtful."

Rafiq sighed. "Then it would appear we have both lost this day."

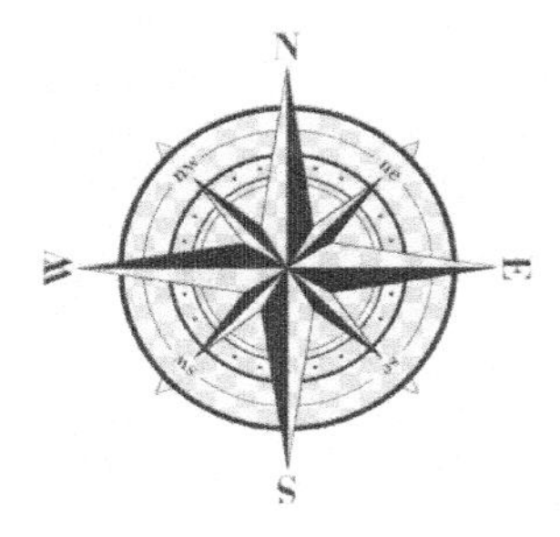

Nobis Hotel

Stockholm, Sweden

Present Day

The expected knock at their hotel room door still caused both of them to flinch. Acton rose, Laura switching to a chair by the window as the knock was repeated. He opened the door to a smiling staff member, a cart with a hastily ordered lunch rolling in.

Acton let the young man complete his spiel, then the bill was handed over for him to sign. He did, adding a generous tip, then before returning it, tilted the bill holder up slightly. "How would you like another thousand?"

The man's eyes bulged. "Sir?"

"I need to use your cellphone."

The man seemed even more confused. "Sir?"

"Both ours aren't working here. American phones, so I guess they're not compatible. I need to send an important text message to a friend. I'll give you an extra thousand kronor for one text message."

A slight smile appeared. "Umm, I suppose so." He reached into his pocket then paused. "This isn't anything illegal, is it?"

Acton chuckled, glancing back at Laura. "He thinks we're drug dealers."

Laura laughed. "Just spies, darling, just spies."

The young man shrugged. "I guess it's all right." He handed Acton the phone after activating it with his thumb. Acton quickly sent as succinct a message as he could to Reading, then once he saw it was delivered, deleted it from the phone. He handed it back then reopened the bill holder, adding a '10' in front of the tip.

"Thanks."

The young man's eyes bulged then he backed out of the room, bowing. "If you need anything, Mr. Acton, you just ask for Elias."

"I'll do that." Acton closed the door, Laura already at the food.

"I think you just made a friend."

Acton shrugged. "He could prove useful, you never know." Laura took her plate and sat cross-legged on the bed. He eyed her. "You can eat at a time like this?"

She shrugged. "Who knows when we'll get another chance. I say we eat as much as we can, then wait for their call. It has to be coming soon."

Acton sighed then joined her. "Let's just pray Hugh gets the message."

And can help us.

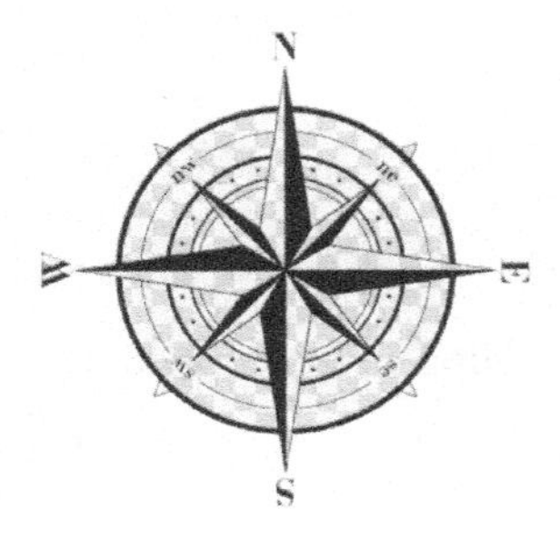

Al Lixbuna, Islamic Iberia

Caliphate of Córdoba

989 AD

Magnus watched Rafiq as the concerned, distraught brother walked away. Guilt racked him at the pain he had caused, though the thought of Fatima, waiting for him, helped ease it. He turned as shouts erupted behind him, another of his ships setting sail. Each of the six vessels under his command had orders to sail the moment they were ready. If the truth were to be discovered, then their lives would be forfeit, and he wasn't willing to see his men punished for something he had done.

This entire situation was foolish, and he knew it. When he returned home, his father would likely revoke his title for having risked everything over a woman. But this woman was unlike any he had ever met, and this woman was to be his wife. He was convinced that once his father witnessed the love they shared for each other, the man would come around.

Yet that all depended on them making it out of port with the deception undiscovered.

He didn't intend to ever return here again. There were plenty of places along the coast where they could trade, and this was a long voyage he would no longer be willing to make once he had a family back home.

Though if he knew his father, he'd probably be forced to continue his responsibilities. After all, one day he was to be King.

He chewed his cheek for a moment as he watched a group of Muslim women pass with their escort, their traditional dress so plain and unrevealing, he found it impossibly enticing. Viking women were never ashamed to show skin. They were strong, willing and able to fight when necessary, and capable of incredible tenderness when not.

He had been in love once, madly, but Odin had taken her from him before they could be married, and he had sworn off matters of the heart from that moment on.

Until he had met Fatima.

There was something about her that he had found alluring, and when he had managed to speak to her for just a few moments, his heart had nearly pounded out of his chest with excitement. Notes had indeed been secretly exchanged, though unlike the story he had fed her brother, they had been mutual and welcome.

Then the clandestine meetings had been arranged, then the forbidden encounter that he would never forget for as long as his lips drew breath. It had been exciting, wonderful, and the love in her eyes as he took what she offered had swelled his heart with joy, and he swore he would do whatever it took to be with her, to protect her, to provide for her, and to be the only man who would ever possess her heart.

That was when the plan to fake her death had begun, though it had been a mere fantasy. He had intended to ask her father for his permission to marry her, and in exchange, grant him the exclusive contract to act on behalf of all Viking trade missions to the port.

It would have made the man very wealthy, enough that Magnus had hoped it might overcome the fact he wasn't Muslim. But with the announcement of the arranged marriage, everything had changed, and what was once fantasy had been thrust into reality.

And it had worked.

Brilliantly.

They had staged their fight, she had jumped from the cliff and been taken successfully aboard one of his ships. At least he assumed so. If something had gone wrong, the ship was to return to port with word, but the fact they had continued north, told him everything was fine.

And the sooner they left this place, the sooner he'd be reunited with the love of his life.

And the less chance their deception might be discovered. For there would be questions. Her family was about to lose everything, and he was gutted with the knowledge.

Perhaps you can make them whole once things have settled.

It was a possibility. When they were safe, he could return, and in the guise of buying more favorable terms, pay Fatima's father back whatever dowry had been lost, and still offer him the exclusive contract. If things worked out perfectly, and they were to get away with their lie, and if he was able to elevate her family to the station they had been hoping for, he wondered if they might not be thrilled to discover that their daughter was alive, safe, and happy in the north.

Could a reunion be possible? Could all be forgiven?

He frowned.

Unlikely.

It was a foolish fantasy. For now, he had to reunite with Fatima and get her safely to her new home. Then the future would unfold as it should, and Odin willing, the actions taken today wouldn't prove foolish.

And deadly.

Hilton Rome Airport Hotel

Rome, Italy

Present Day

Interpol Agent Hugh Reading yawned for the umpteenth time. He had forgotten his CPAP machine at home, and was kicking his proverbial ass ever since the realization at the airport. There had been no going back for it, nor was there any popping into a store in Italy to buy one.

They were expensive, and needed a prescription.

And his idiocy was killing him.

He was so accustomed to the machine now, that without it, he had difficulty psychologically getting to sleep, then when he did manage it, he'd wake up minutes later gasping for breath.

He couldn't believe how reliant he had become on the life-saving device. He had been diagnosed with sleep apnea in time, avoiding the potentially deadly consequences, though he could only keep heart damage, stroke, and a myriad of other things at bay with the machine's constant use.

Next time make a list with it on top.

He yawned again.

Yeah, but you'd have to remember to make the list.

He stared at the hundreds of people surrounding him, a talking head at the front of the conference room prattling on about the importance of international cooperation in the fight against human trafficking, merely rehashing platitudes that everyone in the room was fully aware of.

This was merely an excuse for functionaries to gather and socialize, like so many other junkets governments and NGOs were responsible for.

And he hated every minute of it.

His partner at Interpol, Michelle Humphrey, loved them, convinced they were necessary for her to be upwardly mobile, something he had no interest in. He was at the end of his career, she had yet to peak. But she had the flu, and he had been sent in her stead.

I'd rather have the flu.

He frowned, thinking of the last time he had been erupting from both ends.

Maybe not.

His phone vibrated and he prayed for an alert informing him the world was about to end, instead seeing a number he didn't recognize, but a message that had his heart racing.

It's Jim. Don't reply. Don't do anything official. Interpol might be compromised. Contact KD. Professor Viggo Karlsson of Stockholm University kidnapped by

Saudis at embassy. Forcing us to steal ring he discovered. We think we're being watched. Hugs and kisses. J.

The last few words confirmed it was his friend that had sent it, and because he knew him so well, he knew it wasn't a prank. Since he had met them, he had been under more fire than when he served in the military, had seen more of the world than he ever imagined he would, and made two of the dearest friends he ever had.

He would die for those two, and they would do the same for him.

He just tried his damnedest to make sure that was never the only option left on the table.

KD was their code for Dylan Kane—Kraft Dinner. If they needed his help, then they were up shit's creek, and the fact they were concerned about Interpol meant his hands were tied somewhat. And they were right to be concerned. Saudi Arabia was a member of Interpol, so they had internal access. If the Saudis had indeed kidnapped this professor, then it had to be at the behest of someone in Riyadh.

Nobody bought the BS that Riyadh didn't order the murder in Istanbul, and he had no doubt that whatever had just happened in Stockholm was fully sanctioned.

That meant his friends' lives were in danger.

He excused himself to no one in particular, shuffling down the aisle and out of the room, activating the secure app on his phone that Kane had provided for just such occasions. He forwarded the entire message to Kane, with a brief explanation of how he received it, then figured out how to book a plane ticket on his phone, on his own dime, for Stockholm.

He had access to an account that Laura had set up for him several years ago for these situations, though he didn't want to risk using it as he couldn't be sure of the level of surveillance they were under. Normally, he would use the account in emergencies to buy tickets when they needed help, or just for a vacation if he wanted one. He always felt guilty using it, and never did for a vacation unless they insisted on him joining them on one of their own. His rationalization was that them buying him a plane ticket was like him buying them a coffee.

They were just so bloody rich.

He was envious of his friend. Not that he wanted Laura for himself, though he'd be a lucky man if he did, but because he would never have to worry about money again. Reading rarely did. In fact, he couldn't remember worrying about money since he was a new father. Though to know you could leave your situation if you wanted to, and suffer no financial consequences, had to be a liberating feeling.

And to know you could help a friend or family member in need, without a second thought, would be comforting.

Like his friends had helped him enjoy life a little more these past few years, especially since the disappearance then death of his best friend and former partner, Martin Chaney.

Oh, Martin, you bloody fool, I wish you were here!

He stared at his phone, the confirmation for his ticket to Stockholm confirmed, an alert vibrating a moment later about the unbelievable charge to his credit card.

Bloody hell!

Al Lixbuna, Islamic Iberia

Caliphate of Córdoba

989 AD

Rafiq found himself inexorably drawn toward the cliff where his sister had committed the ultimate sin only hours before. He stared out at the ocean, a ship sailing south in the distance, then froze. He twisted around, staring back at the port where he had just been, another Viking ship departing the inlet's natural shelter from the fury that could be the ocean.

Shelter north of where he now stood.

If they were heading home with a wounded man, why would they have gone south?

He stared back at the harbor, his eyes narrowing as he searched for some explanation as to why the ship would have gone south before going north.

Finding none.

It made no sense. Why had that ship been near this particular cliff? And why had it been sailing away from it, as opposed to past it?

Could she have jumped to the boat?

He frowned, chastising himself.

Fool! She'd die from the fall.

There was no way she could have survived the fall into the waters below. Even the strongest of men couldn't have. And besides, the ship was too far from the shore to have had time to collect her, then sail away from the base of the cliff.

It simply wasn't possible.

He had to resign himself to the fact his sister had jumped to her death, and it had to simply be coincidence that the ship was there for some reason he just wasn't aware of.

"You heard it too?"

"Yes, it was strange, and lasted for quite some time."

"So did her scream."

"What do you mean?"

"Didn't you notice her scream seemed to last longer than you'd expect?"

Rafiq spun toward the voices, startling the two men walking past him. "Do you speak of the girl who fell from the cliff earlier?"

The first man nodded, eying his robes, the men clearly Christian. "Yes, but she didn't fall. She jumped."

His much shorter companion agreed. "It's true. I saw it with my own eyes."

"I wonder what that Viking said to her."

"I'll tell you what he said. He—"

Rafiq held up a hand, cutting him off. "You spoke of hearing something. What was it?"

The taller one shrugged. "I'm not really sure. It lasted for a good minute or two, and it sounded like something rubbing."

Rafiq's eyes narrowed. "Rubbing?"

The man's head bobbed. "Yes. Like one thing rubbing on another."

"An anchor!"

He stared at his shorter companion. "Huh?"

"An anchor! Like when you drop an anchor and the rope is pulled through that ring thing. I don't know what it's called. The sound the rope makes on the ring. It sounded like that, but as if the rope were long enough to reach the bottom of the ocean, let alone the port."

Rafiq stared at him for a moment, processing this new information when his heart nearly stopped and he battled to keep his jaw from dropping. "Come with me, if you would." He marched toward the edge of the cliff before the men could have a chance to refuse. When he reached the site of his sister's tragic death, he knelt, beckoning the men to do the same. They reluctantly joined him on the ground as he lay flat, crawling toward the edge. He looked back at them, waving his hand. "Come closer. It's right here."

They exchanged nervous glances but complied. Rafiq pointed at the post with the hook on it that he had noticed earlier.

"What do you make of that?"

The taller one shrugged. "What of it? They're used to raise and lower goods."

Rafiq stared at the unforgiving sea. "Here?"

The other edged forward, staring below. "Well, perhaps not *here*."

His companion agreed. "No, not here, but you'll find them all along the coast. Normally there's flat land below like a beach." He stared at the ring once again, then the raging waters. "Not sure why there'd be one here." He shrugged. "Maybe there was a beach down there once."

His friend shook his head. "Not in my lifetime."

"Mine either, but maybe long ago."

Rafiq considered their explanation, and dismissed it, pointing at the shiny inner edge of the ring. "Then why does it look like it has been used recently?"

Both men paused then leaned back over the edge to reexamine the discovery. "Huh, will you look at that!"

The taller one nodded vigorously. "Definitely been used recently. You don't get a polish like that without some activity."

Rafiq stared at them. "Like from a rope, a long rope, like what you heard earlier when my sister jumped?"

The short one's eyes shot wide. "She was your sister? Oh no! You have my condolences!"

Rafiq bowed his head slightly, but pressed on. "You heard this noise after she jumped?"

"Yes," they answered in unison.

Rafiq thought for a moment. "And during?"

The men stared at him, the tall one replying. "What do you mean?"

"When did you start hearing the sound? While she was screaming, or after?"

Another shrug from the tall one. "I can't honestly say I heard anything but the scream." He frowned. "Until I heard the rope, of course."

Rafiq remembered something else they had said. "You said her scream lasted longer than you expected?"

Both nodded, the short one beating his friend to the punch. "Yes, *much* longer. Almost as if she were falling twice as long as you might expect."

"And *then* you heard the rope?"

"Yes," they both agreed.

Rafiq stared out at the sea below, where the Viking ship had been. Could she have been tied to a rope? It made no sense. If she was planning to run away with this Viking, why not just do so? Why the elaborate deception? Why fake a suicide?

His jaw dropped and his eyes widened.

Because you don't pursue someone you think is dead!

"What are you thinking?"

He flinched, forgetting he had company. "Nothing. I, umm, must go." He scrambled to his feet, stepping back from the cliff. "Thank you for your time." He hurried back home, picturing how the deception might have been accomplished. If his sister had been tied to a rope and jumped, there was no way the ship could have come close enough to the shore to collect her, then make it out to sea as far as they had been when he spotted them.

And jumping from that height, tied to a rope, would have snapped her in half. And where was the rope? Wouldn't it still be tied to the ring?

That wasn't what had happened, he was sure of it.

She had to reach the boat. That's the only option.

He smiled, his eyes flaring as he realized what had happened. A long rope would have been threaded through the ring from the top, both ends allowed to fall to the waters below. A smaller boat would have collected both ends then carried them out to sea, looping them through another ring on the ship he had seen, then tying them together, creating one continuous rope. His sister, using some sort of harness, would have slid down the rope to the boat, then they would have cut it, tying off one end, then dragging the rope along with them until it was clear of the ring.

Leaving no evidence behind.

Except a polished ring that should never have been there, and perhaps was to have been removed later by their accomplices.

It all made perfect sense. Because she had been moving diagonally toward the boat instead of straight down to the waters below, her scream would have lasted longer. Then the sound the men had heard afterward was the rope pulling through, hiding their deception.

It was brilliant.

And as far as anyone was concerned, his sister was dead by her own actions, his family would be left to mourn, and she could run off with the man she obviously loved.

Rage flared in his stomach at the selfishness of it all. His sister was promised to another man, a wealthy, powerful man about to change all their lives, but only if she fulfilled her duty to her family. This selfish act would put an end to the deal his father had worked out with Sheik Al-Musawi, and not only would they be denied their increased stature, they could very well lose their business should he take out his annoyance on them.

Fatima, you foolish little girl, do you not realize what you have done?

A hatred he didn't know possible grew in his heart, and he didn't know what to do with it. He wanted to tell his parents the truth, yet it would devastate them. He wanted to track down his sister and drag her back by the hair to fulfill her duty.

And another part wanted to simply slit her throat so he could restore the honor to his family that she was about to cost them.

He had no idea what he should do, and decided that prayer and his father might provide the answers. Surely, by now, Al-Musawi would have indicated his intentions toward his family, and perhaps his worrying was for naught.

Though he doubted it to his core.

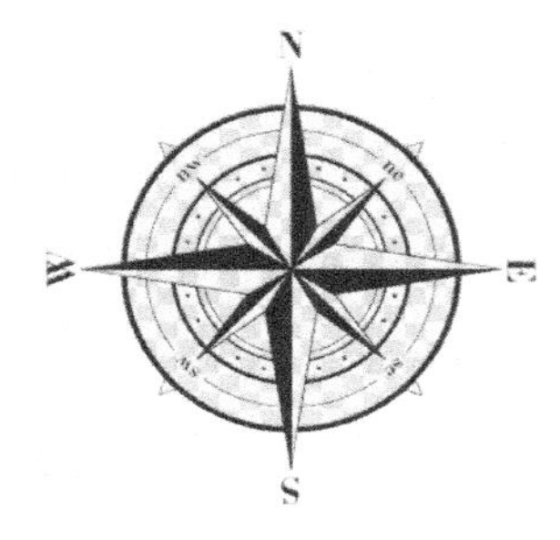

Park Hyatt Beijing

Beijing, China

Present Day

CIA Special Agent Dylan Kane moaned as the gorgeous Zhi Ruo moved her magical mouth from one part of his body to the next. His eyes closed, he imagined it was the love of his life making him feel so good, and not a target he had been pumping for information, literally and figuratively, for years within the Chinese government.

It was part of the job, a part he had always found pleasurable, but now found uncomfortable, despite his girlfriend's blessing. Lee Fang had been in the business as well, though less on the clandestine and more on the Special Forces side than him. They had met when he had rescued her from her own government, and their professional relationship had transitioned to friendship then much more.

He wanted to marry that woman.

He hissed with pleasure, Zhi Ruo knowing everything he liked after all these years, and he felt a touch of guilt that Fang had yet to discover all his sensitive spots.

Though no matter how expert the sexual partner, he'd sacrifice it all for just one night with Fang.

His CIA issued watch, a perfect Tag Hauer replica, sent a coded electronic pulse into his wrist, something only he could sense, and something that would only work when activated on his wrist—take it off, and the signal would never be sent.

He looked down at Zhi Ruo, his choice something most men would never face.

Continue making love to a beautiful woman, or take a call that could mean life or death for someone.

The choice should be obvious, though making it wasn't. How does one interrupt what was happening to take a call that by its very nature no one knew about?

He smiled.

"Ow!" he cried, reaching down to grab his calf. "Cramp!"

Zhi Ruo stared up at him. "Now?"

He shrugged, rolling out of bed and stretching out the calf, wincing in fake pain. "Just give me a minute, and I'll be right with you. I think I'm just dehydrated from all that partying we did."

She grinned. "Drink up, baby, I have plans for you that go way past breakfast."

He limped to the bathroom. "Be back in a few."

He closed the door, entering a coded sequence in the watch by pressing the buttons in a specific pattern, and the message scrolled across the display, indicating a secure communication from Interpol Agent Hugh Reading.

What are the professors up to now?

Reading never contacted him unless it related to his former teacher, and James Acton, along with his new wife Laura Palmer, had a knack for getting themselves into trouble. Quite often they bailed themselves out, but too often needed an assist.

They were just lucky they had good friends in better places, otherwise they'd have been dead years ago.

But they gave as good as they got, and on more than one occasion had returned the favor, using their tremendous wealth to help others, including his former comrades on Bravo Team when they had been disavowed.

He brought up the message from Reading through his secure phone, his eyebrows shooting up as he reread it several times.

What is it with these Saudis? Do they believe their own press?

Unfortunately, there was nothing he could personally do from his current location to help Acton. He was on a mission, and no matter how pleasurable and guilt-ridden it was, he couldn't abort.

But luckily, he had friends too.

Al Lixbuna, Islamic Iberia

Caliphate of Córdoba

989 AD

Rafiq stepped through the door of his family's home to the sounds of Sheik Al-Musawi shouting at the top of his lungs, the servants hidden in doorways, trembling with fear as his mother held his only surviving sister tight against her as tears streaked both their faces.

It was worse than he had thought.

As the eldest son, he had a right to be at his father's side, and decided it was best to exercise that right, as he was the only one who knew the entire truth.

"I will destroy your family! You'll never do business in the Caliphate again!"

His father was on his knees, hands clasped in front of him, begging the powerful man, any shred of dignity he might have had, gone. "Please, sir, be reasonable. I have done nothing wrong! I have a family!"

"You raised a selfish little whore who has dishonored herself and her family, wasted my time, and humiliated me by showing everyone that death was preferable to marriage to me. I may never recover from this!"

Tears streamed from his father's eyes and a wave of shame washed over Rafiq at the pathetic display.

And yet he didn't blame him. He would probably do the same if the roles were reversed. Sheik Al-Musawi had the power to ruin them, and they were powerless to stop him.

His chest tightened with a thought, a last-ditch effort that could backfire horribly. "She didn't kill herself."

The argument immediately halted, Al-Musawi and his father, still on his knees, both turning toward him.

"What did you say?"

It was his mother, appearing in the doorway behind him, that broke the silence.

"She's not dead. At least I don't think she's dead."

His mother rushed toward him, grabbing his arm, her eyes filled with tears and hope. "Wh-what do you mean? She's alive? My Fatima is alive?"

He was committed now, and he chastised himself vigorously for blurting out what might not even be true. And even if it were, was faking her death to escape the arranged marriage any better than committing suicide? Was it any less dishonorable?

If anything, it was more. In fact, it most certainly was. She had not only left her family to think she was dead through suicide, a sin if there ever was one, but she was giving herself to a man who wasn't even a Muslim, without her father's blessing.

It was shameful.

It was dishonorable.

And she should die because of it.

Yet none of those truths could save his family.

And then another, perhaps equally foolish thing gushed from his mouth. "She was kidnapped."

"What?" It was the sheik who reacted first, his face red with rage. "By whom?"

"The Vikings. The one who you've been doing business with, Prince Magnus. I witnessed him arguing with her, then he tied her to something and pushed her over the cliff. They had ropes already in position, and she slid down to one of their boats. I saw the boat with my own eyes, sailing away from the shore, heading out to sea."

His father struggled to his feet, his sorrow and fear replaced with anger. "Why is this the first we're hearing of it? Earlier you said she had jumped."

Rafiq turned to his father, scrambling to keep the lies straight. "I was mistaken. In my grief, I became confused, but after talking to Magnus just a short while ago, I realized his explanation for the ship being where it was made no sense, and must be a lie."

"Explain yourself," demanded Al-Musawi.

"Because the cliff is to the south of the port, and Magnus claimed that the ship was heading home, to the north, because they wanted to return a sick man to his family before he died."

This calmed Al-Musawi significantly. "And what other evidence do you have?"

"Two witnesses who claimed they heard the sound of a rope pulling through a metal loop, like an anchor being dropped might sound like."

His father nodded. "They heard this? At the cliff?"

"Yes. And I discovered a metal loop driven into the side of the cliff, right where she jumped, and it showed signs of having been recently used." He paused for effect as he stared at each of them. "I think they had this all planned."

"But why would she go to meet him?" It was his mother that asked the question impossible to answer.

"I'm, umm, not sure. But whatever the reason, she paid for her mistake with her freedom."

"My poor girl!" wailed his father as he almost collapsed. Rafiq and Al-Musawi grabbed him by the arms and lowered him into a seat, his mother quickly taking over his care, snapping orders to servants.

"We must rescue her."

Rafiq's eyes widened at Al-Musawi's comment.

"She is to be my wife. To do anything less would bring dishonor to my family, and that I cannot abide."

Rafiq's head slowly bobbed, Al-Musawi's anger now clearly directed at the Vikings instead of his family, his impromptu lies working out beautifully so far. "That could be an expensive undertaking. They have at least six ships with a substantial head start."

Al-Musawi sliced the air between them with his hand. "I don't care about the expense. Commission an expedition, follow them, and kill them all if need be. I want her back." He reached into his robes and produced a silver ring with colored glass in the center. "This was to be my engagement gift to her. It has been in my family since the days of the Prophet, peace be upon him. When you find her, give this to her as a symbol of my devotion to her."

Rafiq took the ring and held it up, reading the engraving inside.

For Allah.

He gripped it tightly in his hand. "I shall protect it with my life, and swear I shall return my sister to your side, or die trying."

Al-Musawi stepped closer, staring into his eyes, sending a chill rushing down Rafiq's spine. "I'll trust you to keep your word."

A bead of sweat rolled down his back, fear gripping him, but he was committed now. He took a chance. "And my family?"

Al-Musawi looked about the room, then down at the patriarch. "There has been no dishonor here. You are all victims to these deceitful Vikings, as am I. Bring her back, and all will be forgiven."

"And if I fail?"

"Then your life will be the only payment I demand of your family."

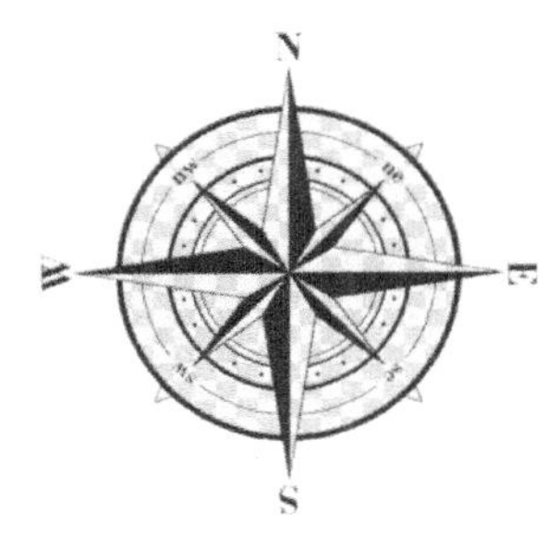

The Excalibur Hotel & Casino

Las Vegas, Nevada

Present Day

"I can't eat that."

The man stared at whom CIA Analyst Supervisor Chris Leroux assumed was his significant other. "Why not?"

"There's something wrong with it."

"What?"

"The chicken. It's too small. It must have been sick."

The man chuckled and Leroux suppressed a smile. "It's a Cornish game hen. It's supposed to be small."

The young woman, Filipino he was guessing, vehemently shook her head. "You eat it."

The man shrugged. "Fine, but you're going to be hungry later."

She poked at her fingerling potatoes, clearly not pleased with much of the meal, the dinner served at the medieval show definitely not designed for Asian palates. "Can we order room service when we get back to the hotel?"

The man frowned. "Ugh! I just paid for this!"

She whispered something in his ear.

"Really?"

She nodded.

"Baby, for that, you can order the Kobe beef!"

Sherrie White, Leroux's significant other as well as a CIA Agent, snorted, and the couple they had been eavesdropping on flinched then looked back. Sherrie smacked Leroux on the arm. "You're too funny, hon."

Leroux sat in mid-chew, his tiny Cornish game hen gripped in front of his mouth, unsure of what to say. Improvisation was never his strong suit. "Umm, thanks?"

The two in front of them flushed then resumed watching the show, their conversation curtailed, something Leroux would have felt guilty about if he were the one that had dropped the ball.

He glanced at Sherrie. "Some agent you are."

She shrugged, ripping a leg off the poor bird. "I'm off duty."

Swords clashed as men raced past each other on horseback, the hooves kicking up the dirt that filled the air with a smell Leroux wasn't accustomed to.

Nature.

He was a geek, dork, nerd, whatever the kids were calling it these days—probably none of the above—whose idea of a good time was the couch and a good sci-fi marathon. Yet when he had landed the outgoing bombshell sitting beside him with the help of his best friend from high school, Dylan Kane, he began to slowly emerge from his shell.

Though his idea of a good time was still the couch and a good sci-fi marathon, except now he preferred it bookended with sex.

Something twitched.

He gazed at Sherrie for a moment, chewing away as she watched the duel, probably hoping for a slipup that resulted in some real blood. She was all action. Badass, kickass, and smartass. She was awesome, way more than he deserved, though she'd kick his ass if she knew he still sometimes felt that way.

My God, I'm a lucky guy!

Leroux's phone vibrated in his pocket and he pulled it out reluctantly. He had no friends besides Sherrie and Kane. She was with him, and Kane was on assignment. That meant it had to be work related, and they weren't to contact him unless it was a matter of life or death.

Unfortunately, in his business, it was always a matter of life or death.

He checked the call display.

It was Sonya Tong, one of his senior analysts. He flashed the display to Sherrie who shrugged. "If you get recalled, I'm going to the Thunder from Down Under. I've got three hours left before I head to Shitbuktu, and I want to enjoy civilization the way it was meant to be. Vegas style."

He gave her a look then swiped his greasy thumb across the display. "This better be good. I've got a girlfriend who's threatening to leave me for a dozen ripped Aussies."

"Umm, I think it's good."

He immediately regretted being so casual. When he was as happy as he was at this moment, it was too easy to forget there were those who hadn't been as lucky as him to find the love of their lives. Especially when the love of their lives was on the other end of the phone.

And their boss.

Tong had an unhealthy crush on him, and as her boss, it put him sometimes in a bit of an awkward position, especially when Sherrie was involved in an op.

"What is it?"

"I've got a message from Special Agent Kane that he needs help with."

Leroux immediately became concerned for his best friend, and leaned forward, drawing Sherrie's attention. She became all business, putting down her food and carefully wiping her fingers as she prepared for a quick change of plans. "What is it? Is he okay?"

"Yes, he's fine. It's the professors that aren't."

Leroux sighed with relief. Though he didn't wish Professors Acton and Palmer any ill will, should anything happen to them, he'd lose little sleep over it. They were acquaintances at best.

Kane's death, on the other hand, would leave a hole inside him that he doubted could ever be filled.

"What have they gotten themselves into this time?"

"They're claiming a colleague of theirs has been kidnapped by the Saudis, and they're demanding the professors steal some ring to get him back."

Leroux's eyebrows shot up.

That's a new twist.

"Okay, I'm scheduled to be back there tonight, anyway, so start the usual checks. Do you have the name of the professor that was kidnapped?"

"Yes."

"Okay, run down everything you can on him, find out if there've been any reports, and see if you can contact the professors."

"They've asked to not be contacted. They think they're under surveillance."

"Okay, find them, see if we can get some eyes on them. I'll contact the Director to let him know what's going on, but let's operate under the assumption we're a go."

"Okay, I'll assemble the team." There was a pause. "Sorry to interrupt your, umm, romantic getaway."

Leroux searched for the right words. "Don't worry about it. It's Vegas, not Paris." He ended the call then turned to Sherrie. "Bad news."

"Professors again?"

"Yup. I've gotta call the Director. I'll be right back."

"You better hurry. Those oiled up racks of ribs are hitting the stage soon."

Leroux patted his stomach. "Not happy with my washboard abs for delicates?"

Sherrie snorted, as did the couple in front of them, and Leroux smiled.

Then wondered just how much they had overheard of his phone call.

Amateur move, moron.

North Sea

989 AD

Magnus stood at the prow of his ship, Fatima at his side, his arm over her shoulders, holding her tight against him. Her warmth was welcome on this chilly morning, though nothing could warm him like the thought of what lay ahead. They were together, their ruse apparently successful, and all six ships were reunited, heading along the blustery coast toward their homeland.

Laden with valuable cargo, the men were in a good mood at the prospect of seeing their families, and his future appeared bright. They had been traveling for what felt like months but was merely weeks, the wind filling their sails the entire way, with the men supplementing their speed with the oars. He was still nervous that their deception might yet be discovered, and the safest place to be would be home, under the protection of his father and the brothers and sisters of the clan.

"How long before we reach your home?"

He smiled at Fatima, squeezing her tighter. "*Our* home."

She returned his smile. "*Our* home."

"Two days, three at most. You're going to love it, though you'll find it colder than you're used to."

She rested her head against his chest. "You'll keep me warm."

"We'll keep each other warm. Once we're wed, we're never leaving the bed chamber until you're with child."

She inhaled deeply, pressing tighter against him. "I can't wait to have children. I hope they have your hair and eyes."

Magnus chuckled. "And I hope they have yours."

She stared up at him. "If it's a boy, then your coloring. If it's a girl, then mine?"

He laughed. "May Odin make it so!"

"Sir! Sails on the horizon!"

Magnus' chest tightened and he let go of Fatima, following his second-in-command, Olav, to the stern of the boat.

"Look!"

He followed the direction Olav indicated and frowned at the crest emblazoned on the sails.

They were trading vessels from the Caliphate.

Fatima joined them. "What is it?"

"It looks like our efforts have been discovered. Those are Caliphate ships."

She gripped his hand tightly, peering into the distance. "Can you be sure?"

"Their markings are unmistakable." Magnus spun toward his crew. "To the oars! We must reach home before they catch up to us!"

The crew immediately manned their stations, the orders relayed to the other vessels, the rhythmic surge of each stroke underway within moments.

Olav stepped closer, lowering his voice. "How did they catch up to us? We've had full sails the entire way, and what I thought was a healthy head start."

Magnus stared at the ships, frowning. "You've forgotten one thing, my friend. We're laden with cargo, they likely are not."

Olav frowned. "Should we dump the cargo?"

Magnus shook his head. "No, I will not have this voyage be for naught because of my foolish heart."

"Then what shall we do?"

"Pray to Odin for a strong wind in our sails and sturdier men than they have at the oars."

Olav smiled. "Then we have nothing to fear, for none are sturdier than our brothers."

Magnus patted his friend on the back, concealing the fear he barely held at bay. "From your lips to Odin's ears, my friend." He turned to face the ships in pursuit, gripped by worry, as their empty holds gave them the edge on speed.

Please, Odin, carry us safely home, and let me alone face the wrath of those I have wronged.

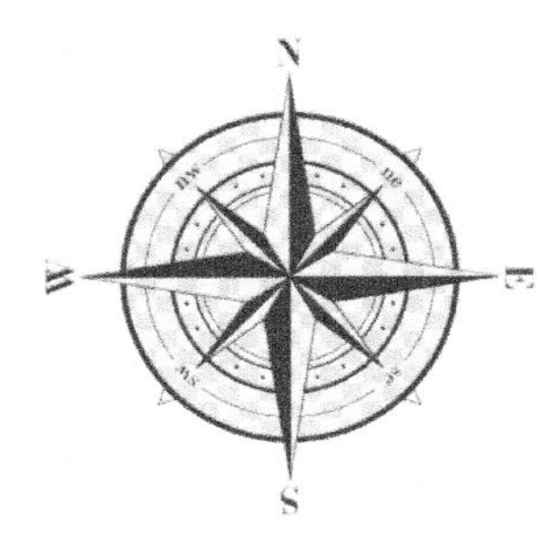

Nobis Hotel

Stockholm, Sweden

Present Day

Acton lay beside Laura on the king size bed, his eyes closed, his hands folded neatly on his chest, holding his phone, just in case he drifted off.

Unfortunately, there was little chance of that.

Laura lay beside him, as exhausted as he was from the non-stop adrenaline rush they had been on for the past few hours, and had just managed to drift off if her rhythmic breathing were any indication, when his phone vibrated.

"I'm up!" she gasped, flipping over as he pushed with his feet to gain a seated position against the headboard. He looked at her.

"Ready for this?"

She nodded, pen and paper in hand.

He swiped his thumb and put it on speaker. "Hello?"

The computer-altered voice sent shivers through his body. "It is time. Open your door."

Acton's eyes narrowed as he stared at the phone. "Why?"

But the call had ended.

Laura pushed him toward the door. "Check!"

He gave her a look. "There could be a man with a gun on the other side of that thing."

She rolled her eyes. "If they were going to kill us, we'd be dead by now."

He climbed out of the bed. "You just remember that in the eulogy. 'My biggest regret is telling him to open the door, where a large Saudi with a gun ended my husband's life.'"

"Look through the peephole, smartass."

He did, finding no one there. Which surprised him. He opened the door, tentatively, and peered through the crack.

No one.

"There's nobody—" He paused, noticing a bag sitting on the floor, directly in front of the door. He opened it all the way and stepped out, checking both ends of the hallway but finding no one in sight. He picked up the bag and stepped back inside, locking the door.

The bag rang and he nearly soiled himself.

"There's a phone!"

He returned to the bed. "Ya think?"

"Hey, I'm nervous."

"So am I." He patted her leg. "Sorry."

She waved off his apology. "Don't worry about it." She pointed at the bag. "Aren't you going to answer that?"

He unzipped the bag and pulled out the simple flip phone, reminding him of the old days when a Motorola Razr was considered the epitome of cool. He flipped it open. "Hello?"

"There are two pins in the bag shaped like American flags. Do you see them?"

Acton began pulling out the few items inside, then found the pins in question. "Yes."

"Each of you pin one to your shirt. Make sure it isn't covered by anything. When you put a jacket on, move the pin. If the pin is ever blocked, we break one of your friend's bones."

"That won't be necessary," said Acton through clenched teeth. He handed a pin to Laura who quickly snapped it in place, then did the same for him as he held the phone to his head. "Why are we wearing these?"

"Everything you hear and see will be transmitted back to us. We will tolerate no deviations and no trickery. Try anything, and your friend dies. Do you understand me, Professor Acton?"

Acton frowned, then wiped it from his face as he remembered Laura's pin was now aimed directly at him. "Yes."

"There is a tablet in the bag. Do you see it?"

Acton held up the tablet sitting on his lap, already removed from the bag, for Laura's camera to see. "Yes."

"On the tablet are instructions, provided by Professor Karlsson, on where the ring is located, and how to get in without being detected.

Follow these instructions, retrieve the ring, then you will be contacted for the exchange."

Acton eyed the tablet, his eyebrows popping slightly.

How could he not know I already found it?

He held up three fingers. "How many fingers am I holding up?"

Laura's eyes bulged.

"Don't toy with us, Professor Acton."

He held up one finger.

"Follow your instructions to the letter, and this will be over soon."

The call ended and Acton flipped the phone closed.

Laura gave him a "what was that about?" look, but he shook his head. While he wasn't convinced they could see them, as he hadn't spotted any lens on the small pin, he had no doubt they could hear them. Their lack of reaction to his finger gestures suggested he was correct in his suspicions, but unfortunately, there was no way to truly test his theory beyond what he had already done.

"What do we do now?" asked Laura, whispering.

He chuckled. "I'm sure they can still hear you." He pulled the pin close to his mouth and raised his voice. "Isn't that right!" He let go of it then activated the tablet computer, the instructions already opened for them to see. He held it up for Laura. "I guess we follow their plan, and hope they keep their word."

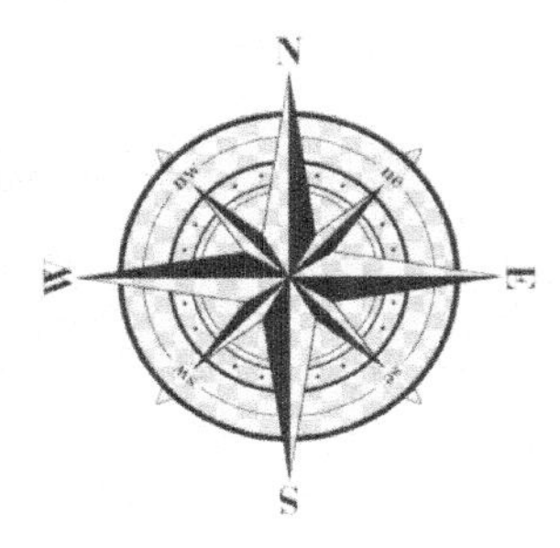

North Sea

989 AD

"Sir, it *must* be them. Six Viking sails, all *knarr* class cargo vessels."

Rafiq peered into the distance, the sails unmistakable, the count accurate. It *had* to be them. They had encountered numerous Viking vessels on their voyage north, and none had proven to be those they were searching for.

And all had fallen, fighting valiantly despite being outnumbered.

He hated killing the innocent, though these were heathen pagans, worshipping false gods, and their brethren had been party to dishonoring his family and threatening its entire future.

Those responsible had to pay.

Or he would die.

Though Sheik Al-Musawi had promised only he would pay with his life should Fatima not be returned, he was the only male heir. If his parents were unable to produce another upon his death, then all they had would be given to their extended family, and what had been built would be torn apart piecemeal.

All they had sacrificed so much for would be lost.

He was supposed to inherit, then his yet to be born eldest son after him. And all of that was now at risk thanks to his foolish sister's selfish actions. And he was faced with a conundrum. If he managed to retrieve Fatima, she likely wouldn't go willingly. Then when she was returned to Al-Musawi, she likely wouldn't back his story that she had been kidnapped. The foolish girl would probably declare her love for this pagan Viking, tell everyone she had gone willingly, faking her own suicide, then his family's ruination would be total.

She couldn't be allowed to tell her story.

And that meant there could be only one outcome here.

And it broke his heart.

Unless you die instead.

His eyebrows rose slightly at the thought. If *he* were to die in the battle soon to pass, then Fatima could remain a "prisoner," and his crew manning what remained of the fleet would return home with news of his valiant efforts, and that Fatima remained an irretrievable prisoner. It could preserve the family honor, and leave her alive.

He sighed.

He loved his sister, and under normal circumstances would have died without hesitation to save her life, but these were not normal circumstances. These were circumstances of her own creation, circumstances she willingly participated in.

And her entire family, *his* entire family, was now at risk because of it.

No, he wouldn't sacrifice himself to save her. Family loyalty only went so far, and she had already demonstrated that this infidel was more important to her than her own flesh and blood.

And that once again brought him back to the same, inevitable conclusion.

He closed his eyes. "How long until we reach them?"

The captain of the vessel stepped forward. "We should overtake them within two days, sir."

Two days. Spend them well, my sister, spend them well.

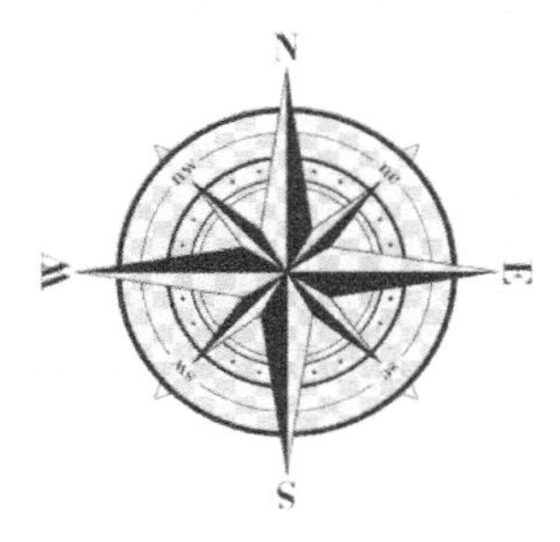

MGM Grand Hotel

Las Vegas, Nevada

Present Day

Leroux shook his head. "This is déjà vu all over again."

"You're telling me," agreed Sherrie, lying beside him, naked as the day she was born, a quick session of send-off sex completed just in time, Sonya Tong interrupting the post-coital bliss only moments after it had begun.

Leroux pointed at the tablet feeding the secure footage from his team at Langley as Tong provided context over the speaker.

"He doesn't look too happy," said Sherrie.

"No, he doesn't," said Tong. "This is Professor Karlsson entering the embassy, and as far as we know, he went voluntarily."

Leroux leaned closer. "Have you reached out to his wife?"

"No, we didn't want to risk that she might be under surveillance. For now, we're hoping the Saudis don't know we know something is going on."

"Okay, so just like Istanbul, we have him going in, and I assume we haven't found anything showing him coming out?"

"Nothing. But about half an hour after his meeting was scheduled to begin, these three SUVs"—the image changed to show the rear gates opening, three vehicles with blacked out windows surging through and out of frame—"leave in a hurry."

"Track them."

"Randy's on it." The footage changed again, the timecode showing a couple of hours had passed. "And here we have the money shot."

Leroux shook his head as the footage showed Acton entering, bold as brass. "Is that a cellphone in his hand?"

"Yes." The image zoomed in on it. "It looks like it's connected to a call."

Sherrie grunted. "Clever guy. He figures they won't touch him as long as someone on the outside can hear everything that's going on."

Leroux agreed. "And I assume he leaves?"

"A few minutes later." The footage changed again to show him leaving, phone still in hand, then climbing into an SUV, Laura Palmer behind the wheel. Leroux pointed at the image, a man on a phone stepping onto the sidewalk, staring at the SUV as it rolled past. "Identify the man on the phone."

"Already done. His name is Abdullah Al-Jubeir. He's the Ambassador's Chargé D'affaires at the embassy, his righthand man."

"See if you can trace that call he just made."

"That's going to be difficult."

"We just need to know where the call was made to. Even just the country will help us narrow down who's pulling the strings."

"Okay, I'll get on it right away."

"Where is Acton now?"

"His telephone shows him at their hotel, the Nobis."

Sherrie looked at Leroux. "Do we call him?"

Tong replied. "I wouldn't. He left Agent Reading specific instructions not to, which suggests they're under electronic surveillance."

Sherrie shook her head. "And this is all over a ring?"

"That's what the message from the professor said. They have to steal the ring to free their friend."

Leroux exhaled loudly, his lips jutting out. "Are the locals aware?"

"No, not so far as we can tell."

"The wife hasn't contacted them?"

"There's no indication she knows yet, though the Actons talked to her before they went to the embassy, which suggests she's the one who told them that's where he went. I'm guessing he was supposed to meet them at the airport and didn't show."

Leroux chewed his cheek. "Which means she knows he didn't, so could be calling the police at any moment."

Sherrie put a hand on his thigh. "She needs to be spoken to."

Leroux agreed. "Yeah, but what if they have her under surveillance?"

"Send someone in undercover."

Leroux thought for a moment, then nodded. "You're right. We need to get a discrete message to her, otherwise she could blow this entire situation up into another international incident."

Sigtuna, Roden

(Modern Day Stockholm County, Sweden)

989 AD

Magnus leaped from the prow of his vessel, his feet splashing in the cold waters, the numbing effect going unnoticed as he rushed toward his family and friends, already gathering at the shore, the word having gone out the moment their sails were spotted.

He embraced his mother, lifting her from the ground as she kissed him on alternating cheeks repeatedly. The crowd parted as his father approached, and Magnus beamed a smile at him before taking a knee.

"Get up, get up! I'm too old a man for you to waste the precious minutes I have left on protocol."

Magnus laughed and rose, exchanging a hearty hug with his father, then standing back and assessing the man's health. "You look well."

"I feel well. It's the season. The cold always brings out the best in me."

Magnus glanced over his shoulder to see Fatima standing at the shore, Olav at her side, having helped her from the boat. "Father, Mother, I would like you to meet what brings out the best in *me*." He held out his hand and Fatima smiled nervously, the entire crowd settling into a hushed silence, all eyes on the love of his life. She took his hand. "Father, Mother, may I present Fatima Halabi, originally of Aleppo, daughter of Najeeb and Abeer, and the woman I intend to marry."

Gasps abounded, even a few shocked utterances erupting in protest. For it was clear from Fatima's appearance that she wasn't one of them. Though most here had never seen a Muslim, they had heard of them and their strange ways. For a future king to take one as his wife, to bear children that might one day rule these lands, was unthinkable to many.

Yet in time, they would grow to love her as he did. And should it come to pass that they didn't, he would readily step aside for his younger brother to inherit. He had no designs on the throne, and never had. He was born into something he had never desired, nor aspired to.

He maintained his smile, though he could tell his mother was shocked, and his father was concealing, unsuccessfully, his own displeasure.

"We must speak." His father spun on his heel, heading back toward their home. Magnus took Fatima's hands in his, speaking in Arabic so she knew what was going on.

"Wait here. I must speak with my father."

"He hates me. They all hate me." Tears erupted and his mother rushed forward, taking Fatima from him.

"You poor girl. Don't mind my foolish husband, he'll come around. Let's get you inside where it's warm and dry. You must be hungry and tired."

"She doesn't speak Norse, Mother."

"Then you know your first task, don't you?"

"Yes, Mother."

Magnus' heart warmed as Fatima was surrounded by the women of his home, their tone friendly and comforting, Fatima's tears replaced with flashes of a shy smile as she was led away.

"Sir, sails on the horizon!"

Magnus didn't bother to look, for there was no doubt who they were, and the fact they were now visible, meant they would be here within hours. "Prepare for battle." His order was barely above a whisper, yet the response was swift as the men and women of his homeland sprang into action, leaving the way clear for him to join his father, and explain why so many were about to die.

Fatima found herself inside a home unlike any she had ever seen. She was accustomed to homes made from stone in Iberia, yet here everything seemed constructed from the forests that surrounded them. It was different, exciting, and a little overwhelming. A hearty fire roared at one end of the long building, and at least a dozen women of varying ages were tending to her. She wasn't used to being touched, and their tongue was foreign, only a smattering of words understood, almost all with no context.

It was overwhelming.

Yet she maintained control. Or at least she thought she had. Her future mother-in-law grabbed her trembling hands then snapped an order that was immediately obeyed, the tent emptying. The old woman said something to her, a smile on her face, but Fatima had no idea what she was saying.

And it was frustrating her.

"I wish Magnus were here. At least he could translate."

The woman's face brightened. "Magnus!" She pointed at Fatima, then her heart, then repeated his name.

Fatima's eyes narrowed then she smiled. "Do I love Magnus?" She nodded vigorously, tapping on her heart with her hand. "Yes, I love Magnus."

"Love."

"Yes, love. I love Magnus."

The old lady smiled, pleased with this revelation, then turned her head and shouted something. Two of the women returned, more subdued this time, and set to providing them both with food and drink.

It was then that she finally noticed the barked words and sounds of heavy activity outside, and a sense of foreboding spread through her body.

They're here.

Rafiq stood at the prow, surveying the shoreline ahead. It was clear they were expected, and that the reception was not to be peaceful. And that they would be far outnumbered by the time they arrived. Their only hope of victory had been at sea.

Yet they had failed.

The men's spirit wasn't in it. These weren't warriors. He had raised a fleet with ease, the sheik's purse deep, but it was manning them with those who could fight that was the problem. He had heard of the Vikings and their prowess at war. They were vicious with an almost gleeful attitude toward battle and even death.

How one could be so willing to die for a pagan god, he had no idea.

And these men he now commanded, though capable sailors, were not battle hardened like those they were likely to face.

We won't make it off the beach.

And he made a decision. "Signal the others to hold their position."

"Sir?"

"You heard me!"

"But we'll be slaughtered for sure!"

Rafiq shook his head, turning to the captain. "No, my friend, going in alone is the only way we won't be."

"I want an explanation."

"I fell in love. What further explanation is there?"

Magnus' father glared at him. "You dare to make light of this situation? We have an enemy approaching our shores. *I* am prepared to fight to the death. The question is, are you? Where do your loyalties lie, my son? Are they with your family? With your brothers and sisters? Or are they with your new bride from a foreign land, with beliefs so strange, they worship only *one* god?"

Magnus' chest ached with the fact his father felt the question was necessary. "You know where my loyalties lie, Father. With you. With Mother. With my brothers and sisters, with our people. Never doubt that. I do not love her people. I think they're backward in so many ways. But she is different from her people. Her spirit is exhilarating, her voice intoxicating, her beauty unparalleled. From the moment I set eyes on her, from the moment I heard her sweet voice, I knew she was the one Odin had made me sacrifice so much for, and would once again make me pay a price to attain. Happiness has been elusive to me, Father, you know that. When Astrid died, I thought I could never love again. That emptiness lasted many years. Until I met Fatima. I love her, Father, with all my heart, and I intend to marry her."

His father regarded him for a moment. "Even if it is without my blessing?"

Magnus' stomach churned, his heart hammering at the words. "Yes, Father, though it would crush my spirit should you not give it."

His father sighed, shaking his head. "I always knew you were going to be trouble, boy, from the moment you tried to come out of your mother feet first. You did everything backward then, and you're doing it again today." He jabbed a finger at the life beyond the walls. "There are dozens, nay, hundreds of women, beautiful and willing, who would give anything to be your bride, yet you choose someone so many will find impossible to accept."

"Then it is their loss. If you desire it, I will renounce my birthright and live the simple life of a commoner. You know I was never one to seek power."

His father shook his head then approached him, placing an arm on Magnus' shoulder. "You are my son, and I love you, no matter how foolish you are. If you love this woman, then I must accept that. How about you introduce me to her, so I can understand who we are about to shed blood for."

Magnus smiled. "Thank you, Father. I know you'll find her worthy."

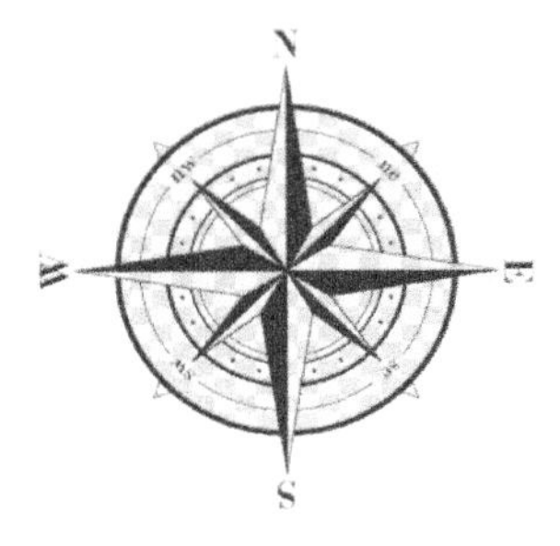

Nobis Hotel

Stockholm, Sweden

Present Day

Acton cursed at a message that had just appeared on the tablet. Laura looked at him.

"What now?"

"I have to call Mira." He showed her the message with the instructions it contained.

"Bloody hell!"

Acton tapped the number shown and the tablet dialed, the call automatically on speaker. Mira answered almost immediately, her anxious voice betraying her state of mind.

"*Hej?*"

"Hi, Mira, it's Jim Acton."

"Oh, thank God, I've been getting worried. Please tell me you found him, and the old fool just forgot he was meeting you."

"I need you to listen carefully, and most importantly, don't panic."

"Oh God! Something's happened! What did those barbarians do to him?"

Acton kicked himself for his poor choice of words. Telling someone not to panic was the best way to make them do just that. "Viggo is okay, but I need you to listen."

Heavy, sobbed breathing was the only response.

"Mira, I need you to go to the front door. There will be a man there. He's going to hand you a pin then leave. Put the pin on. It has a camera and microphone on it. The moment you put it on, everything will be transmitted to the people who have your husband."

"Have? Jim, please, tell me what is going on!"

Acton's heart ached at her anguish. "I'm so sorry, Mira, but you *must* follow my instructions to the letter. Go to the door. Now."

He could hear her footsteps then a door open, an alarm chirping in the background. There was a gasp, but nothing said, the door closing a moment later.

"I-I have the pin."

"Put in on, then we can talk."

Another pause. "Okay, it's on."

"Good. Now listen very carefully. Everything you say from now on will be transmitted to the people who have your husband."

"Who has him?"

"The Saudi government, as far as we know. I can't say much more, because we're being recorded as well."

"Wh-what do they want?"

"The ring he discovered."

There was a quick inhalation of air caught by the speaker. "What? This is all because of a stupid ring?"

Acton understood her outrage. It was ridiculous, yet it was the situation they all found themselves trapped in. "Apparently, it's important to someone. We're going to go get it, hand it over to them, then they'll release Viggo. If everything goes to plan, this should all be over tonight."

"Oh, please God, take care of my Viggo. Do-do you think he'll be okay?"

Acton exchanged a look with Laura, both of them clearly in agreement they weren't at all confident in the outcome. But he had to give the poor woman hope. "Yes, as long as we all follow their instructions to the letter. It's essential you tell no one what is going on. Not the police, not his students, not your friends. Nobody."

"I understand."

"Good. Now, just sit tight and wait to hear from us, and don't worry if it takes several hours. We're not sure exactly how the exchange will play out."

"Okay, Jim, I trust you. Please promise me you'll do whatever it takes to get him back to me."

"You have my word, Mira, we'll do everything we can."

He ended the call, tossing the tablet on the bed then collapsing back on his pillow.

"I noticed you didn't promise her."

Acton frowned, turning his head to face Laura. "Because I'm betting we're never going to see him again."

Her eyes flared at his perhaps too frank assessment, and she glanced down at her pin. "Even after we retrieve the ring?"

He grunted. "I'm afraid *we* may never be seen again."

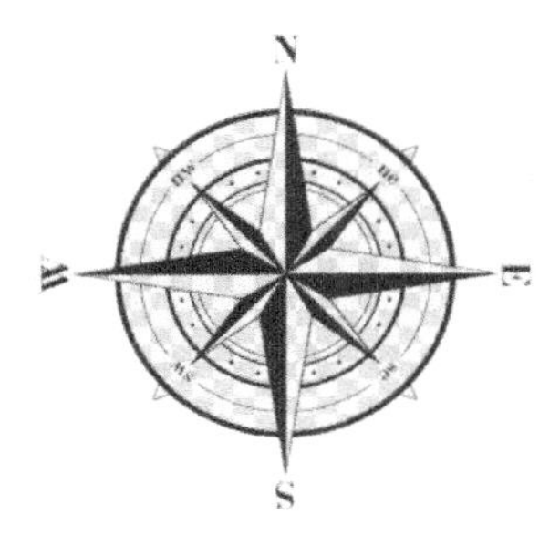

Sigtuna, Roden

989 AD

Magnus stood at the head of an army prepared to tear the new arrivals limb from limb, yet he hoped it wouldn't be necessary. His father's meeting with Fatima had gone well, and he had embraced her as his daughter-in-law before it was through.

It had been the proudest moment of his life.

Though they were not formally partnered yet, with his father's blessing, they were for all intents and purposes husband and wife. The marriage would take place as quickly as possible, perhaps within a few days, once the unpleasantness about to take place was over.

He bowed as Rafiq approached, alone, the man clearly here to talk rather than fight.

"Prince Magnus."

Magnus smiled. "Rafiq Halabi."

"I assume you know why I'm here."

Magnus frowned. "I'm afraid I do, and I apologize. You were never to know. Your family was never to know."

Rafiq's eyes flared, the man clearly keeping a tight leash on his anger. "You say that as if it were a good thing. Do you not realize the dishonor you have brought to my family? The shame? If I do not return with Fatima, then I am dead. *That* is the price demanded by the sheik, my sister's future husband! *I* am to die for your selfish act."

Magnus closed his eyes for a moment, this news unexpected. None of this was supposed to happen. Everyone was supposed to think she had killed herself. Yes, he had expected the sheik to be displeased, and acknowledged that there was a distinct possibility he might seek to quench his anger at Fatima's family's expense, yet there were remedies to that. His intention to give the family the exclusive contract to deal with his people, for one.

Yet no one was supposed to die.

No innocents.

They were to have lived their lives out here, in peace, and her family was to grieve, then move on, also in peace.

"He is determined to have blood?"

Rafiq nodded. "Or Fatima."

"But if Fatima returns, surely he'll punish her, perhaps even kill her."

Rafiq shook his head. "No. I told him that you kidnapped her."

Magnus' eyebrows rose at the revelation. "That's unfortunate." And it was. It likely meant his people would never trade there again. It could mean hostile encounters for years to come at land and at sea.

All because he had been a selfish fool.

Rafiq stared at him, his hand gripping the hilt of his sword. "I'm afraid I had no choice. The sheik was threatening to destroy my father's business. It would have ruined us all. The only way to save us was to deflect the blame."

Magnus nodded at the fleet, holding offshore. "You obviously succeeded."

"Yes. The sheik must preserve his honor by showing he attempted to rescue his future wife."

"And should you fail?"

"Then I die."

"But will he be back?"

Rafiq shrugged. "That, I cannot say for certain, though I think now that she is here, with your people, he will realize any attempt short of war would be futile."

Magnus tensed.

War.

With the discovery of their deception, he had sullied the Viking reputation within the Caliphate. That reputation was one of formidable warriors, yes, but also of fair traders. He had no desire for war, and none was likely to come after the failed attempts to take Iberia years ago.

But if Vikings couldn't be trusted in business dealings, then his brothers might be attacked and killed, whenever they approached a port, for fear that one on board might kidnap *their* daughter or loved one.

He had been a fool.

He should never have let this happen.

"What do you propose?"

Rafiq regarded him for a moment. "A challenge. Your best against my best. The winner keeps Fatima."

"No, this is madness! I'll go with you!"

Fatima rushed from the crowd gathered, throwing herself at Rafiq's feet. "I'm sorry, Brother. I never meant to hurt anyone. I was stupid, I know, but I love him, and I knew there was no way I could be with him as long as anyone thought I was alive. Please, don't hurt him. I'll go with you!"

Magnus' stomach churned and his heart ached with her words. The very idea she would leave him was heartbreaking, though he understood why. Yet he couldn't live without her.

But there was a solution.

"I'll return with her, to face whatever punishment your people demand. I don't want the actions of one lone Viking to affect the relations between our people, perhaps for years to come. I cannot risk war for my own selfish love."

Rafiq drew a deep breath, then slowly exhaled as he stared at Magnus, then down at his sister, at his knees, her hands clasped in front of her chest. "I'm afraid we're beyond that."

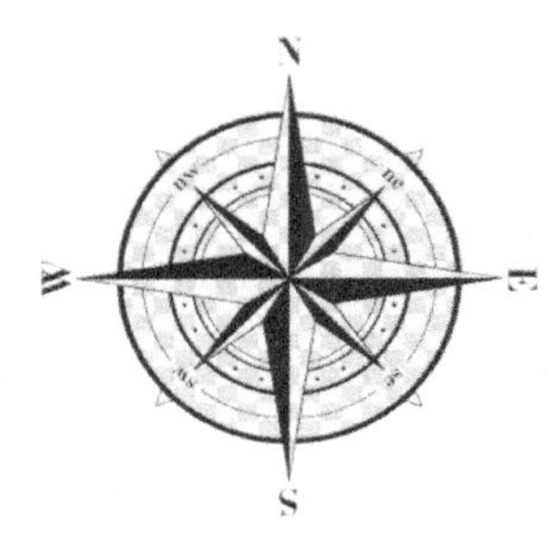

Somewhere over the Continental United States

Present Day

"I've traced those SUVs that left the embassy."

Somebody knocked on the door of the bathroom Chris Leroux had jammed himself and too much equipment into. He was sitting on the toilet, a laptop propped up on his knees, his secure satphone tethered to it to provide him access to Langley's servers, and an encrypted voice connection to his team.

None of which he could take advantage of sitting out in coach with an audience.

"Occupied!"

"Hurry the hell up! You've been in there long enough to work up a second shit!"

Leroux stifled a chuckle. "Sorry! Just returning from Mexico. Montezuma's revenge."

Sympathy immediately replaced the impatience. "Sorry, had that. Good luck, dude!"

I'll have to remember to look like shit when I come out of here.

"Umm, can you repeat that?"

Leroux laughed at Tong's puzzled tone, his live mike forgotten during his exchange with the passenger. "Nothing, just buying myself time."

"Boss, if you need some private crunch time, Sonya's doing a bang-up job here."

Leroux shook his head at his youngest team member's joke. "Thanks, Randy, but I'm fine. Back to business. Where'd they go?"

"Bromma Airport. A private terminal," replied Tong.

"Did they get on a plane?"

"We don't know yet, but a Saudi flagged diplomatic flight left there a few minutes later."

"Headed for?"

"Dubai."

Leroux's eyes widened slightly. "Interesting. I would have thought Riyadh."

"Could it just be a coincidence?"

Leroux pursed his lips, listening to his famous gut. "Could be, but I doubt it. The timing is too tight, and we know he didn't come out of the embassy the way he went in. He's either still in there, or was in one of those SUVs."

"Dead or alive."

Leroux nodded at Randy Child's observation. "Let's hope the latter, but history suggests the former. When does the plane land?"

"Less than three hours."

"Okay, since he's a Swedish citizen, we'll have to hand this over to them, or possibly Interpol."

Child grunted. "There goes the neighborhood."

Leroux suppressed a chuckle, though his underling was right. With the Saudis a member of Interpol, and the regime likely behind the kidnapping or murder, they would be privy to the investigation. "Yeah, I'll talk to the Director, but there's no way Washington is going to authorize anything beyond electronic surveillance with there being no Americans involved."

"What about Professor Acton?" asked Tong.

"He hasn't done anything stupid yet."

Child laughed. "Just wait."

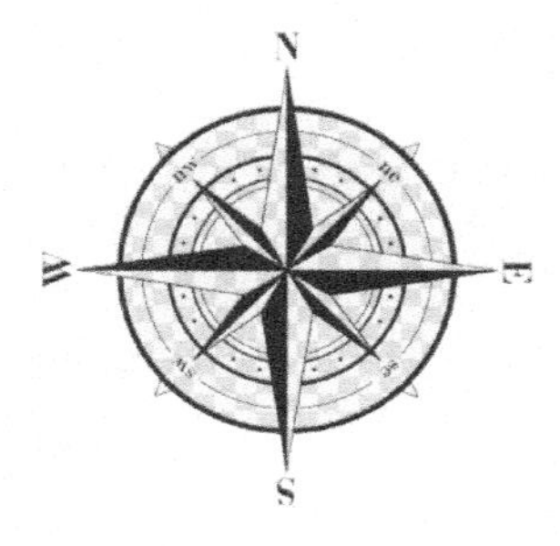

Stockholm University

Stockholm, Sweden

Acton swiped the parking pass included in the package left by the Saudis. There was a beep and the gate rose, clearing the way to the underground parking garage. Laura read out the instructions, guiding them to a secluded spot near an elevator on the lowest level. He backed in, just in case they had to make a quick getaway, then turned off the engine.

He looked at Laura, painfully aware they were both under constant surveillance.

I wonder if they work down here.

They likely did. Many underground garages had their own cellphone signal boosters, and it wasn't worth the risk testing his doubts.

Lives were at stake.

"Ready for this?"

Laura frowned. "Of course not."

Acton grunted. "Me neither." He regarded her for a moment, fear filling him at the prospect of her getting hurt. "It isn't too late to back out. We have no obligation here. Nobody would blame us for just going to the authorities."

Laura shook her head, determination creasing her face. "No. This is the easy part. All we need to do is get the ring and get out. This isn't America. It's not like this place is swarming with armed guards."

Acton nodded, drawing a breath of courage. "You're right. Let's see if we even succeed in getting the ring, then cross the next bridge when we come to it." He jabbed a finger at Laura's pin. "And you guys better hold up your end of the bargain."

He stepped out of the SUV, locking it behind him with the fob. They strode casually toward the elevator, Laura holding the tablet with their instructions.

"Look to the right, then when the doors open, at the floor. When we step inside, keep your head down, turn to face the doors, looking left, then press the button for the third floor."

Acton kept his gaze fixed to the right as they reached the elevator. "They obviously know where all the cameras are." He wondered if that intel came from Karlsson, or from their own people. He had to admit, despite working for years in the same place, he wouldn't be able to tell anyone where the cameras were at his university. No, this level of detail was too specific to be from his friend.

That meant the Saudis here had their tentacles deep within the university, perhaps through exchange students with extracurricular activities that included spying for their king.

He pressed the button to call the elevator, his heart hammering hard. They were about to cross a line where coming back from would be difficult, if not impossible if something went wrong. Yes, they were doing this to save their friend, but they were committing a crime. Legally, they should have gone to the authorities. Instead, they were taking on law enforcement's job for them.

Like too many times in the past.

Every time they got involved in something, he would reassess the situation after the dust had settled, searching for things he could have done differently to avoid getting involved, or minimizing the damage. Unfortunately, other than compromising his own principals and allowing harm to come to others while he stood idly by, he rarely could find fault in his actions, despite the sometimes tragic outcomes.

He just prayed this wasn't one of those times.

A chime sounded and the doors to the elevator opened. As he stepped inside, he dropped his chin to his chest, staring at the floor, then turned around, tilting his head to the side as he reached forward and pressed the number three. The doors closed, and the elevator began to rise, Acton praying for a smooth, uneventful ride.

"When we step out, we go to the left, but we need to cover our eyes."

"Huh?"

"With your hand, I guess."

"That won't look obvious."

"Just massage your temples."

Acton smiled slightly. "My wife, the spy."

The doors opened and Acton stepped out, pinching his forehead between his thumb and middle finger as he bore left.

"We're clear to the door."

Acton eyed a dozen doors ahead of them. "Which one?"

"Three-oh-four. Last one on the left. Use the pass around your neck, then you'll have to enter a code."

"Please tell me you have it."

"No, you'll have to guess."

He nearly wigged out before catching her sarcastic tone. "No joking when we're breaking the law, dear."

"Yes, dear."

They arrived at the door and he tapped the pass against the pad, the security panel activating. "Code?" He entered the sequence as Laura read it from the tablet. There was a click, a green indicator displaying, and he pushed open the door, stepping inside.

Laura closed it behind her. "Okay, there are no cameras here, we're safe for now."

Acton grunted. "As long as nobody got suspicious as to why a man, fifty pounds lighter than Viggo, using his ID, was here with a beautiful young woman after hours."

Laura stopped, tilting her head toward him and batting her eyes. "Aww, you think I'm beautiful."

He grinned. "Jimmy don't marry no ugos."

Laura slapped his ass then guided them to an office at the rear of the lab, half a dozen tables filled with discoveries from the dig site, including a newly arrived body that could be Fatima herself. He resisted the urge to examine her remains, instead forcing himself to focus on the task at hand.

Saving their friend by becoming thieves.

The door to the inner office was unlocked, Karlsson's name proudly displayed above his title, the nameplates white on black, designed to be easily slid in and out, a subtle reminder every time one walked through the door that one could be replaced with the flick of a finger.

Laura pointed. "There's the safe."

He headed for the corner of the room then dropped to his knees. Laura read out the combination and he spun the tumblers, holding his breath when he was finished. "Here goes nothing." He twisted the handle and the safe clicked open.

Laura exhaled loudly behind him, squeezing his shoulder. "It should be in the back, in a sample bag."

Acton spotted it and gently retrieved it from the safe. He held it up for Laura to see, then suddenly realized something. "Why are the lights on?"

Laura's eyes bulged and she spun toward the lab. "Oh my, I didn't realize." She lowered her voice. "Somebody must be here."

Acton gently closed the safe so as not to make a sound, then spun the tumbler as he stuffed the sample bag with the ring in his pocket. He peered through the windows lining Karlsson's office, but saw no one. He wasn't surprised. It wasn't exactly a large area, and he doubted he could have missed someone on the way in. "Maybe they just forgot to turn out the lights."

There was a click at the main door and it swung open.

Just once I'd like something to go right!

He ducked, gripping Laura by the arm and hauling her down beside him, a half-wall filled with books their only cover. He grabbed Laura's pin and glared at it. "No one was supposed to be here, you assholes!" he hissed. He slowly rose, catching a glimpse of a young woman, her back to them, leaning over the remains he had noticed earlier.

They must have just arrived.

It made sense. If the remains had just arrived, this would be the first chance they had to properly examine them, and no self-respecting scientist would wait until Monday when something as exciting as this find was sitting on a table, begging to be studied.

Yet his understanding the young woman's presence didn't help their situation any. If she spotted them, then all would be lost.

Her phone beeped and she pulled it from her pocket. A finger was eagerly swiped. She read the message then tapped a response before quickly leaving the room, the door clicking shut behind her.

Acton looked at Laura's pin. "If that was you, then good thinking."

They rushed for the door, but Laura held out an arm before he could open it. "We have to wait for her to get on the elevator."

Acton cursed. "How many Mississippis is that?"

She shrugged. "Thirty?"

He began counting, but before he could reach Laura's estimate, there was a click then a beep at the door.

Did she forget something?

Laura dropped to the floor behind a lab table as he ducked behind the door.

And frowned at what came through.

A security guard. They were about to be discovered, and Karlsson was about to die.

Unless he used his training without hesitation.

He stepped forward, grabbing the man around his neck, locking his arm into position over the man's throat with his other arm. Then squeezed. A struggle immediately ensued, and Acton held on for dear life, the man more powerful than his compact frame had suggested.

But if he lost his grip, he'd probably be bested, the man twenty years Acton's junior. He could live with that, but there was another, far worse outcome if the man continued to struggle too hard.

His neck might accidentally snap.

Acton was about to err on the side of caution and ease his grip when the struggle finally weakened, then waned to nothing. He gently lowered the guard to the floor then checked for a pulse.

"Okay, he's out. Let's get the hell out of here."

"What's going on here?"

Acton looked up to see the woman from earlier standing in the doorway, her mouth agape, her eyes wide as she stared at him, a man from all outward appearances dead at his feet.

"Professor Acton?"

He cursed, his reputation obviously preceding him.

"Oh my God, is he dead?"

Laura swiftly rounded the table, approaching the woman from behind, then pressed a finger into her back. "Move, and you die."

She gasped then dropped to the floor, out cold.

Laura stared down at her. "What do we do now?"

Acton checked the guard's pulse once again, then shrugged. "We get out of here as quickly as we can and hand this damned ring over. Once we have Viggo, we can come back and explain everything, and hope we're forgiven."

Laura agreed. "Let's move then, before they wake up." She led the way out the door and they ran for the elevator. The doors opened, the car still on their floor from the young woman's arrival, and they stepped inside.

Acton stared at the floor then to the left, cursing as he realized he had forgotten about the hallway cameras. He hit the button for the bottom parking level. "Why the bottom?" he muttered, watching the floors count down.

"Maybe that's where he normally parks?"

Acton decided it wasn't important, instead readying for the doors to open—either at their destination, or on an earlier floor with a dozen guards on the other side.

The quiet weekend was again their friend, and the doors opened in the parking garage. He gently pushed Laura through the doors with a hand on her back, following immediately behind her as he retrieved the fob from his pocket. He pressed the button.

And all hell broke loose.

"Did you do that?" asked Laura as security alarms blared and beacons mounted to the walls flashed. He rushed for the door of their SUV, yanked it open then jumped inside, slamming the door shut, thankful for the reprieve it brought from the cacophony of noise outside the thin glass.

He started the vehicle and put it in gear, hammering on the gas as Laura fastened her seatbelt. "I think we've been found out."

Acton grunted. "No shit."

A security guard emerged from a stairwell to their left, shouting something at them in Swedish. Acton ignored him, turning up the ramp and beginning the winding route to the surface as more guards appeared at each landing. Thankfully, no shots had yet been fired, and Acton wondered if the guards here even carried guns.

It's not back home.

He spotted the exit ahead and gunned it, two guards dashing out in front of them, waving their arms. He floored it and laid on the horn. "Get the hell out of the way!" he shouted, the two men compelled to comply at the last second by his approaching bumper and not his own urgings.

"The gate!" cried Laura.

Acton braced himself with the steering wheel and pressed harder on the accelerator. The gate splintered then broke, and moments later they were clear of the parking structure, racing across the visitor's parking lot then onto the street.

The phone they had been provided rang in his pocket. He eased off the accelerator and fished it out, handing it to Laura. She put it on speaker, holding it up to him. "Hello?"

"You have the ring?"

His eyes narrowed.

How couldn't they know?

"Yes."

"Go to the airport, Terminal Five. You will be met."

Acton tensed. This wasn't part of the plan. At least, not as he had understood it. They were supposed to exchange the ring for Karlsson, and he had assumed that would be happening in Stockholm in a very public place.

An airport meant travel.

And he feared where.

"What are you talking about? We had a deal. We give you the ring, you give us Viggo."

"You were discovered. The deal has changed."

The call ended before Acton could protest, and he cursed, slamming his fist against the steering wheel. "This is getting too serious. We should just go to the police and turn ourselves in."

Laura nodded. "I think you're right."

The phone rang again, startling them both. Laura answered, again putting it on speaker.

"Talk like that, Professors, will ensure your friend dies a most horrible, painful, and prolonged death."

A bloodcurdling scream erupted from the speaker before the call was cut off, leaving a chill to rush down Acton's sweat-drenched back.

"We don't have a choice," gasped Laura, her voice filled with anguish at the sound of agony they had just heard. Acton looked at his wife and reached out for her, squeezing her hand.

"We'll get through this."

He was about to mention that Reading would have received their message by now, and that plans to help them might already be in motion, but he stopped himself in time. He hated the fact they were being listened to, though he still had his doubts as to whether they were being watched. He stared at the road ahead, unsure of what to do beyond follow the plan forced upon them.

And making sure he got his face on every damned camera he could before boarding.

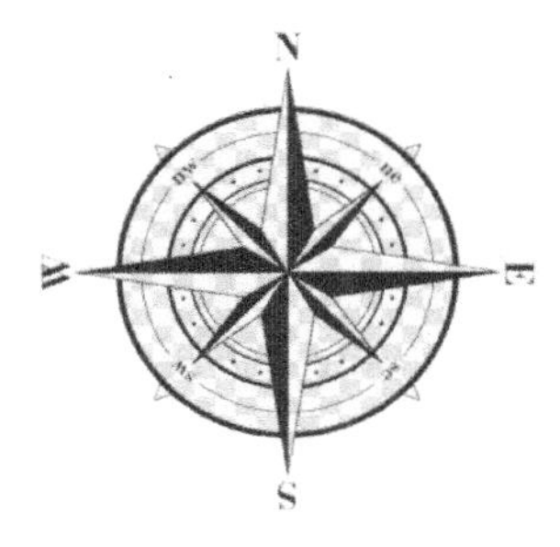

Operations Center 2, CIA Headquarters

Langley, Virginia

"Sir, I've been monitoring Stockholm police reports, and it looks like there was just an incident at the university where Professor Karlsson works."

Leroux rose from his station, having arrived only minutes ago from Las Vegas, Sherrie already en route to Shitbuktu as she had called it, having taken a separate flight. He was thankful to have something to jump into straight away, rather than spend the evening worrying about her.

He stepped over to Sonya Tong's station. "Details?"

She shook her head. "Not much, except that there were two perps, a man and a woman—"

Randy Child spun in his chair, staring up at the ceiling. "Fifty bucks says the professors."

"—and they were armed. They tried to kill one of the guards—"

Leroux interrupted. "That doesn't sound like them."

Child dropped his foot, stopping his spin. "You're right. If those two tried, they would have succeeded."

Tong continued. "And another woman was assaulted before they made their escape."

Leroux shook his head, this escalation unexpected. "What was taken?"

"Nothing on that yet."

Leroux turned to Child. "Where are they now?"

"Their phones are still at their hotel."

Leroux didn't buy it. "See if we can pull some traffic camera footage of the area, see if we have them on video near the university."

Child went to work as Director Leif Morrison entered, National Clandestine Service Chief for the CIA. "What's the status?"

Leroux stood a little straighter. "It looks like our two professors are about to be wanted for armed robbery and attempted murder."

Morrison's eyebrows shot up. "Holy shit!" He glanced about the room. "Pardon my French, people."

Leroux shrugged. "We've all said far worse."

Morrison chuckled. "I have no doubt." He motioned at the large set of displays that curved across the entire front of the operations center. "What am I looking at?"

"I'm not sure yet."

"What does that famous gut of yours tell us?"

Leroux frowned. "That they've just completed the first step of someone else's plan."

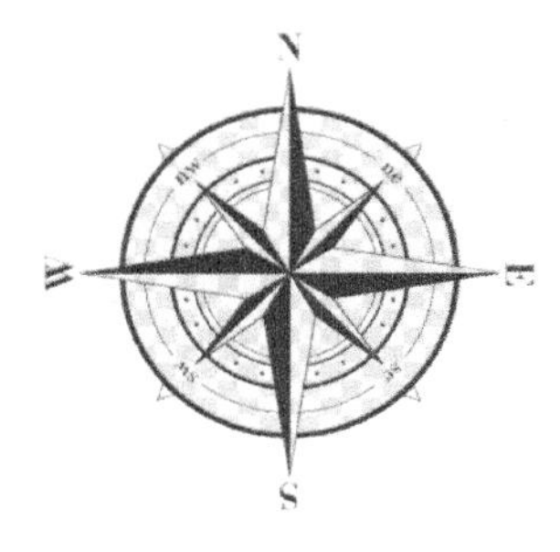

Stockholm Arlanda Airport

Stockholm, Sweden

Acton took a seat in the main terminal, Laura beside him, a cart full of their luggage from the hotel in front of them. A handoff had been made within moments of arriving, their passports and tickets delivered to them by a Middle Eastern-looking man, along with their luggage. Everything had been thought of, as if the Saudis were too experienced at this.

It was disconcerting, to say the least.

He checked the ticket, the destination providing mixed feelings. "Dubai." He held it up for Laura to see.

"Really? I wasn't expecting that."

He nodded. "Neither was I. I would have thought Riyadh, but maybe they're trying to make it look like they're not involved."

Laura frowned. "It's just a hop, skip, and a jump to Saudi Arabia from Dubai. When we land, they could just load us in a car and we're heading down the highway to the Kingdom."

Acton sighed. She was right. This wasn't exactly good news, though it did buy them time. He had to assume Reading was on the case, and if he was, then Kane was as well. If the CIA were involved, and they could very well be because he was an American being manipulated by a foreign power, then they could be watching them right now.

And they'd absolutely notice them catching a flight to Dubai using their own passports.

He frowned.

And so might the Swedes.

"We better get a move on. That girl at the university recognized me. It's only a matter of time before we're flagged." He looked up at the ceiling, spotting one of the security domes hiding the cameras. And made a point of staring at it for several moments as they headed to the check-in counter.

"How long do you think we have?"

"Before our names are on every cop's lips? Not long."

"Then we better hurry."

They checked their luggage without incident, though they were admonished for showing up so late for their flight, Acton giving the excuse of a lemon rental, all forgiven when he mentioned the sportscar's notorious British brand.

As they headed for security, Acton cursed, fishing the ring out of his pocket and removing it from the plastic sample bag as surreptitiously as possible. He slipped it on his pinky finger, disposing of the bag in a nearby trash can.

Laura winked at him. "You look like a mobster."

"I'm gonna make him an offer he can't refuse."

Laura snickered at his horrendous Don Corleone impression. "Don't make me laugh, it'll just draw attention to us."

Acton spun the ring on his finger, his mind racing. If they were arrested here, then the ring would be confiscated, and his friend could die. Though if they made it on the flight, and out of Sweden, there was no way they wouldn't be arrested upon arrival with the same result.

"We're not going to make it."

Laura looked at him. "What do you mean? Onto the flight?"

"We might make it out of Sweden, but there's no way we're not getting arrested at the other end."

Laura squeezed his hand. "Let's just hope they've thought of that."

"Let's hope." His eyes roamed the terminal as they headed for security, then settled on one of the myriad of retail offerings. "I've got an idea."

Stockholm University

Stockholm, Sweden

Elsa Andersson sat on a stool in the lab that had always been a safe place for her, still trembling at what had happened earlier. When she had come to, it was to wailing alarms and flashing lights, then guards at the door. Police had been called, along with paramedics, and all were here now, swarming the crime scene.

A crime scene that made no sense to her.

Why would Professor James Acton be here without Karlsson, why would he have assaulted the thankfully alive guard, and why would his wife threaten to kill her? None of it made any sense. And apparently, it didn't make any sense to the detective now interviewing her, repeatedly asking her if she was certain, absolutely certain, who the suspects were.

"You've never met the man."

"No."

"Yet you can be absolutely certain it was him."

"Yes. Like I said before, I looked him up on the Internet yesterday."

"Why?"

She growled. "Like I said before, because Professor Karlsson said to."

"And why was that again?"

She snapped. "Listen, they're getting away! Why are you wasting time? They tried to kill that guard over there, and she threatened me with a gun!"

"It looks like a sleeper hold was used on the guard."

"That's only because I walked in on them before he could finish the job."

"You said the other one, Professor Laura Palmer, held a gun on you?"

She nodded. "She pressed it against my back."

"Did you see the weapon?"

Elsa paused. "Well, no. But I felt it."

"So maybe it wasn't a gun?"

"Of course it was a gun. They're American! They all carry guns!"

The detective frowned. "We don't exactly let them in the country with weapons."

Elsa grunted. "Well, I don't know about that, but she had a gun."

"Or something pressed against your back."

Elsa glared at her.

"Now, back to this text message you received from Professor Karlsson. You said he asked you to meet him in the lobby, but he wasn't there. Then when you returned, you found Acton and Palmer in here, and the guard unconscious on the floor."

"Yes."

"Don't you think that's a bit of a coincidence?"

Elsa's eyes narrowed. "What do you mean?"

"Well, you receive a message from your professor, then these two show up using his pass."

Elsa's jaw dropped. "You think he's involved?"

The detective smiled slightly. "More likely they have his phone, and used it to send a message to draw you away while they did whatever they did."

Elsa paused, her mouth still agape. "I guess that makes more sense. But why? Acton and Karlsson are supposed to be friends. Why would he take his pass and phone, then break in here?"

"Why indeed. Is there anything valuable here?"

She shrugged. "To academics, maybe. To thieves? I don't think so."

"So, no ancient relics that might be valuable to collectors, jewelry, treasure?"

Elsa's eyes widened. "The ring! It was why they were here. Not *here* here, but in Sweden. Professor Karlsson invited them here to see the ring we discovered."

"It's valuable?"

"To someone like Acton, absolutely. It's over a thousand years—"

The detective cut her off. "Where is it?"

Elsa pointed toward Karlsson's office. "In the safe."

"Show me."

Elsa led her to the office and pointed at the safe. "Huh, it's still locked."

"What's the combination?"

She shrugged. "No idea."

The detective called one of the others over. "We need to get that opened. It's on university property, so get the president's permission so we don't have to wait for the courts." The detective returned her attention to Elsa as her partner walked away. Another officer entered with a tablet in his hand.

"We've confirmed their identities. It's definitely James Acton and Laura Palmer."

The detective smiled, then pulled out her phone, ordering the arrest of Professors James Acton and Laura Palmer for armed robbery and attempted murder, something Elsa couldn't believe was possibly true.

If she hadn't lived through the terrifying experience herself.

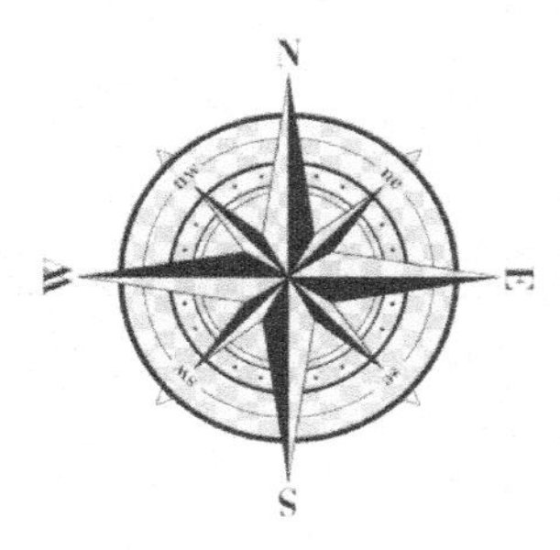

Leonardo da Vinci–Fiumicino Airport

Rome, Italy

Agent Hugh Reading shuffled along in the security line, frustrated with the delay, exhausted from his lack of CPAP therapy, grumpy about the amount of money this flight was costing him, and terribly worried about his friends.

It was eating him up inside.

His phone vibrated and he quickly grabbed it, praying it was good news. The call display indicated his partner back in London, and his hopes surged.

"I thought you were sick?"

"I am, but I've got news you needed to hear from a friend."

His stomach flipped as he expected the worst. "What is it?"

An announcement blared over the public address system.

"Where are you? The conference isn't over yet."

Reading frowned. "Umm, if I told you then I'd have to kill you."

"That's what I thought. Well, this might not come as much of a surprise to you, then. Guess what just came across the wire?"

"What?"

"Your professor friends are wanted in Stockholm for armed robbery and attempted murder."

Reading froze, pressing the phone tighter to his ear. "Bloody hell!"

"I'd suggest stronger words. Their names and pictures have been sent to us."

Reading resumed his shuffle, his mind racing. "Can you stop it?"

"It's already been sent out. There's no way."

Reading cursed. "Then whatever they're up to is about to come to a screeching halt."

"Hugh, what's going on?"

He sighed. "I'm not really sure, but I need to know where they are."

"Aren't we assuming they're still in Stockholm?"

Reading grunted. "With those two, I've learned to never assume anything but the unexpected."

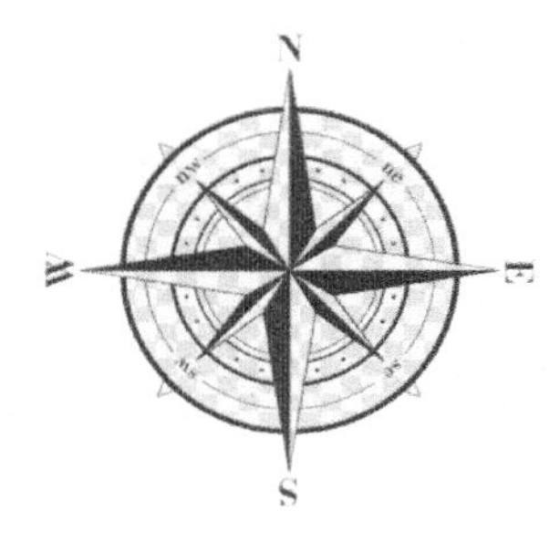

Karlsson Residence

Stockholm, Sweden

Mira Karlsson nearly jumped out of her skin at the doorbell. She had been staring at the phone and her husband's empty chair all day, terrified to do or say anything, the pin on her shirt like an albatross around her neck.

She leaped to her feet then steadied herself, remembering she had to remain calm and not let anyone suspect what was truly ravaging her normally sedate household. She glanced down at the pin as she reached for the doorknob. "Don't worry, I won't tell them anything."

She opened the door, her eyebrows rising at the sight of a delivery man. He handed her a small package. "Oh, I wasn't expecting anything."

The man smiled. "Surprises are always the best! Hope it's something good!" He lowered his voice. "Whatever you do, don't tell the police your husband is missing."

Her mouth opened in shock then she stared down at the pin. "I won't, I swear." She looked at him, her eyes narrowing. "But you've already told me this." She tapped the pin and the man appeared confused for a moment.

He frowned, handing her the handheld computer. "Sign here." She did, her hands trembling as she tried to comprehend what was happening. She signed her name and he smiled, taking back the device. "Have a nice day."

He returned to his truck and she stared after him for a moment before closing the door. She shuffled back to her post by the phone, staring at the small package in her hands.

Should I open it?

She shuddered. With the Saudis involved, it could be a bomb for all she knew. But then why warn her? Why let her know it was them? Surely if they wanted her to open a bomb, they would make it appear to be from someone else.

Her jaw dropped and she drew a quick breath.

It wasn't them!

Someone else must have found out what was going on, and they came to warn her to keep quiet so they could work the case. Her shoulders slumped as her stomach flipped. She stared at the pin, realizing that whoever had her husband now knew someone else was involved.

What do I do?

What could she do? The only instruction she had been given was to not tell anyone what was going on. She assumed everyone else was given the same instruction, but obviously someone had disobeyed.

And whoever that was, might have just cost her husband his life.

She pulled the pin off her shirt and held it up to her face, her entire body shaking as she lost control. "Please, you've heard everything. I never told anyone. Please, I beg you, don't hurt my husband. I'll give you whatever you want. Everything we have. Just don't hurt my husband!"

She stared at the pin, tears flowing down her cheeks, not sure what she was expecting to happen.

And when nothing did, she curled into a ball and wept, praying for the first time in years, to a god her husband didn't even believe in.

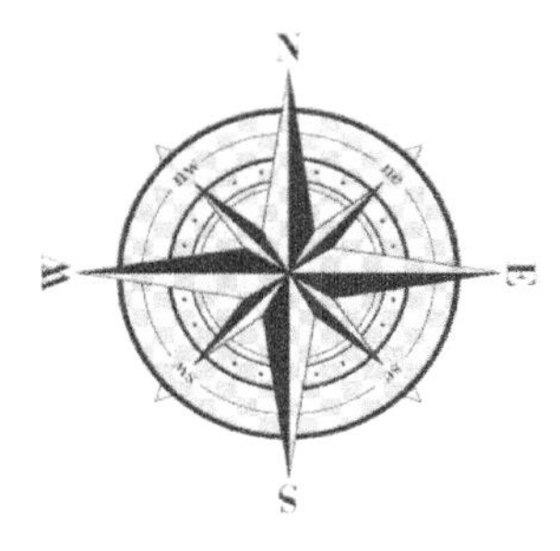

Unknown Location

Viggo Karlsson moaned, his nipples in agony, the bastards that had kidnapped him twisting them with pliers hours ago to elicit a scream out of him when his friends apparently had doubts on whether to continue. While he didn't want to die, he didn't want anyone risking their lives for him, yet he was powerless to do anything.

He had refused to speak to Acton when it was demanded of him, so they had brought out the pliers. He had never imagined such pain was possible, the mere thought of it sending a new surge through his body. At this moment, he would rather die than feel such a thing again, and the very thought devastated him. To think that this could be the end of everything, all over a ring lost for one thousand years, was tragically disappointing. He might be old in some people's eyes, but he still had too much left to contribute before he was cremated and his ashes spread across the fiord where he was born.

And his wife would be wrecked.

She could take care of herself. That wasn't what worried him. The woman took care of *him*. But she was lonely. He still had his work, but she only had him and a dwindling pool of friends, some passing as time was known to cause, others moving to greener pastures or to be with children who had made lives elsewhere.

If only Theo were still with us.

Their only son had passed away almost ten years ago from ALS. It had struck swiftly, taking him in less than a year, and much of that final time was filled with pain and suffering. It had been a blessing and a curse to finally see his suffering end, but it had changed them both forever.

It was almost enough to make him believe in God, if only it would have meant his son would be in a better place, rather than simply dead, his existence finished.

His wife believed, and that was enough. He had always felt that if God were indeed real, he would be loving enough to accept all into His dominion, even those who didn't believe, so long as they led a good life.

And he thought he had, though if the afterlife were real, he'd prefer eternal damnation than his friends dying for him.

But again, he had no control over the situation.

In fact, he had no idea where he was, except that it wasn't the airplane they had woken him on. When he had refused to hand over the ring to the Ambassador, he had risen to leave, but before he could get out of the room, he was grabbed by both arms and jabbed in the neck with something. He assumed it was a needle loaded with some sort of drug, because he passed out in short order, waking on the plane where they demanded he speak to Acton, then provide them with every detail of his university he could remember, including the location of security cameras and passcodes.

What had dismayed him was that they knew so much already. They had the blueprints and security camera layouts in levels of detail far greater than he could provide.

They just asked the questions to make sure you were telling the truth.

It was clear to him they were blackmailing Acton and his wife into stealing the ring in exchange for his life. His fear at first was that they might get hurt in the attempt, so he was reluctant to actually give complete information. If they were to be caught in the act because of a forgotten camera or an incorrect code, then they could be saved from what was to come.

Unfortunately, these men holding him captive had apparently thought he might try something, and instead threatened not only the lives of his friends, but those of his wife and students at the dig site.

And he believed them. These were fanatics. No sane person would go to these lengths just for a ring. And their actions in Turkey removed any doubt that they would make good on their threats. There they had sent a team of fifteen hitmen in a premeditated murder—one doesn't bring a bone saw to a kidnapping—and beat a man to death, then chemically liquified his remains.

Then denied, denied, denied.

And they would do the same to him and his friends.

All for a ring he couldn't care less about right now.

I just want to go home.

But where was home in relation to here? He had no idea where he was. After giving them everything he knew to help Acton steal the ring, they had injected him again, and he had woken tied to what he assumed was a chair, with a hood over his head and tape over his mouth.

And a bladder ready to burst.

He shouted against his gag, not certain if he was alone or not, the hood over his head leaving him completely unaware of his surroundings. He hadn't heard anything since he had regained consciousness. For all he knew, he could be alone in the center of a warehouse, or surrounded by dozens, all staring at him in silence.

"He's awake."

It was said in Arabic, a language he had learned in his youth when his father had been stationed in Egypt as part of the diplomatic core. Things had been more peaceful then, not like they were today. At first, he had supported the migrants fleeing the civil war in Syria, but as his government took more and more in, he, like many Swedes, realized too late the mistake they had made.

They were losing their country.

Yet none of that mattered right now. He'd give anything to be back there, and was about to demand an answer as to what was going on when he decided to keep the fact he spoke Arabic to himself—it might prove useful should they reveal some detail he could use later to gain his freedom.

"Please, is anybody there? I need to use the bathroom."

It was a universal need, shared by everyone, though he wasn't sure if it would be understood through his gag.

Someone approached. Footsteps on carpet.

Not a warehouse.

His hood was yanked off and he blinked rapidly, staring up at the bearded man who stood in front of him. He jabbed him in the chest with a finger.

"Scream, Professor, and you die a slow, painful death."

Karlsson nodded, there no need to convince him of the truth contained in those words. The tape covering his mouth was yanked free, and he drew several deep, gasping breaths, the first he had taken unrestricted in hours, he was sure. "I-I need to use the bathroom."

The man stepped back and pointed to a door on the left. "Five minutes. And leave the door open."

Karlsson stood, the effort required surprising, his joints protesting at not having been used since the embassy. He stepped into the bathroom, turning on the light, and gasped.

It was immaculate.

Based upon the amenities in plain view, wherever he was must be a hotel. He made for the toilet and took full advantage, as he had no idea when he might be given another chance. As he sat, he took in his surroundings, deciding this was a luxury hotel like none he had been in before.

It meant his captors had money.

And of course they did. They were connected with Saudi royalty, and that meant Saudi oil money.

He shook his head.

Why anyone would buy Saudi oil over that available in peaceful countries like Canada, he'd never know. It was why he had a problem with the environmental movement sometimes. By blocking pipelines, they forced companies to buy their oil from murderous regimes like the Saudis and Venezuelans, instead of from those evil Canadians.

Their response?

Leave it in the ground.

Right, and shut down Western civilization as we know it.

Morons.

He flushed a toilet full of what those people were dishing, and headed for the sink, finally staring out the window in the room behind him, reflected in the mirror he now faced.

And gasped once again.

A city, carved out of a desert that stretched as far as the eye could see, was shocking in how far below him it appeared.

Where am I?

Then his eyes shot wide as he realized exactly where he was.

The Burj Khalifa, the world's tallest building, located in the heart of Dubai.

And his heart sank.

Nobody would think to look for him here. There was no hope of rescue, no hope of police that could be trusted to come to his aid. Even if he managed to escape, he would be surrounded by potentially hostile, certainly untrusting people, who would hand him over to authorities likely under the influence of whoever had taken him.

The Saudi government.

I'm doomed.

He dried his hands and stepped back into the room. The man who had removed his gag pointed at a comfortable chair in the corner.

"Sit there and keep your mouth shut. If you try anything, you'll be bound and gagged. Understood?"

"Yes." His stomach growled. "Umm, could I perhaps get some food and water?" He glanced at his watch, his eyebrows jumping.

Eight hours!

"I haven't eaten since this morning."

The man nodded. "I'll have some brought up." He left the room, a conversation between the man and another starting up, again in Arabic, debating whether to bother feeding a man who might be dead in short order.

"Someone could ask questions," protested the other man.

"Who? And what would they ask? Why hotel guests ordered room service? Why would they possibly have questions about that?"

The response was dripping with sarcasm. "Oh, I don't know, maybe why we need a third meal when there are only two of us here?"

The first chuckled. "Is that what you're worried about? Then we'll order something that can be shared. No one will question that."

"I still say we let him starve. Give him tap water if it will shut him up, but every time someone enters this room, we risk being discovered. Sheik Al-Zayani will not be at all understanding if we mess this up."

Karlsson latched onto the name.

Al-Zayani.

He had heard the name once before, this morning. The Ambassador had said the ring belonged to the Al-Zayani family, and they wanted it back. Things had rapidly headed south when he said he didn't have the ring with him, nor was it in his purview to give it to them.

"Why not?"

"Because it doesn't belong to me."

The Ambassador had vigorously nodded. "Exactly! It belongs to us!"

Karlsson's eyes narrowed. "Your country didn't even exist when this ring was buried and forgotten."

"You know what I mean. The ring belongs to the descendants of who originally owned it, one of our citizens. It belongs to the Al-Zayani family, and they want it back."

Karlsson hadn't bought the explanation. "How can they possibly know the ring belongs to them? It's over one thousand years old."

The Ambassador had seemed slightly uncomfortable with the question, leaning forward in his chair and lowering his voice. "I will tell you something, my friend, something you need to understand. When the Al-Zayani family says something, no matter how outrageous you may think it is, you believe it as if Allah himself had said it. Their word is enough. The ring belongs to the Al-Zayani family because they say it does, and they want it back."

Karlsson shook his head. "And again, like I said, it's not mine to give."

Frustrated words had been barked behind him in Arabic. "Enough of this nonsense!"

And moments later he had felt something jab into the side of his neck as he rose to leave, his world fading to black.

This little overheard tidbit at least confirmed who was behind this.

He strained to listen to the conversation that continued in the next room of the suite they occupied.

"That American has the ring," said the first. "It's only a matter of hours before he gets here, then this will all be over."

"Right, and do you think the sheik will want any witnesses left who might be able to talk?"

There was a pause. "Would he care?"

"What do you mean?"

"He's one of the most powerful, richest men in the world. He's untouchable."

An audible sigh sounded. "I pray to Allah that you are right, my friend, otherwise you and I could be sharing a grave with our Swedish professor before the night is out."

"I'll put a bullet in the sheik's head myself before I let that happen."

"You would condemn your family to death just to save your own? I for one would happily accept death, as should you. I just pray that Allah finds our deaths worthy of entry into Jannah."

The first chuckled. "Let's not plan our deaths just yet. I still think the sheik doesn't care if anyone knows. He's simply above the petty concerns of us mere mortals."

The second laughed. "Let's hope you're right." He sighed. "So, we feed him?"

"Feed him, and order extra for ourselves. If we're going to die today, then I refuse to do it on a stomach that isn't bloated with the finest life has to offer!"

Karlsson shivered as his stomach growled. It sounded like Acton had succeeded in stealing the ring, and if he were indeed on his way, he had obviously come through the ordeal unscathed, and he prayed the same was true for Laura.

Prayed.

He sighed, wondering if he were a hypocrite for praying to a god he didn't believe in.

If you're real, then please protect my friends. Don't worry about me.

He suppressed a grunt.

No Atheists in foxholes?

He frowned.

I am *a hypocrite!*

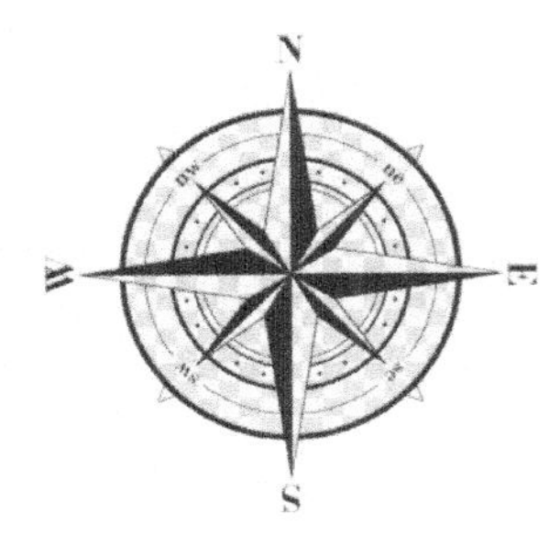

Operations Center 2, CIA Headquarters

Langley, Virginia

"Well, this isn't good."

Leroux stepped over to Randy Child's station. "What?"

"I've been monitoring flights leaving Stockholm and just got a hit. James Acton and Laura Palmer boarded a flight to Dubai earlier."

Leroux's eyes narrowed. "Dubai?"

"Yup."

"Interesting." He gestured to the main displays. "Put it up." Child complied, copies of the boarding passes and passport scans appearing. Leroux read every piece of information displayed, searching for something, for anything that might give them a clue, when he stopped, his gut telling him something wasn't right. "They each checked two bags."

Child shrugged. "So? Maybe they don't like to travel light. They're rich, aren't they?"

"Yes, but why did they have their luggage with them?"

Child's eyebrows shot up. "Huh?"

"And look when those tickets were bought. Just minutes *after* the robbery was reported."

"So?"

"So, why do you bring your luggage with you on a robbery, *then* buy the tickets to leave the country? And why buy tickets? They have a private jet at their disposal."

Child shrugged. "Maybe the jet wasn't available? It's a lease-share network, so there are no guarantees."

Tong attacked her keyboard, then shook her head. "No, there's a jet in their network in Oslo. They could have just reserved that one and it could have been there in time."

Child folded his arms across his chest, regarding Leroux. "So, what are you saying? I'm confused."

Tong cleared her throat. "So am I."

Leroux dropped into his chair. "Think about it. You break into the university, assault two people, then leave for the airport. *After* you leave, and are heading for the airport, you buy the tickets. You have your luggage with you already, because this was obviously your plan all along. But if it was, why not have the tickets purchased beforehand?"

"Because they didn't want them to be flagged?" suggested Tong.

Leroux shook his head. "No, they aren't in the system yet, and they certainly wouldn't have been before the robbery. There was no reason to not book the tickets ahead of time. What if something had gone wrong and they lost their data connection and couldn't purchase the tickets from the car on the way there? There are any number of things that could have gone wrong in purchasing those tickets. Hell, there might not have been any seats."

"So, we have an anomaly."

Leroux nodded at Tong. "Exactly. I think something else happened. There's no way they planned on assaulting two people during that robbery. They're not the type to hurt innocent people. I think they went in, stole the ring, and they were supposed to meet with the Saudis to exchange it for Professor Karlsson." He pointed at the display, the agency used to purchase the tickets shown. "And that's not their regular agent." Leroux shook his head. "I don't think they bought these tickets at all. I think they were bought for them after something went wrong."

"You mean the two people assaulted."

"Exactly."

"But how would they know right away?" asked Tong.

Leroux spun in his chair. "Remember, Acton didn't want any contact. They're obviously under very close observation, and if our man in Stockholm is right, it's in the form of pins stuck to their shirts."

Child frowned. "Yeah, that didn't exactly work out."

Leroux agreed. "No, but we did learn something that will hopefully prove valuable later." He stood, stepping toward the large displays. "But back to these tickets. If they were bought because something went wrong, then that means there was no reason for them to have their luggage with them."

"Maybe they went back to the hotel?" suggested Tong.

Child shook his head. "No time. They definitely went straight to the airport from the university. No stops or detours."

"Then someone must have brought them the bags."

Leroux snapped his fingers at Tong's suggestion. "Exactly! Check the footage, see if you can find them arriving. Maybe we can see who did the handoff to them, and get a face. We need someone we can track, and someone we can link back to the Saudis."

Child continued to be confused. "But why bring the bags? I don't understand. If this is some kidnap for ransom thing, why bring a change of clothes?"

Leroux smiled slightly at him. "Because what happens when a passenger on an international flight shows up with no luggage."

Child leaned back in his chair. "Aaah, that's it! You get flagged!"

"Exactly. They needed their bags to look like legitimate passengers, otherwise they might have been flagged by security, and asked questions they couldn't answer. It could have risked the entire operation."

Tong pursed her lips. "That's what this is, isn't it? An operation."

Leroux paused, considering her words. "Yes, I suppose it is. The Saudis are definitely pulling out all the stops to get this ring and the Actons out of the country. There's just one problem."

"What's that?" echoed Tong and Child.

"They'll be arrested the moment they land."

Child tapped at his keyboard. "Yup, you're right. Their names just went out on Interpol. They'll know pretty soon just where they are."

Tong frowned. "And they'll notify the Dubai authorities, who will arrest them and return them to Sweden for prosecution."

Child cursed. "Aborting this carefully planned operation, and killing Professor Karlsson and any other loose ends that might be still dangling out there."

Leroux tapped his chin, staring at the screen. "Carefully planned is the key."

Child stopped his chair in mid-spin. "What do you mean?"

"There's no way the Saudis wouldn't know they'd be arrested the moment they arrived."

"So, they've planned for this?"

Leroux nodded. "They must have."

"Which means they've got people on the inside in Dubai and in Interpol."

Leroux frowned. "Anything is possible with these people in that part of the world."

"What can we do to help them now?"

Leroux pursed his lips, thinking. "Okay, you're right. The game has changed. We now have an American citizen and a British subject about to be arrested in Dubai, after having committed a serious crime in Sweden that I don't think it takes a rocket surgeon"—Child snickered—"to figure out they were coerced into, and I'm sure after the fact we'll find lots of proof to clear them. Before, it was just Professor Karlsson involved, but now that there's definitely an American, and it's *this* American, we might be able to get some real assets involved." A thought occurred to him, and he smiled. "Where's Sherrie? I mean, Agent White."

Tong blushed, tapping her keyboard. "She just landed in Baghdad." She regarded him, her eyes narrowing. "What are you thinking?"

"I'm thinking if our professors land in Dubai and we don't do something, they're going to be dead before the sun rises."

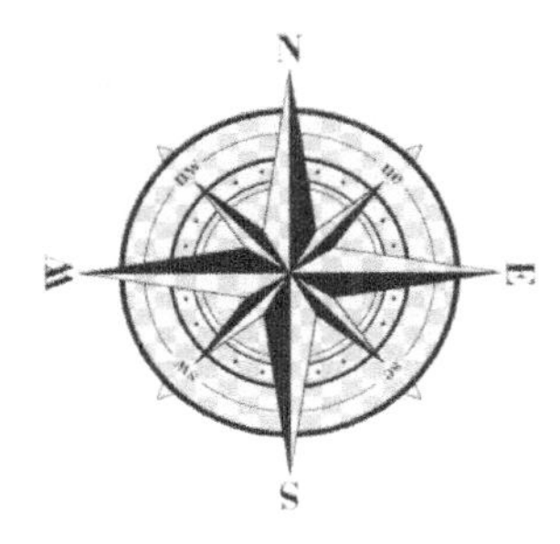

Leonardo da Vinci–Fiumicino Airport

Rome, Italy

Reading sat at his gate, exhausted, waiting for his flight to Stockholm to board. He was debating contacting his partner and having her courier his CPAP machine from London to Sweden, no matter what the cost.

He needed his rest not only for his own health, but to be at his best should his friends need him.

His phone vibrated and he checked the call display, smiling at Michelle's number. He swiped his thumb. "Please tell me you've got good news."

"I'm not sure I'd call it good news, but I've got news."

Reading's shoulders slumped. "Bloody hell. What now?"

"I have them on Emirates flight one-five-eight to Dubai, arriving in five hours."

His eyes shot wide. "Dubai?"

"Yup."

"Why the bloody hell would they be heading there?"

"No idea, but Interpol has requested they be picked up when they arrive. I've pulled some strings and got you a flight there. It leaves in thirty minutes."

He pushed to his feet. "Who'd you have to sleep with to arrange that?"

"Nobody. You, on the other hand, will be putting out for weeks once you get back here."

He chuckled. "Send me the details. Hopefully, I can wrangle them away from the Dubai authorities before anything too harsh is done to them."

"The ticket should be on your phone already. Good luck."

"Thanks." He ended the call, tossing his personally paid for ticket to Stockholm in the garbage.

There's a month's rent gone.

But that wasn't what was bothering him. Something else was. He knew his friends, and they weren't stupid. They had to have known they'd be flagged and arrested the moment they stepped off the airplane. And why would they have left Sweden?

They had to have been coerced into it. For some reason, the Saudis wanted to exchange the ring for the professor in Dubai, instead of Sweden.

And that likely meant they had a plan already in place to address the Interpol issue.

He checked his new flight's arrival time.

And cursed.

They'd beat him by almost half an hour.

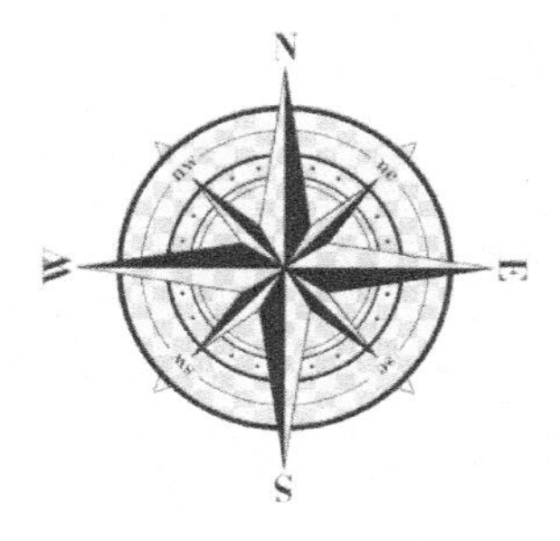

Burj Khalifa

Dubai, United Arab Emirates

A knock at the suite door caused everyone, captor and captive alike, to flinch. Karlsson was eating at a table in the bedroom, with a view of the main room of the large suite, pretending to ignore the goings on, instead consuming not only his food, but the nearly non-stop conversations held in Arabic.

Unfortunately, he had learned little beyond their predictions for the next World Cup.

And they were all wrong.

The man who had removed his hood and gag, a man Karlsson had learned was named Ahmed, rose to open the door, the other, Nasir, standing, his hand behind his back, as if he were ready to pull a weapon. Ahmed stepped back from the door as another man, clearly angry, stormed in.

"Ali! What are you doing here? I thought we weren't supposed to meet until they arrived."

"Someone knows."

Ahmed glanced toward Karlsson who quickly averted his eyes, resuming shoveling the food into himself, a sense of foreboding spreading that this might be indeed his last supper. "How?"

"I just heard a recording of his"—he jabbed a finger in Karlsson's direction—"wife, talking to a delivery man who knew about her husband missing."

"Delivery man?"

Ali smacked Ahmed across the face, causing Karlsson to flinch and drop his fork with a clatter that didn't go unnoticed. "He was undercover, you fool! Police or something." He charged toward Karlsson, spitting his questions at him in Arabic. Karlsson rose from his chair, holding his hands up, and did manage to stop the first blow.

But not the second and third, the smacks thankfully open-handed, though still stinging regardless.

"Who did you tell? Who knows? Tell me how you did it!"

The blows continued to rain down on him along with the repeated questions, when finally he couldn't take it anymore.

"I didn't tell anyone! How could I? You've watched me every second!"

Everyone froze, Ahmed's eyes narrowing. "You speak Arabic?"

And the open hands became fists, and for the first time in decades, Karlsson truly prayed as they slowly beat him to what he was sure would be his eventual death, the unanswered questions forgotten as punishment was doled out instead.

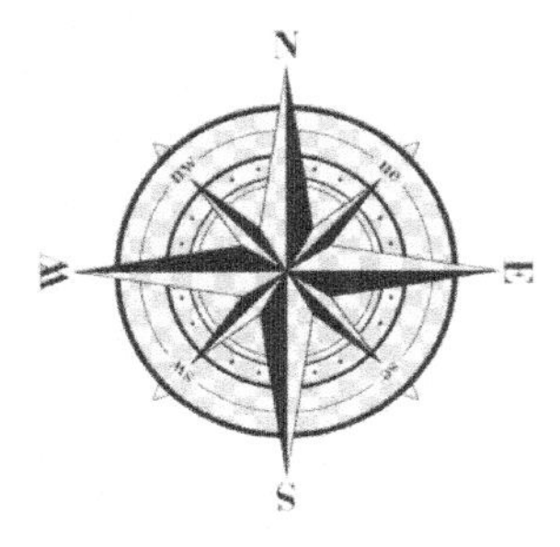

Briefing Room 221B, CIA Headquarters

Langley, Virginia

Leroux paused outside the door to the briefing room, always hating arriving late to a meeting. It wasn't his fault. He had been sent for by Director Morrison after it had already begun, but that didn't lessen the fact he was about to be the center of attention until he found a seat.

And he hated being the center of attention.

He scanned his pass then knocked once, immediately opening the door.

One didn't wait for an invitation to enter a meeting the Director had ordered you to attend.

Morrison was the one speaking as he entered. His boss beckoned him over, pointing at a chair next to him. Leroux took his seat, his eyes flitting around the room as he made note of the attendees while Morrison resumed briefing a man on the display at the front of the room, the metadata indicating he was in Stockholm.

His facial expression suggested he was annoyed.

"According to our agent, she seemed to imply contact had already been made, and indicated a pin that our footage suggests might be a listening device. We've picked up a stray signal from her property. That likely means they know someone's involved, which is why we thought you should know what is going on."

The man on the screen cleared his throat. "We appreciate that, Director, however valuable time has been lost because you didn't share this information sooner."

Morrison maintained a level tone. "I understand your frustration, sir, however our instructions from Professor Acton were to tell no one."

The man leaned forward slightly at the mention of Acton. "And how is it that this particular man, a mere archaeology professor, appears to have a direct line to the CIA?"

Morrison, along with several others, chuckled. "It's a long story, sir. Suffice it to say, he and his wife are of interest to us. I have been authorized to offer any assistance we can to not only return them safely to your country so this matter can be straightened out, but to retrieve your citizen as well, whom we believe is now in Dubai."

"And you're certain of this?"

Morrison shook his head. "No, but you've seen the footage. Professor Karlsson clearly enters the embassy and never exits. Minutes later, a small convoy leaves and a diplomatic flight departs for Dubai. While we haven't been able to find any direct evidence he is in the country, we believe he is, as he hasn't been seen since his arrival at the embassy."

"But you said the student"—the man checked his notes—"Elsa Andersson, received a text message from him."

"Yes, but that could have been sent by anyone. The number could have been spoofed. We haven't been able to trace it yet, which means someone went to a lot of trouble to make us believe it was from him."

The man pursed his lips. "I'll take this to my superiors." He jabbed a finger at the camera. "Do nothing until you hear back from me."

"Of course."

The screen went blank and Morrison turned to Leroux. "Who's in the area?"

He cleared his throat. "Any number of assets, but I think they need a friendly face. Agent White is in Baghdad. We can send her in for the retrieval."

Morrison nodded. "Good. Do it."

"What about the Swedes?"

"We'll wait to hear from them, but we better move some assets into the area. If the Actons are arrested at the airport, Karlsson's probably dead within minutes." Morrison addressed the room. "This is all going down tonight, people, and it's going to be fast. Let's just try to keep ahead of it."

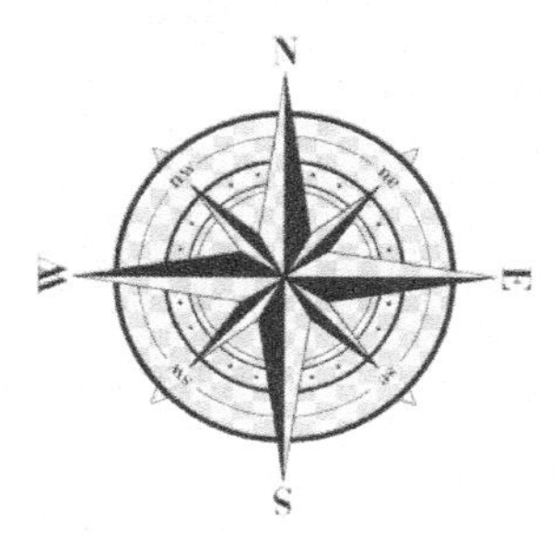

Baghdad International Airport

Baghdad, Iraq

CIA Agent Sherrie White rested her eyes as she rehearsed her cover. It was one she had used before, and if all went well, she'd use on many more occasions. After all, the best cover was well-practiced, and one no one suspected was a cover at all.

And she certainly fit the bill.

Today, she was Claire Masters, an event manager for the truly rich and powerful, those who wanted to throw a party talked about for years, not just until the next one came along.

Yachts, hotels, casinos, venues, landmarks. She could arrange it all, sometimes with a little help from her CIA backers.

Today, she was to meet with a Russian oligarch on the outs with Moscow, who might just have a server loaded with data the CIA desperately wanted. Her job wasn't to steal it, her job was to arrange the party where one of the guests, on the CIA's payroll, would. If she stole it, and it was discovered after the fact, there would be little doubt who did it. But have it stolen when hundreds of guests and staff were in the house?

They'd never know who did it, and her cover would remain intact.

Her phone vibrated and she opened her eyes, the innocuous number one that belonged to Langley. She swiped her thumb as she rose from her seat.

"Are you secure?"

She suppressed a smile at Leroux's voice. "Enough to listen."

"Change of plans. We need you in Dubai ASAP."

"What about my current plans?"

"We're having your flight canceled due to mechanical issues. You won't be able to reschedule until tomorrow."

Sherrie smiled slightly as the board to her right changed, the passengers she had been sitting with groaning in frustration. "You're an evil man."

"Never get on my bad side."

"Who's heading to Dubai?"

"Check your two-o'clock. Woman with a matching purse."

Sherrie casually glanced to her right, spotting a woman approaching with the exact same $4000 red Fendi Peekaboo Mini purse as she had. "Got her."

"Exchange purses. Her name is Gina, you're old friends."

The woman smiled. "Of all the places to see you again!"

Sherrie threw her arms open. "My God, Gina, is that you?"

Gina hurried over and gave her a one-armed hug, the other holding her purse pushed against Sherrie's stomach where her own purse rested. The exchange was made while bodies were pressed together, a move rehearsed a thousand times during her training.

"I wish I could talk, but I have a flight to catch," said Gina, already pulling away. "Call me when you're in New York."

Sherrie waved. "You can count on it." She held the phone to her ear. "Done."

"Good. When you arrive in Dubai, you'll be met by local contacts. Be prepared for anything."

Sherrie smiled. "I'm always prepared, baby."

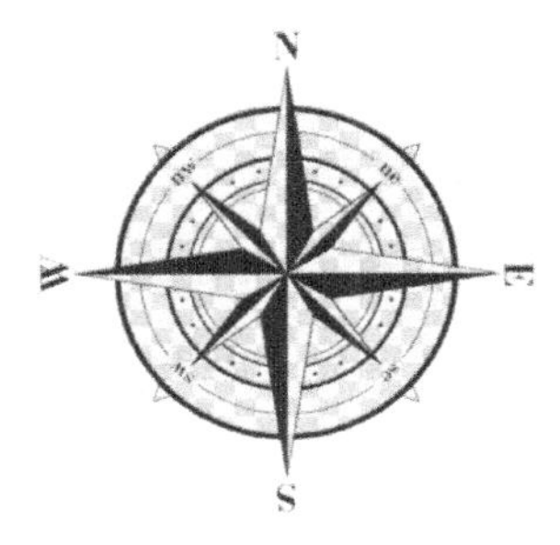

Over the Arabian Sea

"Thank God you were able to make that shot, Niner, otherwise the mission would have been blown."

Sergeant Carl "Niner" Sung eyed Sergeant Will "Spock" Lightman. "Excuse me?"

Spock cocked an eyebrow. "What?"

"You're thanking God? I like to think I had a little to do with it."

Spock gave him the finger. "Thank you, Niner."

Niner folded his arms, Command Sergeant Major Burt "Big Dog" Dawson chuckling at the show put on by his team. "You're welcome." Niner leaned forward. "And on behalf of God, He says you're welcome too."

Sergeant Leon "Atlas" James groaned, his impossibly deep voice echoing through the hold of the MC-130J Commando II transport they occupied the rear of. "So, now you've got a direct connection to God?"

Spock shook his head. "Careful there, we might have to toss you out the back for blasphemy."

Niner shrugged. "I'm Buddhist. I'll just return even more handsome."

Atlas grunted. "And shorter."

Niner flipped him the bird. "Kiss my short, handsome ass."

"In your dreams, shit ball."

Niner stared at Atlas. "You better hope reincarnation isn't real, otherwise you're coming back as something I'd scrape off my shoe."

Atlas regarded him for a moment then shook his head. "You'd still be too short."

The team, all elite operators in 1st Special Forces Operational Detachment—Delta, commonly known as the Delta Force, erupted in laughter at their friend's expense, even Dawson joining in. As the highest ranking among the team of Non-Commissioned Officers, he was in charge, and the mission they had just completed, installing surveillance equipment on several ghost ships being used to illegally sell oil to North Korea, had been a success. They had installed the devices, and nobody knew they had been there.

Except for one crewmember who had spotted them boarding one of the vessels, Niner taking him out while floating on the water. The Korean-American was the Unit's best shot, and he had once again proven his skills, God-given, were as sharp as ever. And the guard falling into the water unnoticed meant those on board would chalk it up to an unfortunate accident.

And if they continued unawares, the US government would be able to provide proof to the UN that the Iranians and North Koreans were violating their respective trade sanctions.

All in a day's work.

Dawson's comm squawked in his ear.

"Zero-One, Control, come in, over."

He activated his comm. "Control, Zero-One, go ahead, over."

"Zero-One, stand by for Control Actual, over."

Dawson held up a hand, silencing the chatter, as Colonel Thomas Clancy came on the line. Clancy was their commanding officer, and a man Dawson implicitly trusted. And respected.

"Zero-One, Control Actual. Change of plans. We've got a situation developing with our professor friends in Dubai."

Dawson shook his head at the mention of two civilians he had been ordered to kill as terrorists several years ago by a corrupt administration, and now counted not only as two of the most solid, reliable civilians he knew, but friends as well. It had been a long, twisted, strange road, but there was little the men of Bravo Team wouldn't do for the two professors who so often found themselves in the middle of events bigger than themselves. "Acton and Palmer? What did they do now?"

The mention of their names had everyone leaning forward.

"Looks like the Saudis kidnapped a friend of theirs in Sweden, forced them to steal some ancient ring, then bring it to Dubai where we think the exchange is happening."

Dawson's eyes narrowed. "Why not just exchange it in Sweden?"

"We're not sure. Langley seems to think the Saudis are panicking, and are either trying to figure out a way to keep everyone alive, or are planning on killing everyone on safer soil."

"How about just not doing stupid shit to begin with?"

Clancy chuckled. "Since when have they ever done that?" There was a pause. "Listen, we're still waiting for the mission to be sanctioned, and what the ROE will be, but I'm redirecting you to the general vicinity immediately. By the time you get there, you'll have your orders, and hopefully a location on your targets. All the intel we have has been sent to your phone. Copy?"

"Copy. I'll brief the men."

"Do that. Control Actual, out."

"What's up, BD?" asked Spock, everyone eager to hear what was happening with the professors. Dawson held up a finger, opening the data file sent from Control, quickly skimming the details, his head shaking the entire time. He turned to the men, the plane already banking, their updated orders obviously received in the cockpit. "Well, it looks like there's no rest for the wicked."

Atlas jabbed a massive finger at Niner. "I blame him for insulting Him." The finger's target adjusted upward.

Niner was about to deliver a retort when Dawson cut him off. "The professors are in a situation again."

Spock grunted. "When aren't they?"

Dawson smiled. "They do keep us employed. Looks like this one isn't their fault. Pop quiz: what's the only type of building you can enter, but never leave the same way you came in?"

Niner shrugged. "A morgue?"

Dawson chuckled. "Close. The correct answer would be a Saudi embassy."

Atlas groaned, Dawson swearing he felt it over the vibration of the airframe. "Don't tell me we've got another Istanbul."

Niner leaned forward earnestly. "Please tell me my future wife is okay?"

Dawson gave him a look. "If you're referring to Professor Palmer, then as far as we know, she's fine. I'll let her husband know you're concerned."

Niner grinned. "Do you think he'll tell her for me?"

Atlas shook his head. "You're going to get your ass waxed one of these days."

Niner stood, dropping his pants to reveal a cheek. "Already done. Feel that. Smooth as a baby's bottom."

Spock pulled his Glock. "If that ass isn't holstered in three seconds, I'm adding a new hole."

Niner pulled up his pants and sat back down. "You're all just jealous that I have the balls to get a Brazilian when it's needed."

Atlas grunted. "That's only because we have man-sized balls and it would hurt too much, not like those giblets you're sporting."

Niner squeezed his boys. "I've had no complaints."

"Why would you. They're yours."

"I meant from the ladies."

Atlas gestured toward Niner's hands. "Why would they? They're—"

Niner spun toward Dawson. "BD, they're picking on me."

Dawson eyed him. "You're the one who cocked a cheek." He became all business. "Here's the situation. A Swedish professor went into the Saudi embassy in Stockholm this morning and never came out. He was supposed to meet the professors but never showed. Acton, in his infinite wisdom, went to the embassy himself—"

"Now *he* has balls," observed Atlas.

"—then came out a few minutes later. We assume he went in looking for his friend. Shortly after he left, Interpol Agent Reading received a message from Acton on a hotel staff member's phone. That message indicated their friend had been kidnapped by the Saudis, who wanted them to steal some ring that had been discovered, and hand it over in exchange for their friend. Reading passed the message on to Dylan, and that's how we're in the loop."

"I miss Dylan," sighed Niner. "He was always nice to me."

Atlas cleared his throat. "That's because he always had a thing for Asian chicks."

Everyone split a gut laughing, even Niner joining in. "Okay, that was a good one."

Atlas stood, taking bows. "Thank you, thank you, I'll be here all week. Try the Pork Rib MREs, they're fantastic."

Dawson regained control and continued. "After that message was sent, there was a police report that there was a robbery at the missing professor's university, and arrest warrants were issued for Acton and Palmer for armed robbery and attempted murder."

This wiped all the joviality from the cabin. "That doesn't sound like them," said Spock. "It must be some mistake."

"Probably," agreed Dawson. "But the fact remains, they're now on a flight to Dubai for some reason, we assume to meet with the Saudis to do the exchange for the professor, and the moment they land, the locals are going to arrest them and send them back to Sweden."

Niner chewed his cheek. "Wouldn't the Saudis know this?"

Dawson nodded. "Exactly, which is why Langley thinks they have a contingency in place. We've got agents on the ground that will try to track them until we arrive."

Niner frowned. "Let's just hope we get there before they've moved them to the Kingdom. I really didn't enjoy my stay the last time I was there."

Dawson smacked his hands together. "Check your gear then get some mental health time. We'll be into the thick of things before you know it."

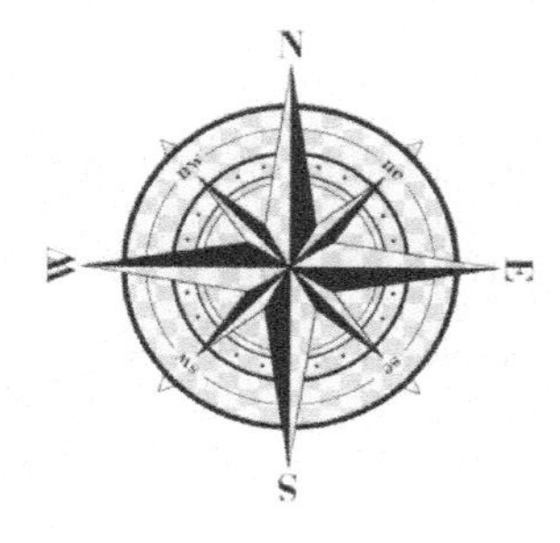

Dubai International Airport

Dubai, United Arab Emirates

Acton leaned into the aisle at the sounds of some excitement up front, then frowned. Four uniformed police were talking to the flight attendants, one of whom pointed in his general direction.

He leaned back in, turning to Laura. "The police are here."

She became concerned. "For us?"

"I assume so."

She sighed. "Even though I was expecting it, I'm still nervous."

"This could be good. It means it's over for us. We can tell them what's going on, and hopefully they can rescue Viggo."

"I'm just afraid they might kill him."

"We still have what they want, remember. If we play our cards right, we can still do the exchange, but it will be the police doing it for us."

Laura's reply was cut off as the four men marched down the aisle, stopping beside them.

"James Acton and Laura Palmer?"

Acton nodded, his heart hammering. Dubai wasn't exactly Yemen, but it was still a part of the world he didn't trust. "Yes."

"You are both under arrest for armed robbery and attempted murder in Sweden. You must come with us."

"Murder?" Laura's eyes were saucers. "We didn't try to murder anyone!"

"Tell that to the Swedish authorities." He stepped back, motioning for them to get out of their seats. "Come with us. Now."

Acton rose, stepping into the aisle, all eyes now on them. It was humiliating, despite being innocent of the charges. Obviously, things were being interpreted incorrectly back in Stockholm. His sleeper hold could have been misconstrued as an attempt to break the guard's neck, and Laura's finger to the back was an obvious misunderstanding.

His humiliation would have been short-lived if it weren't for all the cameras recording them. That was one thing that pissed him off in the modern world—the complete lack of privacy. These videos would be on the Internet for the rest of his life, no matter how innocent they were.

He leaned over and whispered in Laura's ear. "Keep smiling for the cameras as if nothing's wrong."

Laura rose, her eyes widening at the sight. "Bloody hell! We're never flying commercial again."

Acton chuckled. "Good idea." He followed the first two policemen, the others bringing up the rear, a jovial smile on his face as he hammed it up for the cameras. "Someone tell my boss I'll be late for work on Tuesday." This elicited some laughter. "If anyone sees them take us near a Saudi embassy, call nine-one-one." Now the plane was laughing as a whole, and any video that might make the rounds should show an unconcerned American being arrested, and once the story was linked with the truth later, they might just make it out of this with their reputations intact.

"I married him for his sense of humor, not his tact," said Laura behind him, joining in. "I'm beginning to wonder if I made the right choice."

"He's gorgeous, honey, if you don't want him, you let me know."

Acton grinned at the man just ahead who had made the proposal. "I don't swing that way, darling, but if I did, you'd be at the top of my list."

Howls of laughter filled the jetway as they stepped off the plane, the police appearing none too pleased at what had just taken place. They walked about thirty feet before a side door was opened and they were led down steps then out onto the tarmac where two police SUVs waited. They were loaded into the back, and were underway moments later.

"Where are you taking us? I thought we were going back to Sweden."

The man in the passenger seat turned. "Silence!"

Acton regarded him for a moment, his entire body tensing as he reassessed the situation. The men wore police uniforms, were in police vehicles, and had conducted themselves as police officers would, with professionalism and general courtesy.

But as they left the airport, turning onto the busy streets of the city of Dubai, the flashing lights were turned off, and the two SUVs merely merged into general traffic.

He exchanged a glance with Laura, who appeared to have similar concerns. If these were legitimate police, and they were being arrested so they could be sent back to Sweden for prosecution, why would they need to take them from the airport? Wouldn't they just put them back on the next plane to Sweden?

It was possible there weren't any more flights until morning, so they were being taken to a jail where they'd be held for the night. While that prospect didn't bother him much with respect to himself, it bothered him greatly for Laura. He didn't trust the authorities in this part of the world, and he feared for her safety should they be separated.

"Listen, I'm an American citizen, and she's British. I demand we be allowed to call our respective embassies immediately."

The passenger drew a weapon and aimed it at Acton's chest. "One more word, and you die."

Acton raised his hands, leaning back in his seat, only then noticing he hadn't been cuffed. Wouldn't police have cuffed them? Wouldn't that be normal procedure? And police wouldn't point a gun at him to shut him up. Would they? He had experienced encounters with all types of police around the world, and had to admit being drawn on had happened too many times to keep count. Why would Dubai be any different?

Yet it was supposed to be.

Though was it?

Yes, this was supposed to be a safe haven for Westerners in the Middle East, where as long as you were respectful, you could expect to be left alone to enjoy yourself. But in the eyes of the law, they were both criminals, so perhaps that courtesy didn't extend as far as he might have hoped.

Or, as he was beginning to suspect, these weren't police at all, and they had just been kidnapped by the very people who had Karlsson, the very people who had put them on that flight, and knew exactly when they were to arrive.

"You're not police at all, are you?"

A font of Arabic curses erupted and Acton held up his hands again.

"Fine, I'll shut up."

It was when they pulled up in front of the Burj Khalifa that he knew his suspicions were correct. There was no way the Dubai authorities would put two criminals up in the finest luxury hotel in the world, just to await their flight the next day.

The passenger turned toward them. "Say a word, and you die, your wife dies, and your friend dies. Horribly. Understood?"

Acton nodded. "Crystal."

The man's eyes narrowed. "What does that mean?"

Laura leaned slightly in front of Acton. "He means it's crystal clear. He understands." She raised her hands slightly. "And so do I."

"Good." Acton's door opened, revealing two men in suits standing nearby. "Go with them."

Acton frowned but climbed out then helped Laura down. They followed the two men into the hotel, and Acton couldn't help but be in awe of their surroundings. It was an incredible site, an oasis carved into the desert, rivaling anything he had ever seen around the world. If it weren't for the amount of hate surrounding it geographically, it was a lifestyle he could get used to, and could certainly afford.

If one were willing to sacrifice true freedom.

And he was never one to allow that.

He glanced over his shoulder to see the courtyard behind him, and frowned at the sight of two more suits following them.

There would be no escaping.

With Karlsson's life on the line, he had no designs on doing anything beyond obeying their instructions for the moment. One good thing was that they were at least not on their way to Saudi Arabia, though that could change in a heartbeat.

And he had no illusions that they'd be safe here. In the privacy of a hotel suite, anything could happen to them, the Saudis repeatedly proving over the years that life meant little to them, and consequences little more.

They boarded an elevator and Acton caught his breath as they shot up to the 142nd floor. Arriving in about a minute, no one else having been allowed to board by the wall of suits that had blocked the doors the moment they stepped on, they were soon at corporate suite 142E.

A single knock and the door opened immediately, those inside obviously expecting them. Acton stepped through the door, quickly taking in the room, then gasped at the sight of a severely bloodied Karlsson in one of the bedrooms.

"Viggo!"

He rushed toward his friend but a behemoth in a suit stepped in front of him, blocking the way. "What the hell have you done to him?"

"Nothing that concerns you," replied one of the men already in the room.

"This wasn't part of the deal. Nobody said anything about doing this"—Acton gestured with anguish at his moaning friend—"to him. This isn't right! He needs a doctor!"

"Give us the ring, and you can tend to your friend."

Acton spun on the man. "Who are you people? Why are you doing this?"

"We are the people who want the ring. Give it to us, and this is all over."

Acton regarded the man. "And what assurances do we have that you'll let us go?"

Guns were produced by everyone, though not aimed at them. "None. Give us the ring now, or we shoot you and take it ourselves." The man smiled slightly. "Either way, Professor Acton, we get the ring."

Acton scratched behind his ear, cocking his head slightly as he eyed the man. "Umm, that's going to be a problem."

The man's eyes narrowed. "What do you mean?"

"We don't have the ring."

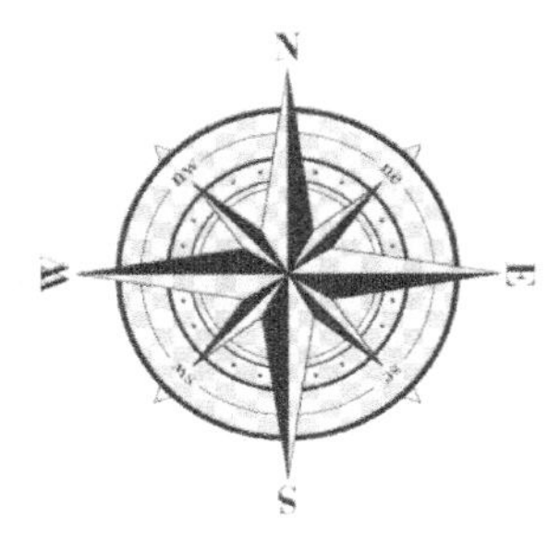

Operations Center 2, CIA Headquarters

Langley, Virginia

"Well, they've been picked up, but they weren't held at the airport like they were supposed to be."

Leroux frowned at the expected news as he reentered the room after being informed by Director Morrison that Delta was a go. "Where are they?"

"You're going to like this," replied Randy Child, pointing at the displays. "I've been able to track them leaving the airport then arriving at the Burj Khalifa."

Leroux's eyebrows shot up. "Really? Why the hell would they bring them there?"

Child shrugged. "These are Saudis. I don't think they really look at things the way we do."

"Obviously." Leroux gestured toward the displays showing Acton and his wife escorted into the hotel by four men in suits, none of whom wore the police uniforms of the men that had arrested them. "Where'd they go?"

Child manipulated the display. "They boarded an elevator, went to the 142nd floor, then entered room 142E. There are no cameras in the rooms, so that's as far as I can take it."

Leroux frowned. "So, you're telling me all you were able to do was track them to their exact final destination?"

Child threw up his hands in mock apology. "I know you're disappointed."

"Tremendously. You're fired."

Child grinned. "I'll pack my things."

"Do that." Leroux raised a finger. "But not until after your shift." He became serious once again. "Do we know who rented that room?"

Child tapped a few keys then laughed. "Oh, this is too good."

Leroux smiled, turning toward him. "Let me guess. They didn't bother hiding it."

Child shook his head. "Nope. Department of Ancient Antiquities, Kingdom of Saudi Arabia."

Sonya Tong shook her head, her arms folded across her chest. "How sheltered from the real world are these people?"

Leroux sat at his station, shaking his head. "Let's just hope their idiocy keeps up. Right now, they just keep digging their own grave."

Child held up a finger. "Now, now, they are after an ancient ring, so at least they've got the right department renting the room. Let's give them that."

Leroux chuckled. "The problem is they honestly think this makes everything look legit." He leaned back and stared at a data file on the building, cycling through what the CIA knew about the structure, things that the average civilian wouldn't consider, such as HVAC ductwork, window types, door thicknesses, and more.

Anything anyone would need to know to breach any part of the massive structure standing over 2720 feet tall.

Leroux sighed. "Well, at least we now have a target for Delta. Get every piece of intel you can over to them. They're going to need it if they're going to come up with a plan that gets our people out alive."

Child shrugged. "Seems pretty easy to me. Hit the room, kill the bad guys, grab the targets, get out."

Leroux turned his chair to face Child. "You're forgetting one thing."

"What?"

"That room is on the 142nd floor. The elevator alone takes a minimum of one minute to get to the bottom. That assumes the elevator is already there when they need it, and that it doesn't slow to stop on any other floors on the way down. By the time they get there, a couple of hundred police could be waiting to greet them."

"Huh. Didn't think about that." Child chewed his cheek for a moment, scrunching up his nose. "So, maybe I should get to work on those elevators?"

Leroux nodded. "Figure it out, and you might just keep your job."

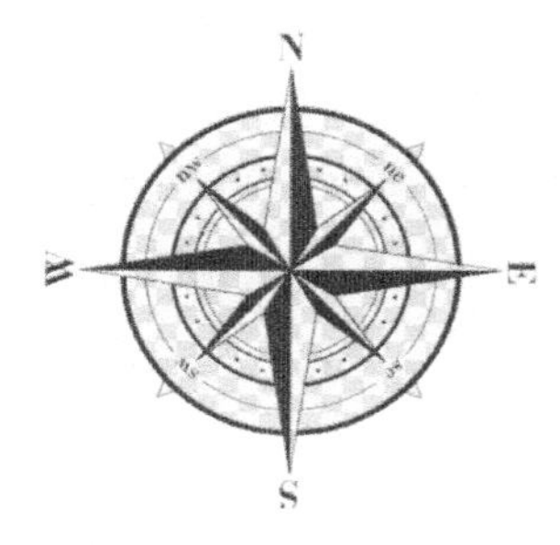

Approaching United Arab Emirates Airspace

"There's no way I'm Tom Cruising it on the outside of that thing."

Atlas agreed with Niner's assessment. "You do have to be a special kind of crazy to do some of the stunts that man does."

Spock batted a hand. "Bah, it's all safety harnesses and shit like that. I'd pay good money to see him in the real world doing that stuff." He looked at the others. "Seriously, I would. How much do you think it would cost to get him here to help out?"

Atlas grunted. "More money than you've got."

Niner's eyes widened with a childlike expression. "Maybe if we pool our money? Pitch it to him like a Middle Eastern King Kong."

Atlas stared at them. "You two have got a lot of good money to spread around." He pointed a meaty finger at Niner. "And you still owe me ten bucks for pizza last week."

Niner grinned. "I'm good for it."

"Only if you survive the mission."

Niner's eyes narrowed. "Why? Are your Spidey senses telling you something?"

"Only that if a little man like you were seen on the side of that building, our targets could be forgiven for thinking you were just a bug."

Niner flipped him the bird. "Have you seen the size of the insects they've got here?"

Atlas dropped to a knee, holding one hand at Niner's feet, the other at his head. "They're about this big."

Dawson joined the others in laughing at their friend's expense, Atlas on fire today. Niner shoved the big man off balance, Atlas recovering with a shoulder roll before returning to his seat. Dawson raised a hand, silencing everyone. "Fortunately, I've got a better plan that doesn't involve Tom Cruise or any of you swatting at planes from the side of the building."

Niner frowned. "Color me disappointed."

Spock grunted in agreement. "Me too. So, what's your non-Hollywood plan?"

"Wingsuits."

Niner's eyes shot wide. "Please tell me you're not going to have us drop from thirty-thousand feet and land on that thing."

Dawson shook his head. "No, none of you are as good as Tom Cruise."

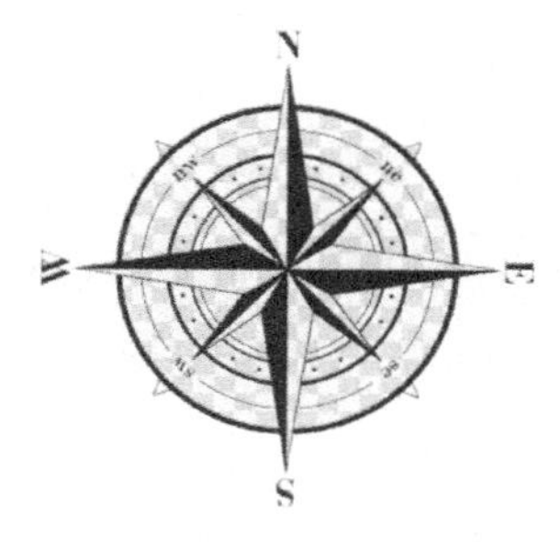

Burj Khalifa, Room 142E

Dubai, United Arab Emirates

"What do you mean you don't have the ring?" The man swung his hand toward both Acton and Laura. "Search them!"

Acton held his arms out to the sides as one of the men approached, a quick pat-down ensuing before he moved on to Laura. She frowned at the man.

"Do those feel like rings to you?"

The man glared at her then removed his hands from her breasts, Acton struggling to control his temper as the groping session continued. Finished, the man shook his head.

The man in charge stormed forward, jabbing a finger into Acton's chest. "Where is it? Tell me now or she dies!"

Acton stepped back, putting himself between the irate man and Laura. "Like I tried to tell you, we don't have it. *With* us."

The man's eyes narrowed. "What does that mean?"

Acton reached into his pocket and produced a piece of paper. "I took the precaution of couriering it before we left Sweden."

The man's eyes widened. "What? Why would you do that?"

Acton stared at him. "Ahh, because I don't exactly trust you, now, do I?" The man opened his mouth to deliver what Acton was certain would be something poetic, but Acton cut him off with a raised hand. "I will give you the tracking number so you can track it. You'll let us go, with our friend, and you'll get the ring when it arrives at its destination."

The man was fuming, pacing back and forth in front of them. He finally stopped, spinning toward Acton. "Unacceptable!"

Acton shrugged. "You have no choice."

The man stepped forward. "I do. I can kill you now."

"Then you'll never find the ring."

The man pointed at the paper in Acton's hand. "I kill you, I take that paper, I collect the package, I have the ring."

Acton held up the paper. "Oh, this isn't the tracking number."

The man threw up his hands, exasperated. "Then what is it?"

"It's a Western Union receipt."

"What?"

"I sent your accomplice in Stockholm, the Ambassador's Chargé D'affaires Al-Jubeir, a five dollar birthday gift. This is the claim number."

"I don't understand."

"Well, if you actually lived like most in your country do, you'd understand that when you send money through Western Union, you can also send a short message."

"I still don't understand."

"Well, when your man collects his birthday gift, he'll be given a message. That message is the tracking number for the courier company."

The man reached forward, snatching the paper from Acton's hand, holding it up triumphantly for the room to see, smiles and head bobs acknowledging his prowess.

Acton shrugged. "That will allow you to identify the message, but not pick it up."

"Why?" It almost sounded like a whine.

"You need the password, which only we know." Acton tapped his temple. "And I only tell you it when we're all safe."

The man glared at him, frustrated. He shook the paper. "So, you give me the password, and that allows us to get the message you sent. That message is the tracking number for the courier company. We can then track the package and pick it up, and it contains the ring."

Acton smiled. "Now you're getting it."

The man pulled a weapon, pointing it at Laura's head. "Tell me the password or I kill her. Now!"

Acton raised a finger. "Oh, was I not clear? We each gave the agent half the code while the other was out of earshot." He smiled. "You need us both. Alive."

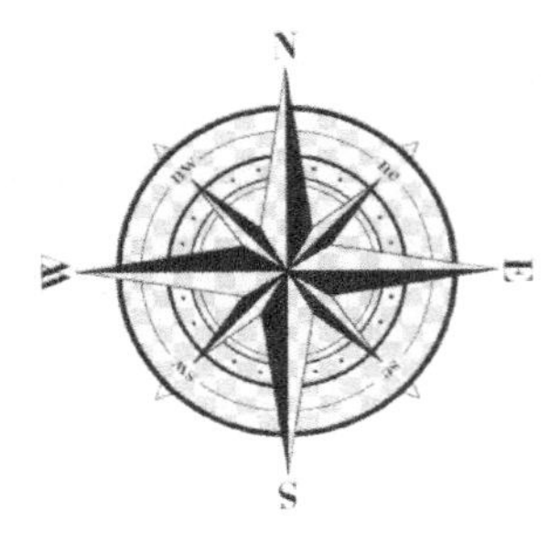

Outside Dubai, United Arab Emirates

Sherrie White stood next to one of two idling SUVs, holding a locator beacon for the cavalry about to arrive from the sky. She had never jumped using a wingsuit, though had trained extensively on how to be inserted into hostile territory via parachute.

This was just an extension of those principals, and she was envious of the team now winging in from international airspace, unbeknownst to the UAE.

She had been collected at the airport by one of the Agency's contacts, and was now fully equipped with enough weaponry that if caught, would ensure her an extended incarceration in a cold, dark cell.

But that was the job.

A job she absolutely loved.

Her parents had died when she was a teenager, and in college she had been approached by the Agency after filing an application on a whim.

Apparently, they liked young recruits who were proven survivors with few family ties.

It was the best thing to ever happen to her. The Agency was her family now, and through it, she had found Leroux, and through him, Kane and Lee Fang. She had her little circle, a cocoon of caring that she had been desperately missing.

And she got to kick ass for a living.

Life is good!

She had a terrific boyfriend whom she loved and trusted, a job that was challenging and exciting, and a few good friends.

The only problem with it was that she could be killed at any moment, her career choice not one that meant someone had her back at all times.

Not like these operators about to arrive.

She sometimes envied the comradery a unit like that must provide, the security of knowing your brothers in arms were there for you at all times, but more often than not, she preferred to be on her own, her only connection to help an earpiece linking her to a security apparatus unparalleled in the world.

"There!"

She squinted at where her partner was pointing, seeing nothing but stars, stars that were brighter than anything she had seen in years, the air clean of pollution, both industrial and light.

Then she saw them, stars that had been twinkling misinterpreted. She smiled as she spotted the first chute, the Delta team she had worked with previously about to arrive.

A chute flared to her right, startling her, the first touching down unexpectedly. She handed the beacon over to her partner then rushed over to greet the first arrival.

"Welcome to Dubai."

The man removed his helmet, and she smiled in recognition.

"Sergeant Major."

Dawson shook her hand. "Good to see you again, Agent White. Sitrep?"

"Nothing has changed. We believe they're still in the room with the hostiles."

Dawson stripped from his gear as the others landed around them. "Nothing on Professor Karlsson?"

"Nothing confirmed, but a large bag was brought into the hotel shortly after their diplomatic flight arrived. We believe he was in the bag, probably drugged."

Dawson bundled up his gear then tossed it in the back of the SUV, the others doing the same, all dressed impeccably in suits.

"Well, aren't we a handsome bunch?"

Niner adjusted his tie. "Some more than others."

Sherrie flashed him a sexy wink then returned her attention to Dawson. "We've managed to book you a room one floor below the target, but unfortunately we couldn't get you something directly below. It's about thirty meters over."

Dawson nodded. "No problem. Let's get in position before they decide to move them. The last thing we need is a ground pursuit on the streets of Dubai."

Operations Center 2, CIA Headquarters

Langley, Virginia

"Any sign the Delta insertion was detected?"

Child shook his head. "Negative. All's quiet on the Middle Eastern Front."

Leroux sighed. "Good." He turned to Tong. "Evac is ready?"

She nodded. "The USS Newport News is off the coast, waiting for the go ahead."

Leroux clasped his fingers over his stomach, staring at the displays, satisfied. Everything was going according to plan so far. Delta was on the ground, en route to the Burj Khalifa, Acton and Palmer, and they assumed Karlsson, were all still contained within a single room, and their evac plan was in place. If all went well, they might effect the rescue with no one knowing.

After all, the Saudis wouldn't run to the UAE authorities complaining their kidnapping plot had failed.

Unfortunately, from his experience, there were simply too many variables in play, and all it took was for one thing to not go according to plan for everything to head south quickly.

Child pointed at the display, two red dots tracking the SUVs led by Sherrie. "They're almost there. Let's hope this goes nice and smooth."

Tong frowned. "Not a chance. Maybe if they had time to plan something, sure, but they've only had maybe an hour to slap something together."

Child spun in his chair. "Yeah, but that's what these guys train for."

Tong waved a finger. "Oh, don't get me wrong, they'll succeed, but my money's on ugly."

Sherrie's voice interrupted them. "Control, this is Coyote-One. The foxes are in the henhouse, over."

Leroux chuckled at the unorthodox update from the love of his life. "Getting creative, are we?"

"Numbers are just so boring. Heading to Point Alpha. Out."

Leroux watched the tapped security footage as the four-member Delta team boarded an elevator without incident.

And so it begins.

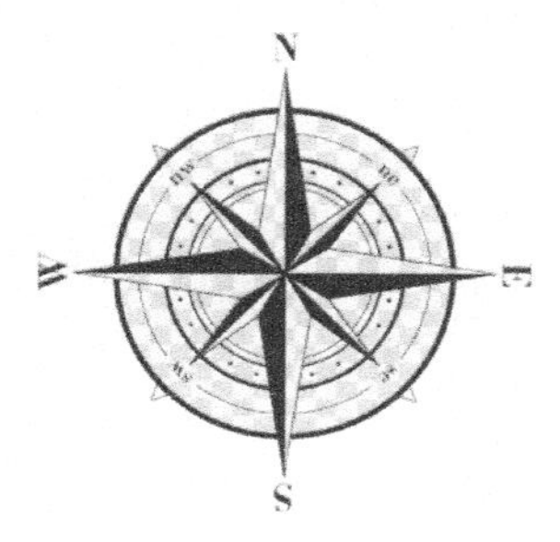

Burj Khalifa, Room 142E

Dubai, United Arab Emirates

Acton stood with his back to the window, Laura beside him, Karlsson still in the next room, the sounds of the beating he was receiving gut wrenching.

"Please, stop!" cried Laura, tears streaming down her face. "You're killing him!"

"Give us the code, and we'll stop."

Acton shook his head, struggling to control his own anguish. "If we give you the code, we all die." He pointed at the crime being committed in the next room. "If he dies, then you'll never get it."

"Then you'll die as well."

"Like I said, that's happening regardless."

The man sneered at him. "Professor, there's dying, then there's *dying.* A bullet to the head is blissfully painless. What your friend is going through is horribly agonizing." He stared at Acton for a moment, as if assessing him. "You're a fit man. I think it would take days before you'd die." He stepped over to Laura, a leer spreading. "And she could take months."

Acton stepped between them, glaring at the man. "Lay a finger on her, you die."

The man laughed, stepping back. He motioned to one of the others, laughing with him. "Go ahead. Test him."

The man smiled then stepped forward, extending a single finger in front of him.

He touched Laura's breast, a huge grin on his face.

Acton's hand darted out, crushing the man's windpipe with a single blow. He collapsed backward, clutching his throat, gasping for breath as the room erupted in anger. Guns were immediately trained on them, the men surging forward, but their leader waved them off.

He pointed at the gasping man. "What did you do?"

"He'll live. The next one won't. Stop beating our friend, and let's settle this. You can have the ring, you just need to let us go."

The man smiled slightly, eying him. "And how can we possibly trust you now?"

"You can't, just like we can't trust you. But there's a difference between you and us."

The man's eyebrows rose slightly. "Oh? And what's that?"

"We're not murderers. You have nothing to fear from us. We can't touch you. But we have everything to fear from you, which means we won't renege on our deal. Let us go, and once we're safe, we'll give you the code."

The man stepped closer, staring into Acton's eyes. "I think you are operating under the false impression that you are far braver than you actually are." He stepped over to Laura, running his hand through her loose hair. "When you watch what we do to your wife, day in and day out, I think you'll be begging to give me the code."

Acton struggled against the bile filling his mouth, his stomach churning and his heart hammering at the prospect of everything going south. He drew a slow breath. "Perhaps, but I think you're just a pawn here, like me. I think you're working for someone else who wants the ring, and if you put it at risk, *you'll* be the one that will face his wrath, not us."

The man stared at him for a moment, removing his hand from Laura's hair before stepping back. He appeared slightly rattled, but Acton couldn't be sure.

Then he snorted and spun on his heel, barking orders in Arabic. Two men rushed forward and grabbed Laura, hauling her kicking and screaming into the second bedroom of the luxury suite.

"Laura!"

Acton rushed after her, his worst nightmares about to come true as his bluff was called. Two of the henchmen immediately grabbed him. He stomped on the foot of one, the recipient's grip loosening, and he wrenched free then drove the other man's nose into his brain with the heel of his palm. He spun, kneeing the other man in the face as he hunched over, grabbing for his aching foot.

Acton turned to resume his path to the room where Laura continued to scream, when a hand swung toward him, the grip of a pistol clutched in it. He ducked, but too late, the blow excruciating, and enough to take him to the floor, those that remained swarming him, their blows raining down on him as Laura cried out in the next room.

He had been a fool.

He had been overconfident.

And now his arrogance would cost the woman he loved everything, but not before he'd be forced to watch.

He had lost.

He stared up at the man in charge as blood trickled down his face, and played the only card he had left. "Fine, I'll tell you what you want to know."

The man sneered at him. "I thought you might."

Burj Khalifa, Room 141B

Dubai, United Arab Emirates

"So far so good."

Atlas stepped out of the bathroom as the team cleared the room, nodding at Niner. "Yeah, but getting in is always the easy part."

Dawson had to agree. Gaining access to their room had been easy, and judging from the duffel bags piled on the bed, it had been fully prepped by the CIA contacts here in Dubai. He activated his comm. "Control, Zero-One, do you have eyes on the target yet?"

"Zero-One, Control. Micro-drones are coming into position now. We'll have eyes and ears—oh, God. Stand by, Zero-One."

Dawson could hear the horror in Leroux's voice. Though the guy was young, he was skilled, and Dawson had worked with him on multiple occasions.

And he couldn't recall him losing his cool like he just did.

He pointed at the bed with the equipment. "Something's wrong. Let's gear up."

Atlas, Niner, and Spock went to work, emptying the bags, a quick inventory completed.

Niner gave a thumbs up. "Everything we asked for is here."

Spock shook his head. "You have to love the fact we have enough arms to start a war in pretty much every country in the world, conveniently stored in those countries."

Niner chuckled. "God bless America!"

Atlas picked up an MP5. "Amen."

Dawson pointed at the large window providing a magnificent view of the city below, the sun long set, the bright lights of the metropolis twinkling from this height. "Prep Plan B. I have a feeling—"

"Zero-One, Control. You have to move now. Karlsson is being beaten and appears near death, Acton has a gun to his head and is bleeding, and Palmer is in another room, and it looks like they're about to…"

Dawson didn't need to hear the rest of it. "Understood. Bravo Team proceeding in sixty seconds."

Niner and Spock made quick work of prepping Plan B as Dawson and Atlas geared up.

"Rules of Engagement?" asked Atlas.

Dawson growled. "Take the bastards out. Rape is an automatic death sentence."

Atlas smiled. "With pleasure."

"Done!" announced Niner. Dawson didn't bother inspecting the job. He trusted Niner and Spock's skills as he trusted his own. He headed out the door and toward the stairwell, the others on his heels. They were committed now, their gear in plain sight. He only hoped Langley was able to provide them with some cover by manipulating the security cameras.

But hotel guests were another thing.

They made it to the stairwell, rushing up the steps to the next floor, then paused at the door.

"You're clear on target floor. Cameras overridden."

Dawson shoved open the door and sprinted toward the target room. Atlas readied the entry ram as Dawson reached the door. He pointed and Atlas didn't miss a beat, swinging the thirty-pound device away from the door, then slamming it into the lock, splintering it open.

Dawson kicked it open the rest of the way with his foot as Atlas stepped back, tossing the ram aside as the team surged inside.

Both of Laura's hands were gripped tightly, her arms stretched across the bed in preparation for being tied down, spread-eagled, so these bastards could take their turns.

But her legs were still free.

She snapped out her right foot, catching one of her accosters in the side of the head, and he stumbled backward as two more advanced, their eyes eager with the anticipation of what was about to happen.

Not if I can help it!

She pulled both knees up then let a double-footed kick out, catching another in the chest. He fell backward, his head slamming into a mirror, the glass shattering as another loud bang in the main living area of the suite brought everything to a halt.

And as her would-be rapists paused, she took advantage.

She swiveled her hips, her right leg swinging toward the man holding her left hand, his head turned toward the shouts in the next room. She nailed him in the face. His grip broke and she rolled in the opposite direction, preparing to do the same, when the barrel of a gun greeted her instead.

Acton, defeated, sat on his knees, praying for the assault on his wife to stop, his captor making no effort to halt any of the horrors happening in the suite despite his capitulation. Instead, the man just continued to smile at him while he made a call, probably to inform his puppet master of his success.

Then the door to the suite flew open, four men with guns drawn surging inside.

Four men that were the most beautiful sight he could imagine right now.

Dawson led the way, his weapon belching lead, everything he aimed at dropping. His trained eye swept the room, ignoring Acton, then he broke off with Niner, heading for Laura's room as Spock and Atlas rushed into Karlsson's. Gunfire erupted from both rooms, the suppressors taking the edge off the shots, *all* the shots, indicating their captors never stood a chance.

A round of "clears" sounded from both rooms, and Acton struggled to his feet as Dawson reappeared, holding Laura. She pushed from their friend's arms and rushed into his, uncharacteristically sobbing. He held her tight, saying nothing as she let the emotions pour out as they should.

For there was nothing he could say beyond platitudes.

From the struggle in the next room, he was fairly certain nothing had had a chance to transpire beyond the terror of what was to come.

Their Delta friends had arrived just in time.

Suddenly she stopped, pushing back slightly, tilting her head up, concerned with his still bleeding head wound. "Are you okay?"

He chuckled. "I think that's supposed to be my line."

She sighed, patting his chest. "I'm fine. My foot's a little sore from where I hoofed one of the bastards, but I'll live."

He gave her a quick squeezing hug. "That's my girl." He tore off his pin then hers, handing them to Dawson. "They're listening in on these, maybe watching us."

Dawson pulled a small case out of his pocket and placed them inside. He snapped it shut. "That'll block any signals. Langley can analyze them later." He motioned to Niner. "Check the Doc's noggin."

Niner quickly grabbed a med kit from a bag near the door that they had dropped on their way in. He sat Acton in a chair then wiped the blood away, examining the wound. "It's deep, but you'll live." He squeezed an expanding foam wound sealer into it, temporarily halting the bleeding. "We'll look at this when we're safely out of this shithole."

Acton looked at the opulence surrounding them.

Niner frowned. "Okay, maybe not *shit*hole." He turned to Laura. "Did they, umm…"

She shook her head. "No, you guys got here just in time."

His shoulders slumped as a heavy sigh escaped. "Thank God." He flashed a smile. "Due to the circumstances, I won't hit on you." He winked. "At least not until I patch the Doc up a little better."

Laura gave him a quick hug. "Don't ever change, Niner."

Atlas appeared from Karlsson's room. "He's in really bad shape. I don't know how we're getting him out of here through the main lobby."

Acton's jaw slackened as he realized they weren't safe yet, and this was just the beginning of their rescue. He stared at the phone on the floor and cursed. "I think we might be getting company."

Dawson spun toward him. "Why?"

Acton pointed at the phone.

Dawson cursed. "Was he on a call?"

"Yes. And I heard someone shouting after you shot him."

Dawson activated his comm. "Control, Zero-One, what's our status?"

He cursed again.

Operations Center 2, CIA Headquarters

Langley, Virginia

Leroux shook his head as his team kept firing updates at him, the map lighting up with additional icons representing local law enforcement converging on the Burj Khalifa.

But that wasn't what concerned him.

It was the hotel security heading for Bravo Team's position.

"Bravo-One, Control. You've got locals en route, ETA less than five minutes. You've got hotel security on its way to your floor now. Less than one minute before they arrive, over."

"Armed?"

Leroux peered at the display showing men in a combination of uniforms and business suits, too many preparing weapons. "Affirmative."

"Can you delay them?"

Leroux snapped his fingers at Child who threw up his hands. "I can't stop their specific elevator!"

"Then stop them all!"

"But how will our guys get out?"

"Just do it!"

Child hammered some keys and the security cameras quickly revealed the results as buttons were jabbed by those now trapped inside the high-speed elevators.

Leroux smiled. "Good work. How long will that hold them?"

"Maybe two minutes."

Leroux activated the comm. "You've got two minutes, Zero-One."

"We'll take them. I've got a phone you need to trace."

"Now, or can it wait until you're clear?"

"Can't wait."

Leroux pointed at Tong. "Get on it."

Tong took over the conversation, the subject phone dialing into a secure local number in Dubai that she was tapped into. "I've got what I need, Zero-One." She worked her magic and cursed as she looked up at the main display. "A call was just placed to a phone in the city." She pointed. "Blue icon, heading for their location now."

Leroux frowned. "Cameras?"

Child brought up the traffic camera feeds, a convoy of half a dozen SUVs racing into view then just as quickly out of it. "That can't be good."

Leroux agreed. "No, it can't." He activated his comm. "Zero-One, Control. You're about to have more company."

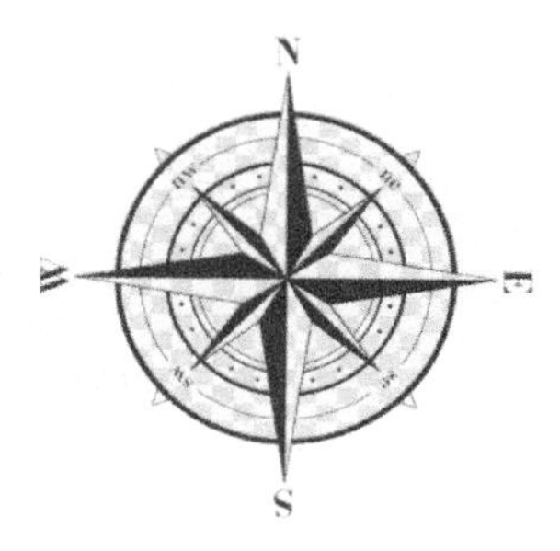

Burj Khalifa, 142nd Floor

Dubai, United Arab Emirates

Dawson led the way toward the stairwell with Spock, Niner covering their six with Acton as Laura provided additional cover for Atlas, cradling Karlsson in his massive arms. Acton and Laura were two of the few civilians he would trust with his life, the two of them not only well-trained by her ex-SAS head of security, but proven in battle, neither hesitating to put their training to effective use.

And she's one hell of a driver.

He never hesitated to take advantage of their abilities in situations like these, whereas most civilians he'd never dream of giving a weapon to—the risk of getting one of their own asses capped by a panicked misfire was too great.

But Acton was ex-National Guard, and the two of them had been under more fire than any civilians he knew, and always managed to survive either by dumb luck or mad skills.

He wagered it was a bit of both.

An elevator chimed behind them and Dawson cursed. "Let's go!" he hissed, urging them toward the door. Spock reached it first and held it open. Laura rushed through, Atlas on her heels, but it was too late.

Shouts erupted and four security guards rushed their position, weapons rising.

"Suppression fire!" ordered Dawson.

Niner spun and opened up on the ceiling above the new arrivals who immediately hit the deck, clearly unaccustomed to actual gunfire. He backed toward the door, Acton's hand on his shoulder guiding him to safety, as Niner fired several supplementary bursts to keep the innocent heads down.

Dawson shoved the door shut behind them, then pulled a small metal wedge from his pocket, jamming it into the doorframe before following the rest of his team down the steps to the floor below. "Niner, execute Plan B."

Niner grinned, holding up a detonator. "With pleasure."

He flipped the cover clear then pressed the switch. A deafening rumble filled the stairwell, and within moments, alarms blared as the power flickered then failed. Spock pushed open the door to their floor, dust and smoke rolling past him. They pressed forward, the screams and cries of confusion from the guests migrating from their rooms and into the hallway as the evacuation began.

Dawson kicked their door out of the way, already off its hinges, ushering the rest in before pressing the door back into place. He surveyed the damage. "Do you think you overdid it a bit?"

Niner shrugged as he and Atlas pulled on the rope they had attached to the window earlier with breaching tape, preventing it from falling onto the unsuspecting pedestrians over a thousand feet below. "Hey, those were blast reinforced window frames. You wouldn't want me having to try blowing it a second time while we're on the run, would you?"

Atlas grinned. "Go big or go home."

Dawson shook his head, but had to acknowledge the man was right. "Everyone out of the monkey suits." He stripped out of his business suit, revealing jet black fatigues underneath as the others did the same. He turned to Acton. "Have you ever done any skydiving?"

Acton nodded. "Yeah, we both have." His eyes bulged. "Are you kidding me?"

Dawson grinned. "I never kid when I'm talking about jumping out of a perfectly good hotel."

Spock emerged from the bathroom where the CIA had stowed specific gear in the event Plan B was enacted, dropping seven parachutes on the floor. He pointed at Karlsson, lying on what remained of a couch. "He can't jump by himself. Not in his condition."

Dawson agreed. "Tandem."

Spock held up the harness. "Way ahead of you." He quickly went to work hooking Karlsson up as everyone else donned their chutes.

Dawson inspected Acton's then Laura's. "You two ready for this?"

They both nodded, Acton replying. "As ready as anyone could be for something as insane as this."

Dawson chuckled. "You'll do fine. Spock will go first with the professor. Atlas will go next, providing cover, then you two. Follow them. Don't worry about what's happening on the ground—"

Acton's eyes narrowed. "Why? What's happening on the ground?"

Dawson ignored the question. "Like I said, don't worry about it. Just follow them. Niner and I will have your six. Understood?"

Acton exchanged a nervous glance with his wife. "It's not like we have a choice."

Dawson laughed, smacking Acton on the shoulder. "That's the spirit!"

Spock was already at the window, Atlas helping him with the barely conscious Karlsson. Shouts in the hallway from men who sounded like they meant business hastened their exit.

Dawson activated his comm. "Control, Zero-One. Executing Plan Bravo now."

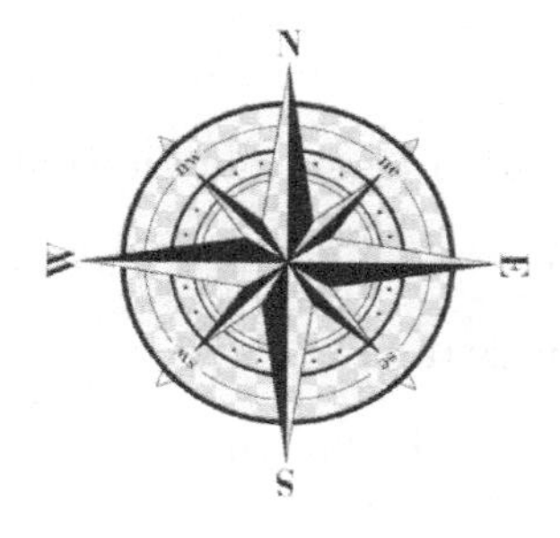

Dubai International Airport

Dubai, United Arab Emirates

Reading shuffled down the aisle of the plane, always marveling at the chaos that ensued the moment the plane came to a halt from the impatience of people desperate to get into line.

Like his seatmate tonight.

What was the point of standing, hunched over because you were too tall to be upright with a luggage rack over your head, just so you could eventually squeeze into a line of people barely moving, when you were at the back of the plane?

Just sit tight, let the herd clear, then stand up, grab whatever you had stowed in the overhead bins, then stroll off the plane.

But no, jackhole at the window seat had to be up and in the line, and with Reading's height, there was no way the man was getting by him without Reading getting into the aisle.

I see why Jim and Laura are always flying private jets.

And again, he was envious.

He was tempted to pull an asshole move and yank out his Interpol ID, ordering everyone out of his way, but it wouldn't work. There were hundreds of people in front of him, with nowhere to go.

Besides, he was halfway there.

He checked his messages, finding an update from his partner Michelle informing him that his friends were not in custody.

He froze.

They should have arrived over half an hour ago.

He quickly fired a text back.

Was flight delayed?

The reply was almost immediate.

No, still checking. Stand by.

Someone shouted, giving him a bit of a shove. He looked up to see the line had moved on, and was about to move when he received another poke and angry shout in what he assumed was Arabic.

He pulled his ID and turned, inflating his chest as he did so.

And glared into the eyes of a five foot nothing grandmother.

He smiled. "My apologies."

He turned back, catching up to the line, shaking his head the entire way as he smiled at what he had planned on saying.

Control your temper, Hugh!

Finally in the jetway, he had some room to maneuver, and hurried past the less swift passengers, emerging in the terminal where an old colleague of his waved.

"Hugh, over here!"

Reading smiled and strode over to the man he had met several times at Interpol over the years, and extended his hand, heading off the cheek kisses the man preferred. "Khalil, so good to see you!"

"You too, my friend!" Khalil Zakaria smiled broadly, taking Reading's hand then moving in for the kiss. Reading placed his left hand on the man's shoulder, patting it and keeping him at bay without his intentions being obvious. Denied, he grabbed Reading's bag instead. "Do you have any checked baggage?"

Reading shook his head. "No, I'm traveling light. I figured I'd just be taking custody of our suspects then getting the next flight right out."

"No! Stay the night. I'll show you the city, we'll have a great time. You can leave in the morning with them."

Reading regarded him for a moment when four heavily armed soldiers jogged by. He surveyed the area and frowned. "Is this level of security normal?"

Zakaria frowned. "No. There's been an explosion at the Burj Khalifa."

Reading's eyes widened. "Terrorism?"

Zakaria shrugged. "No idea yet."

They resumed walking, Zakaria using his ID to expedite Reading's clearance through customs. "My partner seems to think you don't have the suspects in custody."

Zakaria frowned. "No, we don't."

Reading stopped, suddenly very concerned, though forced to hide it. These were suspects, not friends, as far as anyone here was concerned. "Explain."

"The two suspects arrived as scheduled less than an hour ago. They were supposed to be picked up by my partner and local law enforcement." He became somber. "My partner's body was found in a toilet stall in the main terminal about fifteen minutes ago. He never made it to the security station to coordinate their arrest."

Reading's chest tightened. "Then who has them?"

Zakaria shook his head. "We don't know. We have footage of a team arresting them and taking them to vehicles that were in a secure area. Whoever they are, they're *very* well connected."

"Where did they go?" Reading closed his eyes, holding up a hand. "Wait, let me guess. The Burj Khalifa."

"You know your suspects well. Any idea what's going on?"

Reading regarded Zakaria for a moment, wondering how much he could trust him. They weren't exactly friends. They had met on several occasions, and had gotten along well—two old fogies in an agency of youngsters obsessed with advancement and power.

Reading's only problem with the man was that he wouldn't hoist a beer with him. Other than that, he seemed honest and reliable.

He sighed, a leap of faith about to be taken he hoped wouldn't backfire. "I'm going to let you in on a little secret."

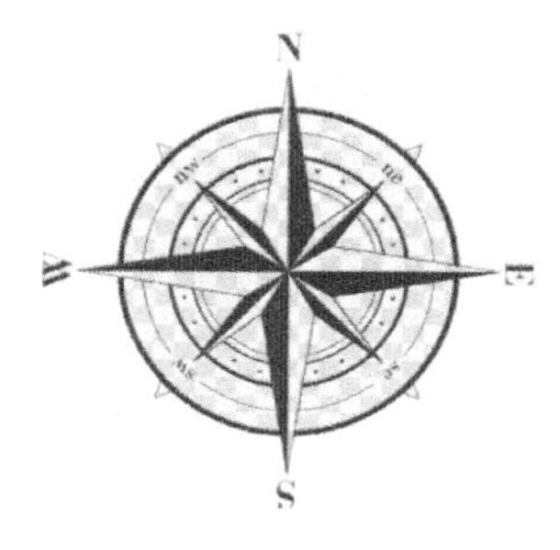

Burj Khalifa, Room 141B

Dubai, United Arab Emirates

Wind howled through the room, tossing about the debris caused by Niner's explosive takeout of the window, and Acton struggled to maintain his balance. Laura flashed him a smile then stepped out into space, tossing her pilot chute out behind her the moment she was clear.

Dawson slapped him on the back. "You're up, Doc."

Acton stepped up to the window, peering down below, relaxing slightly at the sight of three good chutes, including Laura's. "Here goes nothing." He stepped forward then pushed off the lip of the window frame, shoving away from the building as he arched his back, throwing his pilot chute behind him. Moments later, he felt a tug and he looked up to check for a good chute, finding everything in order, the black material above him camouflaging him against the night sky, though not against the bright lights of the massive building he had just regurgitated from.

He grabbed his toggles, velcroed just above him, and got his bearings. He took a bead on Laura's chute and adjusted his path to follow her. He didn't care where Spock and Atlas were heading, he would land wherever she did, though fortunately for everyone, it appeared she was on target.

Why would you expect any less?

She never ceased to amaze him. After everything they had been through, after everything done to them, their relationship continued to grow stronger. He couldn't imagine life without her, and though it was tempting to sometimes consider cocooning in Maryland and avoiding the big bad world they so often found themselves in conflict with, he knew they'd both become bored.

Though he couldn't imagine they'd become bored with each other.

He frowned at the sight of scores of flashing emergency lights below them, police, fire, and paramedic vehicles swarming the area. He was impressed with their response time, and it was easy to forget the wealth contained within this tiny oil-rich nation.

And he had no doubt the Burj Khalifa was a priority target. The first hint of anything amiss would demand a swift response to keep the foreigners calm.

But Spock was guiding them away from all that, the height they had giving them enough time to put some not insignificant space between them and the scene of the crime.

He sighed, looking down at Laura's chute. He had been a fool. They should have immediately gone to the Swedish authorities. This was too big. What had made him think they could deal with this themselves? Yes, they had threatened Karlsson's life if they did, but why was it their responsibility to get involved?

You're going to get her killed one of these days.

A burst of frustrated air erupted from his lips. While it was easy to blame himself, she was just as eager to help, and she didn't even know Karlsson.

She's an amazing human being.

It was one of the many reasons he loved her—she, like him, couldn't just stand by and see innocent people suffer.

The devastating thing was that while he would hate to lose her, he would hate even more to see her defiled like she was about to be, gang-raped by filthy men for days on end.

He'd rather see her die, and that selfish thought almost brought him to tears.

A sound overhead had him looking up. He cursed as one of the chutes above him flared, the diver rapidly losing lift and dropping toward him. The operator lifted his arms, his chute refilling with air as he reached Acton's altitude.

It was Dawson.

"Look down at your three-o'clock."

Acton did, spotting the emergency vehicles, and was about to question what Dawson was concerned about when he cursed. A long line of flashing lights was leaving the Burj Khalifa, and heading their way. "Are they for us?"

"Looks that way. Somebody obviously spotted us. They're going to try and beat us to our LZ."

"Do they know where that is?"

"No, but they just need to follow us. When we land, get out of your chute and into the vehicles. Whatever you do, do *not* open fire."

Acton's eyes widened slightly. "And what if they do?"

"They're local cops. They've done nothing wrong. Just hit the deck and surrender if you have to. We'll sort it out later."

Acton frowned, staring at the Delta operator. "You guys can't be caught here."

"You let us worry about that."

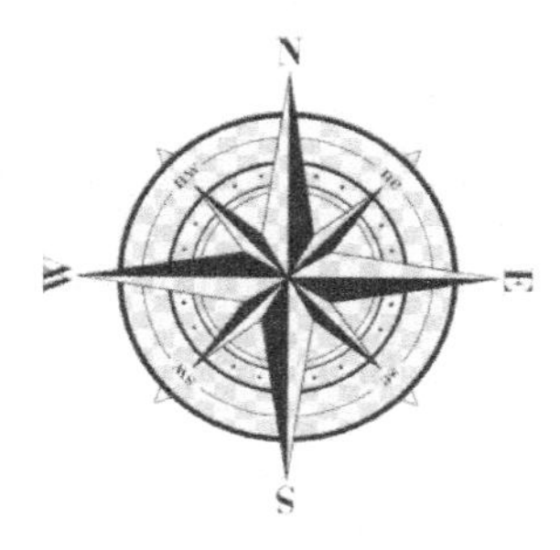

Operations Center 2, CIA Headquarters

Langley, Virginia

"Locals have spotted them by the looks of it."

Leroux cursed as he watched footage from their micro-drones deployed earlier by Sherrie and her local contact. "Do the math. If they guess right, who gets there first?"

Child responded. "Our guys do, but by a hair."

"And our convoy of assumed bad guys?"

Child tapped his keyboard, footage of the six-vehicle convoy shown from overhead.

Blasting past the Burj Khalifa.

"Well, they clearly have someone on the inside."

"You have a gift for stating the obvious," retorted Tong. "An Interpol agent is dead at the airport, the professors are collected by men wearing police uniforms, driving police vehicles allowed in a secure area, and the locals knew nothing about it? My ass. They're so corrupt, it's a wonder there's any law and order there."

Leroux had to agree. The locals were definitely infiltrated, and that could cause complications they hadn't considered, depending on how deep the penetration went. If the locals caught up with Sherrie and the others, several unfortunate outcomes could result. Delta, the CIA personnel, and the professors, could get into a gunfight that they could win or lose, either way causing an international incident. Alternatively, they could be simply arrested, and under normal circumstances, that could prove awkward for Delta, but they'd be alive and eventually handed over.

Yet these weren't normal circumstances. If these police were corrupt, they could hand them over to those in that convoy, to never be seen again.

Their only hope was to get their feet on the ground and reach the extraction point.

But deep down he knew that was impossible. The Dubai authorities had access to the same traffic camera footage they had tapped into, and they would follow Sherrie with ease.

And there was one thing his training told him.

You can't outrun a radio.

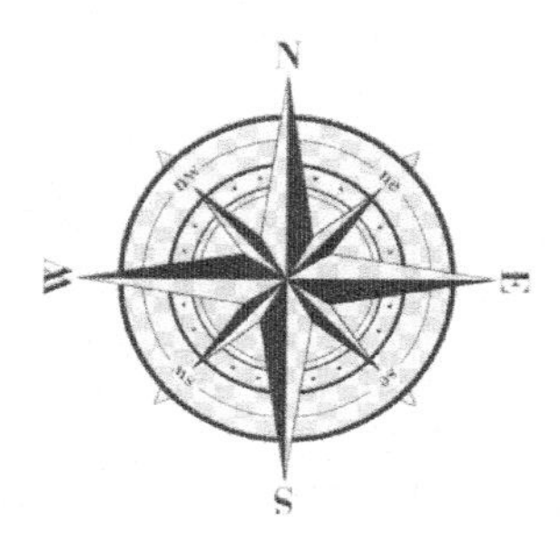

Southeast of Burj Khalifa

Dubai, United Arab Emirates

Sherrie stood beside her idling vehicle, peering up at the sky, her locator beacon in hand as she watched the six chutes rapidly approach, the sounds of too many sirens in the distance.

"Here they come," said her local contact, standing by the second vehicle.

Sherrie frowned, pointing to the flashing lights that were too close for her liking. "Yeah, and here *they* come." She activated her comm. "Control, Coyote-One. We've got company closing in on our LZ."

"Copy that, Coyote-One. Just recover them and head for the evac point."

Sherrie shook her head. "I don't think we're going to make it. Like they say at the farm…"

She could almost hear her boyfriend frown. "You can't outrun a radio."

"Exactly. I think it's time for Plan C."

"Understood."

Acton flared his chute, killing his speed just before his feet touched the ground. He spun around, hauling it in as he checked for the others. Dawson landed beside him, shrugging out of his harness instantly with a chest thrust, letting the chute blow away, time clearly of the essence here rather than proper policing of the equipment.

Acton did the same, mimicking the motions of the experienced operator as the wail of uncomfortably close sirens in the distance continued to become not so distant.

"Let's go people, they're going to be on top of us at any moment!"

Acton recognized the CIA Agent, Sherrie White, who was evidently in command on the ground. They exchanged quick smiles, and Acton rushed over to Laura, already standing by Sherrie's vehicle.

Sherrie pointed at the back seat, the door already open. "Jim, Laura, get in, quickly."

They jumped in, Spock joining them in the back with Dawson in the front. Niner and Atlas, along with Karlsson, were in the second vehicle, and within moments, both were underway, Sherrie hammering on the gas as if Laura were driving.

Acton turned in his seat, staring out the rear window at the flickering lights of the police in the distance, sighing with relief as they turned a corner, putting them out of sight. "I guess now we see who's the better driver."

Sherrie killed his spirit. "Not a chance. Even Dale Earnhardt can't outrun a radio."

Dawson apparently agreed. "Plan C?"

"Yup."

Dawson activated his mike, announcing it to the other vehicle.

Leaving Acton to wonder what Plan C was, and how many more there might be.

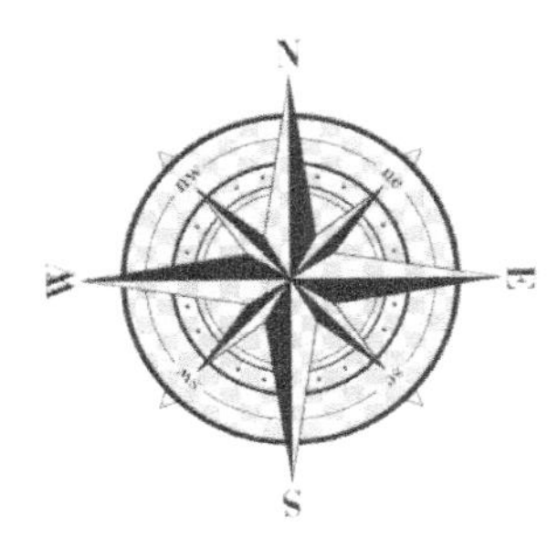

Operations Center 2, CIA Headquarters

Langley, Virginia

Leroux's heart pounded as he watched Sherrie expertly navigate the streets of Dubai, Tong providing her with updates and guidance as they monitored the actions of the locals. Fortunately, for now, there appeared to be little ahead of them, though there was no way they were going to reach the extraction point.

They were going to be caught.

There was no doubt of that.

The question was who would catch them.

Honest police, or those on the payroll of the man pulling the strings, a man they assumed was in the convoy of SUVs.

We need to know who he is.

"Any luck tracing that phone?"

Child shook his head. "It's a burner. Unfortunately, they didn't get stupid on that front."

Leroux cursed. If they knew who he was, they could perhaps apply leverage, yet until they did, they were powerless to do anything but hope Plan C worked.

"They're almost in position," said Tong, covering her live mike.

Leroux rose, stepping closer to the displays, the locals finally getting their act together, deploying other units in a bid to cut off the fleeing suspects of what they were treating as the first terrorist attack on their pride and joy.

The Burj Khalifa.

His eyes darted over to the pulsating icon indicating Sherrie's destination. It was tantalizingly close, though several police units were about to get in their way. He turned to Tong. "Do you see that?"

"Yes, sir."

"Get them around it."

"I might not be able to."

Leroux spun toward Child. "Can they redeploy?"

Child shook his head. "It's too late."

Leroux cursed.

Come on, sweetheart, you can do it!

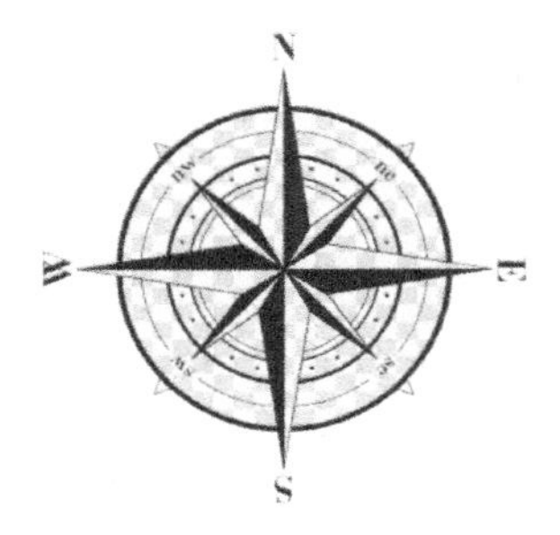

Outskirts of Dubai, United Arab Emirates

"Coyote-One, you've got two vehicles approaching from your left, one from your right. Your path ahead is about to be blocked."

Sherrie cursed as she leaned forward, spotting the vehicles on her left racing toward the intersection she was about to cross. "Check right!"

Dawson frowned. "One vehicle. Small. Is this company issue?"

Sherrie nodded. "Yup." She cranked the wheel to the right, skidding into the intersection and sideswiping the first police vehicle arriving ahead of her. Its driver lost control, careening into a street light, collapsing its bumper, the airbags deploying.

But that was the past. Sherrie gunned it directly toward the oncoming compact car, her massive SUV's engine roaring in anticipation.

"Umm, you know you're playing chicken with someone who thinks he's getting seventy-two virgins if he dies in the line of duty?"

Sherrie ignored Acton's observation from the back seat, instead focusing on the car ahead of her, watching for any telltale signs of what the driver was about to do.

And by all outward appearances, he wanted his virgins.

He swerved, hopping the curb and putting his front end into a glass-fronted shop closed for the night.

Dawson whooped, slamming his fist on the dash. "Balls. Of. Steel."

Sherrie grinned as she took a sharp left, getting them back on track, their final destination less than a mile away. "Never discount lady balls."

She checked her rearview mirror to confirm the second SUV was still with them, having benefited from her clearing the way with her CIA customized vehicle that wouldn't pop airbags or cut off fuel unless it was a truly horrific collision.

Unfortunately, two police units were still behind them, and she could see the flashing lights converging from all directions now that they were on the outskirts of the city, and the buildings they had been surrounded by dwindled.

"Coyote-One, you'll be at your destination in five seconds. Our recommendation is to negotiate your way out of this. Good luck."

Sherrie frowned at her boyfriend's recommendation. "I'm not sure that's going to work out too well for us. Better tell State to warm up their lips, because I think there's going to be a lot of ass kissing needed to get us out of here."

"Copy that, Coyote-One. We'll get you out, no matter what."

She smiled as she slammed on the brakes, bringing them to a halt in the middle of a sand-swept parking lot of an abandoned development.

The second SUV slid to a halt just behind her, creating a V that if necessary, could provide at least some cover.

And they were going to need it.

The first two cars arrived, lights flashing, sirens blaring, and came to a halt directly behind them. Within minutes, another dozen were surrounding them, the occupants out of their vehicles, all aiming their weapons at the two SUVs.

"Coyote-One, the convoy of suspect vehicles is less than two minutes out. We recommend putting yourselves in local police custody for your protection."

"Copy that." She turned to the others. "Langley recommends we surrender to the locals. Those other guys are going to be here any second."

Acton's eyes narrowed. "What other guys?"

Dawson turned to face him. "That call your guy was making went to someone in a convoy of six vehicles. They're going to be here in less than two minutes."

Laura stared toward the road they had just been on. "There's no way we want to be leaving here with them."

Acton nodded. "Agreed, but even if we surrender, we're not out of here in two minutes."

Dawson tapped his Glock. "I'm not sure we want to be unarmed when they arrive."

Sherrie regarded him for a moment. "So, you're thinking we shoot our way out of this?"

Dawson shook his head. "No, but we are *here* for a reason."

Somebody on a bullhorn started blaring orders.

"Did he just say what I think he said?" asked Sherrie.

Dawson nodded. "Yup. And though I'd love to sit here and test the difference between bulletproof and bullet-resistant, I'm thinking it's best we at least step outside."

Sherrie sighed. "Fine. But who's going to do the talking?"

"I will." All eyes were on Acton.

Dawson regarded him. "Good idea. You're civilian, and you have a legit kidnapping story."

"But how do I explain you?"

"We're part of your private security team. We found you, came to get you, made our escape, didn't know who to trust, so tried to make a direct extraction rather than contact the authorities."

Acton smiled. "I like that."

Dawson looked at Sherrie then Laura, appearing apologetic for what he was about to say. "You two should try to keep quiet. There's no telling how they'll react to a woman talking out of turn."

Sherrie grinned. "This is one Charlie-Foxtrot I'm happy to leave to you boys."

Acton chuckled. "Everyone ready?"

Sherrie nodded. "Let's do this." She activated her comm. "Coyote-One to Control. We're about to exit the vehicle, over."

"This is Control. Hostiles are about to arrive, over."

Sherrie cursed. "Company's here."

Acton stuffed his weapon in the back of his pants, not sure of what was about to arrive. The police didn't necessarily scare him, though one panicked officer could turn him into ground beef. It was these new arrivals that were of concern, and like Dawson, he was worried about being unarmed when they injected themselves into the situation.

He opened his door, stepping out slowly with his hands up, the others doing the same. He kept Laura between himself and the SUV, so he'd hopefully take any first shots, perhaps giving her time to jump back into the bullet-*resistant* vehicle, buying her enough time for cooler heads to prevail.

"I'm an American citizen that was kidnapped!" he shouted to no one in particular. "Does anyone here speak English?"

The second vehicle slowly emptied out, taking their cue from the first, and Acton winced as he spotted his friend, Karlsson, held between Niner and Atlas, his face bloodied and swollen, though appearing much better than he had just a few minutes ago, Niner's expert medical care already breathing life back into the man.

That and the halt to the never-ending flurry of blows.

"Identify yourself!" came the reply over the speaker.

"My name is Professor James Acton. This is my wife Professor Laura Palmer," he said, motioning toward Laura. "The injured man is Professor Viggo Karlsson. He was kidnapped and brought here against his will. We were coerced into coming here to negotiate for his release. The others are part of our private security team. We're the victims here."

His words had little effect, and he wondered if they were even understood.

But it didn't matter, the conversation over as engines roared and six large SUVs rolled up on the scene, fanning out then stopping in a solid line of headlights, illuminating the situation and blinding everyone as to what was happening.

Doors opened then slammed shut, the beams cut by silhouettes of the occupants advancing. Acton held up his hand to block the glare when Dawson shouted a warning.

"They're armed!"

The new arrivals walked through the cordon of confused police, marching toward Acton and the others, weapons raised.

"Prepare to defend!"

Acton's heart hammered as the Delta team all drew their concealed weapons, aiming them at the new arrivals and not the police. Acton pulled his own weapon, Laura doing the same as she advanced to take position at his side.

"I think this is about to get ugly."

Acton agreed, the police now shouting at the new arrivals to lower their weapons, and too many of the officers were beginning to panic, several aiming their guns at one group of what they considered hostiles, then the other. "If someone panics, get back in the SUV and hit the deck."

"After you."

"Oh, I'll be right on your ass, don't you worry."

Dawson approached from his right, stopping between Acton and Sherrie. "We've got a Mexican standoff here, ladies and gentlemen. These rarely end well."

The hostiles continued advancing, ignoring the police and the barked orders from the Delta team to halt.

Dawson activated his comm, whispering something.

Two bursts of sand erupted at the feet of the hostiles, followed by two more, the report of sniper rifles reaching them a split second later.

Bringing the advancing horde to a halt.

Two more shots, slightly closer, had them backing away, and Acton suppressed a satisfied grin at the fear now on display as they looked about, trying to figure out where the shots were coming from.

Dawson winked at Acton. "You didn't think we came alone, did you?"

Acton grunted. "A little heads up would have been nice."

"Where's the fun in that?"

A door opened behind the wall of light then shut, a man in traditional Saudi robes striding into view, a level of arrogance and confidence on display that Acton had rarely seen.

It made him want to punch the man in the face.

Repeatedly.

For his demeanor left little doubt he was the man behind everything.

He walked up to them, ignoring all the weapons trained on him, then stopped, his eyes roaming from man to man, the women ignored. "Who is Professor Acton?"

Acton bowed his head slightly. "I am."

"You have something that belongs to me."

Acton shook his head. "No, I have something that belongs to everyone."

The man stared at him, slightly puzzled, as if he weren't used to being contradicted. "I don't understand."

Acton regarded him. "What makes you think that a ring, discovered in Sweden, dating back over one thousand years, belongs to *you*?"

The man's lip curled slightly. "I don't *think* it belongs to me, Professor, I *know* it does."

I have to hear this.

"How?"

"It is a story handed down from generation to generation, a shameful one meant to remind us of how selfishness can destroy everything, and of how thinking of ourselves before others can result in punishment from Allah that lasts generations."

Laura stepped forward, her weapon at her side. "Fatima Halabi was your ancestor?"

"Yes."

"And she dishonored your family by marrying a Viking?"

The man was clearly annoyed at being addressed by a woman, but he replied, keeping his eyes on Acton. "It went beyond that. Perhaps she might have been forgiven if it were simply that. Instead, as the story is told, she was betrothed to another of a higher family, and before they could wed, her suicide was faked as a prelude to kidnapping by a Viking prince. Her husband-to-be was enraged and sent a fleet of ships to rescue her. In the end, it was a member of my family, her eldest brother, who discovered the truth."

Acton lowered his weapon. "That she faked her own suicide and was in love with this Viking, and that there was no kidnapping."

The man frowned, but nodded. "There was a challenge to settle the matter, lives were lost, and so was the ring that belonged to Fatima's husband-to-be. What my family didn't know, what they couldn't have known, was that this ring was not only a precious family heirloom, handed down from generation to generation, but it was a gift from the Prophet Mohammed himself, peace be upon him. Because of my ancestor Fatima's selfish actions, for a millennium, my family has carried that shame, and no matter what level of success we've attained, only the ring's return can right the wrong from so long ago, and completely restore our family honor."

Acton shook his head. "Why didn't you just ask?"

The man stared at him. "We shouldn't have to ask for what's rightfully ours."

"That very well may be, but if you had applied through proper channels, it would have been returned to you, I'm sure."

The man regarded him for a moment. "Perhaps in time, but how many infidels would have touched it in between? How many blasphemous fingers would have been thrust through this sacred artifact before it was returned?"

Acton ignored the hate in the man's voice. This was clearly a zealot, the very worst of what Islam had to offer, and unfortunately, far too common to be excused. "Some, perhaps, though never with the intention of dishonoring it."

The man spat. "For a thousand years it has been dishonored simply by being on your corrupt soil. Now, it will be returned to holy land, to sacred land, where it will never again be seen by the likes of you."

Acton sighed. "You know, it was a symbol of love, not hate." The man seemed unmoved. Acton played another card. "We have Fatima's remains. If you would like, we can have her returned so she can rest in peace with your family."

He spat again. "Any woman who would lay with an infidel is not worthy of returning to sacred land." He stepped closer, his eyes boring into Acton's. "All I want is the ring."

Acton shook his head. "So many have died, so many have been hurt, all for something as trivial as a ring, as trivial as family honor for a sin committed over a thousand years ago. Don't you see anything wrong with that?"

"No, I don't, and frankly, Professor, I don't intend to be lectured by you. Though you may have snipers positioned strategically around us, you are vastly outnumbered, and you *will* die."

"So will you."

"Perhaps, but I'm prepared to meet Allah. Are you?"

Acton decided he had pressed his luck far enough, his thirst for answers quenched. He turned to Karlsson. "It's up to you, Viggo, what do you want to do?"

"G-Give him the damned thing."

Acton nodded, returning his attention to the sheik. "What assurances do we have that you'll let us go?"

"None beyond my word."

Dawson stepped forward. "I'm not sure that's enough."

The man regarded the Special Forces operator for a moment. "I am not my government. When an Al-Zayani gives his word, it is enough."

Dawson turned his back on the man, lowering his voice. "Your call, Doc. This operation is a Charlie-Foxtrot at the moment. My orders are to get you three out, but once you give up that ring, we have no leverage beyond the sniper teams."

Acton drew a deep breath. "I'm guessing those orders included not getting captured operating on Muslim soil?"

Dawson grunted. "It was definitely implied."

Acton eyed him for a moment. "How *were* we getting out?"

Dawson shook his head. "Best you don't know."

"*Can* we get out?"

Dawson glanced over his shoulder at the throng of police and the sheik's men. "Yes, though maybe not without some casualties."

Acton regarded him for a moment. "You seem rather confident."

"I have two sniper teams that these guys aren't even looking for, and if you notice, the positioning of the cars is intentional. We have cover from two of the three sides, and the doors are reinforced, covering much of the third side."

Acton glanced uncomfortably at their own position, outside the protected area. "So, we're the only casualties?"

Dawson smiled slightly. "If the shit hits the fan, hit the ground and roll under the SUV. We'll provide cover fire. Whatever you do, make sure you concentrate your fire on the sheik's men. The police are not our enemy here. When our enemy has been eliminated, we'll surrender to the police if we have to." He leaned closer. "That all being said, I think the best way out of this is a negotiated one."

Acton nodded. "I agree."

Everyone turned as an engine roared, a police car racing onto the scene, a man in full regalia stepping out of the rear, approaching as if he were accustomed to being in charge.

His eyes seized on Acton. "You are Professor James Acton?"

Acton bowed his head slightly. "I am. And you are?"

"I am Chief Al-Numairy. You are under arrest."

Acton's eyebrows rose slightly. "On what charge?"

"Armed robbery and attempted murder. I have orders to escort you to the airport for repatriation to Sweden, where you will face these charges." He paused, and for the first time seemed to notice the sheik and his men. "Who are you?"

"I am Sheik Mohammed Al-Zayani."

Chief Al-Numairy took a step back, his head lowering in near reverence despite the fact Muslims didn't bow, all considered equal in the eyes of Allah. This was fear, not respect, and a chill rushed through Acton as he realized why the name sounded familiar. The Al-Zayani clan were an integral part of the Wahabi sect, a sect of Islam responsible for much of the world's troubles today with their deep pockets and extremely strict interpretations of the Koran.

They were dangerous, and that fact could change everything.

"I'm sorry, I did not realize you were here," said Al-Numairy, his voice bereft of the confidence it had only moments before. "What, umm, business do you have with these people?"

"They have something of mine."

Al-Numairy spun toward Acton. "Then give it to him!"

Acton smiled slightly. "It's not that simple."

But it could be.

Acton eyed the Delta operators for a moment, thinking of everything they had done for each other over the years, and how their being caught here could cause serious problems not only for them, but their country.

And he came to a decision.

"I will happily return the item, under several conditions."

Al-Zayani glared at him, his jaw clenched. "And those are?"

"First, that Chief Al-Numairy is allowed to fulfill his sworn duty and arrest myself and my wife and return us to Sweden."

"And?"

"And that you immediately let my friends leave. Their only crime was trying to save us from your men." Acton chose his words carefully, family honor clearly important to the sheik. "None of this would have been necessary if those you trusted had handled the situation better. I'm certain you didn't want any of what has happened to actually occur. I'm certain you gave clear instructions to recover the ring, and those instructions were executed poorly. If we're all willing to acknowledge that it was those you hired, who now lie dead at the Burj Khalifa, already facing Allah for His judgment for their misdeeds, then this can all be settled peacefully. Agreed?"

Al-Zayani regarded him for a moment, while Al-Numairy stared at both him and Acton, unsure of what to make of the proceedings, but wisely keeping his mouth shut.

Al-Zayani finally sighed. "You are right, of course, Professor, that my family did not want any of this to occur. As long as it is agreeable to

Chief Al-Numairy, then I will agree to your request that your friends may leave."

Dawson put a hand on Acton's shoulder and a mouth to his ear. "What are you doing? We're not leaving without you."

Acton turned his head, lowering his voice. "We don't have a choice. You guys leave and get clear. These police officers have nothing to do with what's been happening. They're going to arrest us, take us to the airport, and put us on the first plane back to Stockholm."

"Assuming everyone keeps their word."

"Yes, but if they don't, then they were never going to, and we're probably all dead regardless. If we did manage to survive, it would be to spend the rest of our days in some prison somewhere."

Dawson shook his head. "I can't agree to this."

"You have to." Acton patted him on the shoulder. "Save your men. And if things go south, don't risk your lives to save us. This is my stupid decision."

Laura leaned into the conversation. "Ours. Get out of here, but take Viggo with you."

Acton turned to Al-Zayani before Dawson could object further. "I want you to let them take my friend. Professor Karlsson has no idea where the ring is, and needs medical help. Let my friends provide that to him."

The sheik turned to Al-Numairy. "Is he under arrest?"

Al-Numairy shook his head, still confused. "No, just these two."

"And the others?"

"If they're responsible for what happened at the Burj Khalifa, then I can't—"

Al-Zayani cut him off. "Those that were killed worked for me. I understand they had an internal dispute and turned on each other."

The chief's jaw dropped at the ridiculous story. "Umm, okay. And the, umm, explosion?"

Dawson cleared his throat. "A gas leak, I would assume."

Al-Numairy's head bobbed rapidly, pleased with the lie being spun. "Yes, yes, of course. If this is the case, which I'm sure it is, then no, we have no reason to arrest these men. They may go." He waved his hands at the Delta team. "They *must* go."

Acton turned to Dawson and pointed at Karlsson. "Take him and your men, and get to safety."

Dawson shook his head slowly. "I still think this is a mistake."

"It may be, but just tell your superiors that I refused to cooperate." He grinned. "They know me, it isn't exactly out of character."

Dawson chuckled. "You do have a point." He became serious. "Are you sure?"

"Absolutely."

He turned to Laura. "And you?"

"Save yourselves. I couldn't live with myself if something happened to you or your men because of us."

Dawson chewed his cheek for a moment. "Fine. We'll do it your way."

The tension in Acton's shoulders eased slightly. "Good. Now get out of here before they change their minds."

Sherrie shook Acton's hand then Laura's. "Good luck, Professors." She climbed into the driver's seat as Dawson pointed at the SUV Karlsson had arrived in.

"Get him inside. We're leaving, now." He shook both their hands. "Just remember. If the shit hits the fan, hit the deck."

Acton nodded. "Good advice at any time."

Dawson slapped him on the shoulder then climbed into Sherrie's SUV as Atlas and Niner helped Karlsson into the back seat of the second vehicle. Within moments, both SUVs were slowly pulling away, the crowd of police parting for them, nobody quite believing what was taking place.

Acton held his breath, silently praying for this minor miracle to not fall apart, then suppressed a smile as they added a bit of speed, clearing the area, their taillights disappearing in the distance.

Laura took his hand, squeezing it, as they now stood alone, facing far too many guns, with no cover to hide behind should the sheik not keep his word.

Al-Zayani turned to him. "Now, Professor, it's your turn."

Acton nodded and Laura pulled a piece of paper from her pocket. He took it and stepped forward, holding it out for Al-Zayani. The man snapped his fingers and one of his men rushed forward, snatching it from Acton, then handing it to his master.

He doesn't even want indirect contact with us infidels.

"What is this?" asked Al-Zayani, holding up the paper.

"The claim number for the message we sent."

"And how do I claim it?"

"Just go to Western Union, give them the name of the Chargé D'affaires in Stockholm, Abdullah Al-Jubeir, as well as that claim number, and the password."

Al-Zayani growled. "I don't have time for this."

"You'll have to make the time. This is the deal. It takes you time to get the ring, and that allows us to get to the airport and on a plane to safety. Everybody wins. Eventually."

"What is the password?"

Acton smiled. "Charlie-Foxtrot." It had been a lie that they had split the code, an on the fly bluff that had become necessary when it was clear things weren't going to go their way back at the Burj Khalifa. "Now you have all you need. Can we go with the police chief?"

Al-Zayani ignored him, one of his men stepping forward, his phone in hand. Words were exchanged, then the paper was taken and a call made. He returned a few minutes later as Acton and Laura stood, the tension in the air palpable as no one spoke, and Acton's question remained unanswered.

His heart sank as a piece of paper was handed over, and he realized what was going on.

They were doing everything over the phone, and not in person as he had expected.

And it made sense.

Everything was done over the phone now, so why not message retrieval? With the claim number and the code, there was no reason for anyone to suspect anything untoward was happening. He should have thought of that, but was a product of his generation, forgetting there was an app for everything.

There goes a perfect plan.

Al-Zayani held up the paper. "What's this number?"

Acton sighed, deciding it was best to go with the truth. "It's a FedEx package number. Just have your man track it, and it will tell you where I sent the package. Mr. Al-Jubeir can pick it up. It's in his name."

The phone expert once again took over, and his eyes widened. "It's at the Nobis Hotel in Stockholm."

Acton smiled slightly as Al-Zayani realized the ring had been at the hotel they were staying at the entire time. Before clearing security in Stockholm, they had hatched their plan, deciding couriering it to their hotel's front desk was safest—not to mention it was the only address they knew in the city. "That's right. It's being held at the front desk. Mr. Al-Jubeir—"

Al-Zayani barked orders in Arabic, and a wave of trepidation washed over Acton. He had expected things to flow much slower than they were, giving them time to get to the airport and the hell out of Dodge, but none of that was happening.

His plan was failing.

Spectacularly.

"They're calling Stockholm," muttered Laura.

"Yeah. Do you think they have someone at our hotel?"

"I wouldn't put it past them. And the embassy is only a few minutes away regardless. What do we do if they get the ring before we get a chance to leave?"

Acton shook his head slightly. "I'm not sure. Hope he keeps his word?"

"Do you think he will?"

"I have no idea." He lowered his voice further. "I still have my gun."

"So do I, but neither of us have enough bullets and enough luck for that to work out."

Acton grunted. "It all depends on how scared this police chief is of the sheik. He has more guns here."

"I think he's petrified of the man. He'll be useless if this goes sideways."

Acton frowned. "Agreed." He was now regretting sending Dawson away, though in his heart of hearts he knew it was still the right thing to have done. Karlsson was safe now, and so were the operators who had become such good friends. If anyone was dying tonight, it would only be him and Laura. He took her hand and squeezed it three times.

I. Love. You.

She returned the discrete message, leaning a little closer to him as everyone waited. A shout of triumph erupted from the man on the phone, and smiles abounded as apparently the ring had been retrieved successfully.

Acton stepped slightly closer to the police chief, bringing Laura with him. "I assume you have what is yours?"

Al-Zayani nodded. "We do."

"And we're free to go?"

Al-Zayani pursed his lips. "I'm afraid I can't allow that."

Acton tensed. "I thought we had a deal."

Al-Zayani laughed. "Professor Acton, what do you think is going on here? When your friend was invited to the embassy and refused to hand over the ring, his fate was sealed. He was on a plane here before you even knew he was missing, thus avoiding any problems like were encountered in Istanbul. He was our leverage to get the ring. We hadn't yet figured out who we were going to use, then you stormed into our embassy, inserting yourself into the situation. The moment you did that, your fate was sealed as well."

"If that fate is death, then why did you let Karlsson go?"

"Did I really let him go? I have many followers in Sweden. One word from me, and he's dead."

Acton shook his head. "I thought the word of an Al-Zayani was enough?"

Al-Zayani smiled. "When dealing with a Muslim, yes, but as the Koran teaches us, lying to the kafir is permitted." He snapped his fingers as he turned, heading for his vehicle. "Kill them."

Weapons rose as Acton spun, diving toward Laura and knocking her to the ground. The sand between them was suddenly torn apart by dozens of rounds, sending police and hostiles alike scattering. Acton took advantage, grabbing Laura by the hand and racing for the cover of the police chief's vehicle parked nearby.

And as they took cover, his chest ached with the pride he felt at this very moment as he realized Dawson and his men had never abandoned them, and were instead still nearby, protecting them as they so often did.

Another siren wailed in the distance and Acton glanced over his shoulder to see several police vehicles speeding toward the scene as the gunfire stopped, the police chief giving orders for his men to hold their fire, the hostiles peering into the darkness, trying to find the Delta team, made all the more difficult by six sets of headlights illuminating everything.

The new arrivals skidded to a halt, the doors opening and a new set of police arriving.

And one familiar voice.

"What the bloody hell is going on here?"

Acton's chest heaved with relief at the sound of their friend, Hugh Reading. His booming voice silenced the confusion that threatened to erupt into an all-out gun battle in the Mexican standoff in which they found themselves.

Someone with Reading began shouting orders in Arabic as their friend spotted them.

But there was no smile, just a glare.

He marched over to them. "Professors Acton and Palmer, at the request of the Swedish Police Authority, and under the authority granted me by Interpol, I am hereby placing you under arrest for armed robbery and attempted murder."

Acton, still taking cover behind the police chief's car with Laura, stared up at him, not sure what to say.

"Get on your bloody feet!"

Acton stood, his gun gripped in his hand.

"Drop that, you daft bastard!" hissed Reading.

Acton complied, kicking it under the vehicle as Laura did the same with hers. Reading motioned to some of the new arrivals, who quickly cuffed them. He leaned closer, his voice low. "Keep your mouths shut. You don't know me."

Acton said nothing as they were led to Reading's car, an argument erupting behind them. A shot rang out and Reading shoved them both to the ground, covering Laura with his body as more weapons opened fire behind them.

Acton twisted to see what was happening, his view blocked by the chief's car, all he could see were the feet of those still alive, and the bodies of those already taken out.

Sniper rifles belched deadly lead in the distance as Bravo Team joined the fight, and Acton watched as man after man of the sheik's team were felled, the gunfire dwindling until there was none.

Reading immediately rose, still crouched over, and ushered them into the car. "Let's get to the airport, now!"

The driver stared at him, clearly unsure of what to do. One of the men Reading had arrived with shouted at the driver and the car was put into gear. Within moments, the scene was behind them, the surviving police left to deal with the mess and the lies that had been told to save them.

But they weren't safe yet.

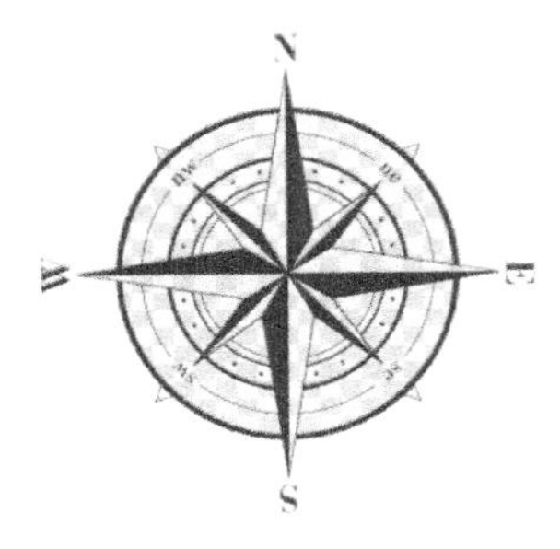

Dubai International Airport

Dubai, United Arab Emirates

Reading sat beside his friends, both handcuffed, both sitting in silence as they all waited for the plane to take off. They had made it to the airport without incident, and his credentials and some phone calls on his behalf from his Interpol contact Khalil Zakaria, had greased the wheels enough to get them on an Emirates flight to Stockholm.

It had been hours since the firefight, and he was still expecting this to all fall apart. According to Zakaria's last update, the sheik and his entourage were dead, as were over a dozen police officers. Acton's "security team" had taken out most of the sheik's men, but not before they turned their weapons on the police surrounding them. Nobody knew exactly what had happened, beyond a story apparently woven by Acton and the deceased satisfying enough people to delay things long enough for their escape.

Yet it wasn't exactly an escape.

His friends were innocent of any crimes here in Dubai, though they were definitely guilty of something in Stockholm. He was dying to know what had happened, what they had been thinking.

Attempted murder? Armed robbery?

None of it sounded like his friends, yet here he sat, his friends in handcuffs, awaiting delivery into Swedish law enforcement's hands.

The door finally closed and the jetway pulled back. He spotted Laura's hand grip Acton's, and he resisted the urge to give them an encouraging look.

For he didn't have any to give.

He still wasn't convinced they were getting away with this. In fact, he wouldn't be until they landed in Stockholm. Until then, it was still possible they could be turned around, as it was an Emirates flight, under control of the UAE, not officials in Sweden who could be trusted.

The plane began to taxi and he gripped the armrests, praying for an uneventful takeoff. He felt Laura's hand on his and he squeezed it, the entire plane vibrating as they roared down the runway. A sigh of relief escaped as the nose gear lifted off the ground and moments later they cleared the runway and roared into the night sky.

He opened his eyes and looked about to see who was within earshot, finding everyone concerned with their own business. He leaned closer to his friends. "Now, what the bloody hell happened that I've had to arrest my two best friends?"

Acton frowned. "You mean this is serious?"

Reading's eyes widened. "You think this is a joke? This is dead serious. Those charges I said are real. You're wanted for armed robbery and attempted murder back in Sweden. When this plane lands, I have to hand you over."

Laura's eyes bulged. "But that's not what happened at all!"

Reading drew a deep breath through his nose. "Then what did?"

The story spilled out as they gained altitude, and when he had finally heard it all, his questions answered, he wasn't convinced his friends wouldn't yet see the inside of a courtroom.

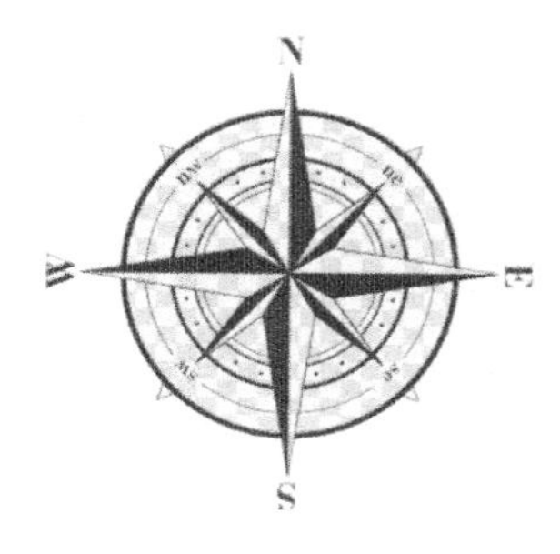

Holding Cell, Stockholm Arlanda Airport

Stockholm, Sweden

Acton sat with Laura in a holding cell at the Stockholm Arlanda Airport. They hadn't seen Reading in hours, though were being treated well. As soon as they had explained to their friend what had happened, he had spent much of the remainder of the flight on the phone with his partner in London, and his contacts elsewhere.

And yet despite that, they had still been escorted off the plane by Swedish authorities, though not until the rest of the plane had been emptied, saving them the embarrassment of yet more footage uploaded to the Internet.

Though there was still the footage from Dubai.

As soon as it hit YouTube, it would live on forever, and despite their antics during the arrest, it was still humiliating.

How am I going to explain that *to my students?*

He grunted.

Or Greg?

"What?"

He turned to Laura. "Just thinking of what Greg's going to say when he finds out what happened."

Laura chuckled. "I wonder what the Smithsonian is going to say."

He sighed. "Hopefully we can get this straightened out." He cursed. "If only I hadn't put that guy in a sleeper hold. I think they're going to say I tried to break his neck, but only stopped because that woman walked in and interrupted me."

"Well, I'm the one who pretended to have a gun and threatened to shoot her if she moved." Laura tossed her head back in frustration. "What was I thinking?"

Acton frowned. "We were both putting on a show for the Saudi cameras." His shoulders slumped. "We're both screwed."

The door opened and Reading stepped in.

Acton leaned forward. "Please tell me you have good news."

Reading dropped into a chair opposite them, the poor man looking haggard, as tired as Acton had ever seen him. "You two are going to be the death of me."

Acton grinned. "You love us and you know it."

Reading eyed him for a moment then shook his head. "Here's what's happened since I've been gone. Your friend, Professor Karlsson, arrived in Stockholm on a civilian charter."

Acton sighed, exchanging an excited hug with Laura. "Thank God! That means the guys got out despite the bastards tricking me."

Laura smiled. "We're lucky BD had a better read on the sheik than you did."

Acton frowned. "I was an idiot."

Laura patted his leg. "Your instinct is to trust. That's not a bad thing."

Acton grunted. "With the number of *un*trustworthy people we've met over the past few years, I'd say I'm a fool for sticking with that habit."

Reading leaned back in his chair, folding his arms. "And I'd agree. But lucky for you, the woman who walked in on you, who claimed you were trying to kill the guard, and that *you*"—he gave Laura a look—"put a gun to her back, is actually a grad student of Professor Karlsson's, and once she found out what was really going on from him, she recanted her entire story."

Acton's eyebrows shot up. "Huh?"

Reading grinned. "She said she never actually saw a gun, and that she realized after the fact that the guard was already on the floor when she walked in on you. The guard has agreed to drop the charges now that he knows you were trying to save the professor."

Laura gripped Acton's arm. "So, what does this mean?"

Reading shook his head. "It means, thanks once again to me, that your asses have been saved, and you're free to go."

Acton threw his arms around Laura, giving her a hard hug, then rose to give Reading an exaggerated kiss.

The big man held up a finger. "Don't you dare."

Acton grinned then stepped aside. "Laura, kiss the man."

Reading grunted. "Now that's more like it."

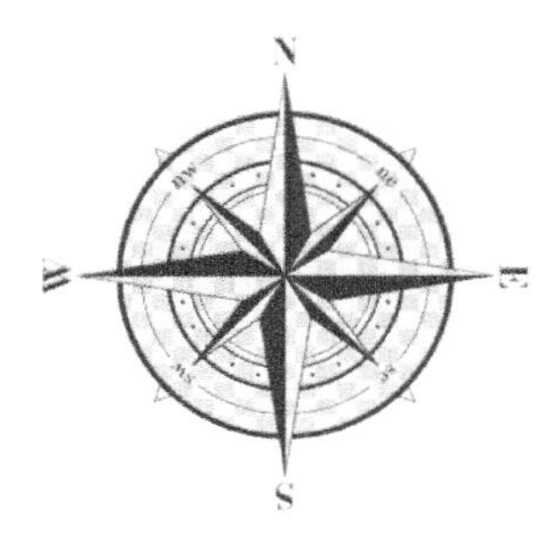

Karlsson Residence

Stockholm, Sweden

"How do I look?"

Acton regarded Karlsson for a moment, his face bandaged, several stitches in sight. "You won't be winning any beauty contests, that's for sure."

Karlsson groaned. "There goes my post-retirement plans, then." He patted his wife's hand. "I guess you're the beauty in the family now."

"Beauty and the beast, darling."

Karlsson laughed then moaned in pain. "Okay, nobody make me laugh. It hurts too much."

Elsa Andersson poured him a glass of water, and was about to help him take a sip when she hesitated, looking at Mira uncertainly. She held out the cup for her.

Mira shook her head. "You go ahead, dear."

Elsa smiled then positioned the straw for Karlsson, who took a few drags.

"Thanks."

Elsa stepped back then turned to Acton and Laura. "I'm so sorry for all the trouble I caused. If only I hadn't fainted, you could have explained everything to me."

Acton felt his collar for the pin that had been his constant companion. "I'm afraid it would have only made things worse. We weren't allowed to tell anyone what was going on, and we were under constant surveillance."

Mira shuddered. "That pin they gave me. I felt like a prisoner in my own home."

Karlsson squeezed her hand. "We're all safe now, that's what's important. It's just too bad the ring was lost."

Acton frowned, the pickup at the front desk confirmed, and Al-Jubeir long gone, apparently no longer assigned to the embassy. "In today's climate, it ultimately might have been returned regardless. If we're to believe the sheik's story, then the ring will be returned to its rightful owners. In the end, I guess I don't have too much of a problem with that."

"And what of Fatima?" asked Elsa. "What becomes of her?"

Karlsson shook his head. "It sounded to me like her family didn't want her remains, so I guess she stays with us."

Laura sighed. "Such a tragic story. I just wish I knew what happened. She faked her suicide to be with the man she loved, somehow married him, was buried with him, and had the ring on that her groom from her arranged marriage gave her. There are so many missing pieces to the puzzle."

Acton agreed. "Unfortunately, I don't think we'll ever know what happened to Prince Magnus and his wife, Fatima."

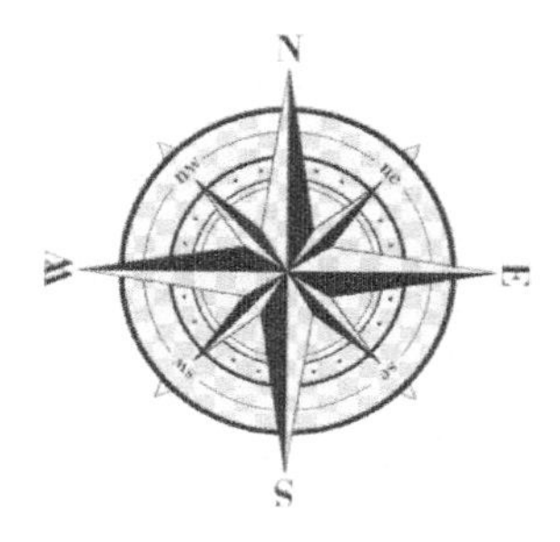

Sigtuna, Roden

989 AD

"Why?" cried Fatima. "I said I'd go back."

Rafiq stared down at his sister, his heart breaking at the sorrow on her face, yet burning at the situation her deeds had forced him into. "My lie has compounded the dishonor to our family. No one will believe she didn't willingly participate in your deception, because she faked her suicide. I told the lie in the hopes that the sheik would blame you, Magnus, instead of my family. And he did. He sent me on this mission, likely knowing full well that I would fail. And his price for failure was clear. My life. Blood must be spilled to save his honor, and that blood must be either mine, or Fatima's."

He reached out for his sister and she took his hand in hers, clasping it to her lips. His voice cracked. "I cannot bear to see you suffer for our greed." A single tear rolled down his cheek. "It wasn't a good match. Not for you, my sister, not for you. For us? Yes. But not for you." He stepped back, pulling his hand away, then with a flourish, freed himself of his cloak, his hand returning to the hilt of his sword. "I'm afraid we must fight, Viking, to the death. But I swear this to you, my friend, that should I be victorious, I will never let my sister marry that man."

Magnus bowed. "And should I be victorious, I will have word sent that you fought valiantly, and with honor worthy of your family's reputation. And I will honor your sister by loving her as no man has ever loved a woman."

Rafiq drew his sword. Magnus held his arms out, shouting at those gathered to back off, quickly explaining what was happening, for no one here spoke Arabic, and Rafiq had chosen not to speak in Norse for fear those gathered might not be as reasonable as Magnus.

Though clearly not happy about it, those gathered backed away several paces, and Rafiq turned toward those on his ship. "This is a fight to the death, between this man and me, and no one else. Should I be victorious, we shall leave in peace together with my sister. Should I not, then *you* will leave in peace, without her, and report to the sheik that I died fighting for his honor."

His men all bowed their heads, and he returned the honor before turning back to face Magnus, a man he suspected would be a formidable opponent. Magnus drew his sword, and the two circled, Fatima sobbing at the sidelines, held by an older woman Rafiq wondered might be her future mother-in-law, judging by the concern on her face.

He also wondered if Magnus believed he was facing a simple trader, one with no experience with the sword, one who would be easy to defeat. If he was laboring under that assumption, he was about to be surprised, for Rafiq had been training with the sword since he was old enough to hold one.

Though he had never drawn blood.

"Please, Rafiq, stop this madness!"

Rafiq's eyes darted toward his sister for a brief moment as he and Magnus warily circled each other, each sizing up the other, searching for any weaknesses, any tells.

Magnus lunged, a tentative, probing exploration, merely designed to garner more information. Rafiq parried it easily and with enough of a flourish to reveal he was no novice. Magnus nodded, as if to acknowledge the fact.

Another thrust, another parry, repeated several times, the crowd gathered gasping with each exchange, a chant building, urging Magnus to victory.

"Please, stop this!"

Magnus stole a glance at the sobbing Fatima, then turned back to face Rafiq, staring him in the eyes.

And Rafiq knew what was about to happen.

He swung from the side, a long arc steadily approaching his opponent's stomach, a blow so deliberately obvious it should have been easily parried. The entire crowd of experienced warriors halted their chant, gasping as Magnus raised his sword over his head, gripped tightly with both hands, exposing his midriff.

Rafiq, on instinct, almost halted his swing, but didn't, knowing his opponent's desire.

You're a better man than I, Prince Magnus.

He cried out in shame as he sliced open the belly of the bravest man he had ever encountered, a man who had willingly sacrificed himself not only for love, but for the future of his people, and for a family from a foreign land that barely knew him.

He sacrificed himself to restore the honor to both houses, to restore the peace between their people, and to allow his sister to live out her days in peace, with her new family, and not married to the man who had killed her brother.

You are a far better man than I.

"No!" cried his sister, surging toward Magnus, her arms outstretched.

And to his horror, directly into the path of his still swinging blade.

Her cry was cut off and she collapsed into his arms as he dropped his sword, his shame, his dishonor, complete.

"Fatima, no!" he cried as he held her tight, her flowing blood soaking his robes, the warmth it provided in these frigid lands a disturbing comfort.

"My love!" gasped Magnus, holding out his hand, his own blood staining the ground as those witness to this horrendous outcome inched forward.

"Magnus!" moaned his sister. And though he wanted to be the one to comfort her in her final moments, Rafiq knew it was no longer his place. He carried her over to Magnus, laying her weakening body by his side, and placed her arm across her lover's chest as with his last ounce of strength he wrapped his arms around her.

"I love you."

Her smile was weak, yet the most content Rafiq had ever witnessed. "And I love you."

Rafiq dropped to his knees, his tears flowing freely, and he placed a hand on his sister, another on Magnus, and prayed to Allah for both their souls, and despite being so different, that Allah grant them both entrance into Paradise, so they could enjoy the rest of their days together, away from the shame all of their actions, including his, had brought into their lives.

"I'm sorry, my sister. And my brother. I never meant for any of this to happen. Please find it in your hearts to forgive me for the lie I told, a lie meant only to benefit my selfish, greedy self, to preserve a future I never deserved, not at the expense of my little sister."

Fatima reached out for his hand and squeezed it briefly. "I forgive you."

And with that, she sighed her last breath, and Magnus cried out, his anguish fading into silence, the only sound left the waves on the shore, and his own pounding heart.

Rafiq reached under his robes, retrieving the ring given him by the sheik, and gripped it tightly in his hand before placing it gently on his sister's finger. He leaned over and kissed her on her forehead, then pushed to his feet, a broken man, a shattered brother, a shadow of his former self, with no will left to live.

A man came through the crowd, his eyes red and burning. He knelt by Magnus and gripped his hand for a moment, before rising to face Rafiq.

"Does this satisfy your family's honor?" asked the man in Norse.

Rafiq bowed, his tears continuing to flow freely, though his voice steady. "I'm ashamed to say it does." He gestured at Magnus. "Your son?"

The man nodded as the woman who had been comforting Fatima finally broke free of those holding her back, throwing herself over both the bodies, as if she had lost not only a son this day, but a daughter, and the knowledge that in such a brief time with his sister, that this woman had already embraced her, had already accepted her into her family, crushed him. How could these people, who he knew so little about, who never knew his sister, care more for her happiness than he had?

"Your son..." He had to stop. He drew a breath. "Your son was a good man. A far better man than I. He fought valiantly for honor, for his people, and for love. I shall pray for him."

The man bowed his head. "And I shall pray for her. Your sister?"

"Yes."

"Then we are family."

Rafiq stared at the man. "We are?"

"I already blessed their union. As far as I'm concerned, they are married, and will be honored as such, and buried as such."

Rafiq collapsed to his knees, his shoulders slumping as he was racked with sobs. He stared up at the man, anguish written on both their faces. "I am so sorry for what I have done. I shouldn't have told the lie I did. If I hadn't, they would both be alive, and I would be back home, with my family. We would have survived somehow, we would have gotten past the shame of what she had done." His head dropped. "I told myself that what I did was for my family, but it wasn't. It was for me."

"Family is everything."

"It is." He drew a deep breath, raising his head and meeting the painful gaze of the old man. "My life is already forfeit. If I return alive, I will be forced to lie once again to save my life, and should it be saved by further treachery, Allah Himself will condemn me on my day of judgment." His fists clenched, his fingernails tearing into his flesh, as his eyes burned. "But if I die here today, on the battlefield, I won't be forced to dishonor myself once more, and my family's debt to the sheik will be paid."

The man stepped closer, now directly in front of him. "I understand."

Rafiq stared up at him. "Please, rid me of my burden, and avenge your son."

"As you wish."

The man stepped back, drawing his sword, and Rafiq closed his eyes as the blade whipped through the air, severing his head from his shoulders, and restoring the honor of not only his family, but that of Magnus' as well.

THE END

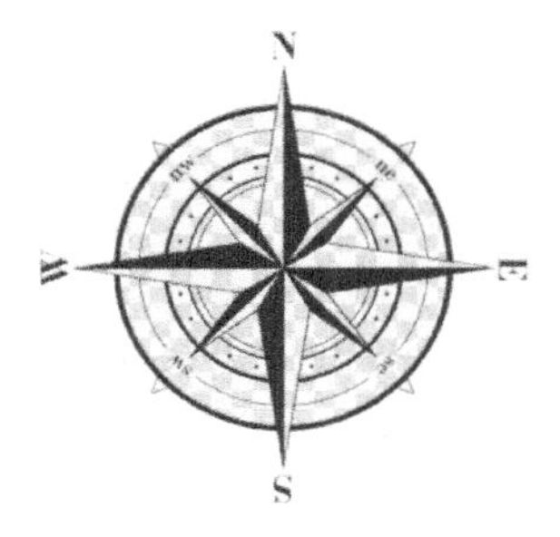

ACKNOWLEDGMENTS

Most people know about the tragic events that took place on October 2nd, 2018. Jamal Khashoggi entered the Saudi consulate in Istanbul, and was murdered in cold blood, with a ridiculously unbelievable series of lies spun that dumbfounded the world in their idiocy.

While the idea for this book came to me several years ago with the announcement of the discovery of the very ring featured in this book, the challenging aspect was figuring out how to link the past to the present. What I was blocked by was how I could believably have someone today, a thousand years later, care that a ring had been found, beyond it being yet another example of Islamic fundamentalists behaving badly.

Enter the Saudi regime itself.

For them to do what they did in Istanbul, proved that pretty much anything was possible with these people. It suddenly became completely believable that they could act on behalf of someone, fabulously overreact to the situation, then think they could get away with it.

If the events of late 2018 had been a work of fiction, I doubt anyone would have believed it. And now, thanks to those sad events, *this* work of fiction becomes plausible.

The ring is real, and the kidnapping from the embassy has been proven plausible. I hope you enjoyed the tale woven in these pages tying them together.

And one more quick note. The couple having the conversation about the Cornish game hen? That would have been my wife and I. She won't eat Cornish game hen or turkey for that matter. In her culture, if the chicken (because they're all chickens) is too big or too small, there's something wrong with it.

So, we eat ham for Christmas here.

And I'll never say what was whispered in my ear.

As usual, there are people to thank. My dad for all the research, Ian Kennedy for some "blowin' shit up" help, Susan "Miss Boss" Turnbull for a grammar save, Fred Newton for some NASCAR info, Brent Richards for some terminology help, Sue Bucksey (she was the first of several on Facebook to provide an answer!) for some Queen's English help, Sue Bucksey again via Facebook for Sherrie's spicy description of the Thunder from Downunder, and, as usual, my wife, daughter, and mother, as well as the proofing and launch teams.

To those who have not already done so, please visit my website at www.jrobertkennedy.com then sign up for the Insider's Club to be notified of new book releases. Your email address will never be shared or sold, and you'll only receive the occasional email from me, as I don't have time to spam you!

Thank you once again for reading.